WATER DAYS

WATER DAYS

A Novel

SUNDAR SARUKKAI

Published by Tranquebar, an imprint of Westland Books, a division of Nasadiya Technologies Private Limited, in 2025

No. 269/2B, First Floor, 'Irai Arul', Vimalraj Street, Nethaji Nagar, Alapakkam Main Road, Maduravoyal, Chennai 600095

ISBN: 9789360457204

10 9 8 7 6 5 4 3 2

Typeset by Mukul

Printed at Nutech Print Services, India

Pre-logue

A CITY HAS ITS OWN LANGUAGE. IT IS NOT THE LANGUAGE that the people in the city speak. It is not the language of the majority of the people in a city. A city is not produced by a majority, it is not a measure of numbers. A city is a quality, is yet another language.

So how does one write in the mother tongue of the city? This does not mean the mother tongue of the writer. The mother tongue of Bangalore is not Kannada; Kannada speakers do not constitute even half the population of this city. Neither is it Telugu or Tamil or Hindi, even if one of these languages becomes the spoken majority sometime in the future.

The language of the city is not another human language that we can speak. It may have a relation to it but it is not that in its entirety. It rises in the way the rain falls on crooked tin sheets over uneven walls, in the sound of sliding slippers on slushy roads. It contains the whisper of light under street lamps in early morning vigils, and the musky sound of breathing dogs under the haze of rainy days. It has the clatter of the vegetable carts, the crumpled sound of a bitten puff by hungry teeth.

Our languages—English, Kannada, Konkani, Telugu, Tamil, Malayalam, Hindi—cannot capture the sounds of these languages. They cannot represent the senses of the city since we have banished our senses into individual, distinct and non-intersecting organs. We think that our eyes only see, but this is the fault of our language. In the language of the city, the eye hears and smells as much as it sees. We too have this synesthetic capability but have lost it under the dictates of those who regulate a language, afraid to let language run free.

The city inspires me to write its story. Especially this story, for this is my city. I don't know exactly what it means to say 'my city'. The city is never mine. Never yours. Not Raghavendra's, not even Poornima's. Nevertheless, it is mine, just like it is yours. Just like it is theirs. We only have to find a language for our belongingness.

A city does not speak to us in the way humans do. We establish a relationship with the place we live in. It changes our life and influences our moods. It is a place that holds our cherished as well as traumatic memories. Walking through old haunts is not to remember what was then but to discover bits of ourselves scattered through the city. The geography of a city produces our histories. Our memories and emotions are sedimented on a park bench, a movie theatre, a corner spot in the darshini with a particular smell of masala dosa, and the fragrance of a coffee wafting along with the smell of sampige flowers on a busy, noisy road. These constitute the existential moments of a city, when it comes alive just for us, so that we can be part of its beating heart.

The mother tongue of a city arises in the moments of its existential crises. You can hear it if you pay attention to it. These are crises of existence that it shares in part with its inhabitants. The anxiety of a city becomes the anxiety of its people. Our languages change, we stutter, produce new words, forget old ones. We hide in cafes, outside bakeries, inside pubs, with the hope that all the noise around us will drown out what the city is trying to tell us.

It told me this story. It gave me a language. Not its own, but one that was mediated and sanitised by the demands of many forces. It gave me images that are recognisable, common, and give a sense of comfort. But it also produced words, twisted sounds, and the images of a young woman's death, along with a drying tap from which parched alphabets drip slowly, so slowly that it seems as if you can write a whole novel before a few of these drops fall to the ground or, in this case, into the waiting mouth of the lurid plastic vessel. You cannot waste water even when they are only alphabets formed as dew in early morning Bangalore. The city does not like that.

The death is incidental. It is time that controls us as well as the city. This story exists only for thirteen days. Nobody has more time than that to deal with death and liberation. The city has even less time. It is that existential crisis of the city that reached me as a murmur, in its own language, which I twisted into English. The city spoke to me of its truth, but I don't know how to write truths in languages that are in principle false. I found the words to write about these lies in my previous novel, *Following a Prayer*, although the truth of that story lay in its silence.

So, like an anthropologist, after decades of growing up *with* the city, I recorded what the city told me. I confess I have not been true to the words of the city. I can blame it on its language or perhaps it is just that I like mysteries. But within these human sounds, perhaps there lies one true story of Bengaluru.

Others helped me hear this story. Dhanu has lived it, and because she was at the taps at 3 a.m., the city has allowed me to tell this story. V.K. Karthika lent her ears and Srinivas Bhashyam his artistic squiggles on the cover and the pages in beween. I am grateful to them. The city is grateful to them.

1

It was past ten in the night and Raghavendra had not yet reached his house. He walked hurriedly, trying to escape hesitant water drops from a sporadic drizzle that gathered to pat his head and shoulders before slithering down. The smell of frying fish suddenly invaded his nostrils and Raghavendra's hunger, even though he was a vegetarian, welcomed the smell and washed it down to his stomach. Home was just a few meandering lanes away, and he knew that hot food would be waiting on the wings of a gas stove.

The rains had started a few weeks earlier; a torrent at first, then reduced to an incessant trickle. Like a prolonged parting, it had reached a stage where the pauses said more than the words. Many of the residents in Mathikere

Extension had tired of this continued intrusion, although some old-time residents spent their days staring into the drizzle, as if trying to remember the city they loved. They had begun to realise that Bangalore, which had once been a city inside a garden, was now a city whose gardens were becoming dried little mounds.

Much of the rainwater had flowed down the mud-tar roads and collected at the entrance of the local temple, where a new compound had been recently built. Raghavendra looked tentatively over the walls, his eyes blinking, trying to keep the rhythm of the rain. Under the mighty pipal tree sat, as always, Marimuthu. He had dug a small canal from the gates of the temple so that water flowed into the hidden roots of the tree. Parrots that spoke the language of the presiding deity—an anthill—were supposed to chatter evening prayers, but in the midst of the rain and mist, they had suddenly vanished, leaving their voices behind in the shade of the leaves. When it rained, it seemed to Mari that these voices fell as drops to the ground, each singing its own song.

Raghavendra turned the corner and was about to pass the temple when, out of habit, he turned his head towards the inner sanctum. He rarely entered this temple, which he felt was too unorthodox for a Brahmin to visit. Actually, it was the sight of the giant anthill that frightened him.

Years ago, Marimuthu had constructed a small room around the anthill. A forty-watt bulb teetered above the door, spreading pale yellow light in oscillating patterns of shadows. Marimuthu saw Raghavendra and went up to meet him. Mari's forehead was anointed with a thick line of kumkum right over his nose. When he performed prayers to the anthill, it seemed to glow brighter.

Whatever the 'Bangalore weather', a term that had come to be commonly used as a quality to define the city, Marimuthu wore only a towel over his shoulders and a saffron dhoti. In December and January, when cold mist blanketed the city and everyone spoke in whispers, as if whispers had something in common with the chill, Mari strutted around with a bare torso. The towel would be casually thrown around his shoulders, and on some occasions, tied around his head. If anyone asked him if he felt the cold, he would ask back, 'Does the snake feel the cold?' Implying that he and the snake were cousins of the flesh. A hidden suggestion, untested so far, was also this: *snakes and I have poisoned fangs*. Only he knew for sure that no snakes came out of that anthill, although he told people that snakes from the anthill curled up at his feet in the night.

Raghavendra would have liked to step into the shelter of the pipal tree, but crossing the gate of the temple implied a tacit acceptance that would have forced him to visit it again. And, if the need arose, with his wife and children. He decided to wait in the drizzle and let the cool drops snuggle into the crevices of his tired mind.

Mari stood leaning on the gate, exhibiting his rights over the temple by placing his leg on it.

'Nagaraj went looking for you,' he said. His voice was reedy, surprising for a man who oozed a powerful presence. His Kannada was excellent. He had become one of the many native speakers of Tamil in Bangalore who could speak that language with a Kannada accent.

'Nagaraj? In this rain?' Raghavendra felt his hunger collapsing into little flutters in his stomach. He had no wish to speak to Nagaraj, let alone meet him. And what was Nagaraj doing in the rain at this time of the night? He liked his hot food, blurry dance programmes on TV and Indian-made whisky at ten.

'Yes. Standing as wet as you, asking me if I had seen you. Not looking happy. No, not at all.'

In saying this, Mari was asking: What made Nagaraj so perpetually unhappy, even though he strutted around the streets of Mathikere Extension as if he owned even the gutters in them?

'If you had asked me earlier, I would have told you. But you don't ask me. You don't come to the temple. Your wife should be coming here on Fridays, bringing milk for the snakes. But you people are so big. If you had asked me, I would have said, be careful of Nagaraj. He is not the kind of man you take as a partner.'

Raghavendra wanted to reply, 'He is not the kind of man for anything.' But he kept quiet.

'If you ask me . . . lots of people ask me about so many things . . . but what can I say to big people like you? Still, if you ask me, I will only say, stay clear of that fellow.'

There were times when . . . No. There were only times. And then there were events.

There were times when Raghavendra would have liked to strangle Nagaraj. Or at least had the courage to ask him to leave. Or tell him, man to man, nose to nose, to quit the 'partnership' so loaded with his silence and Nagaraj's aggression. There were times when he dreamt of leaving Bangalore and going back to Udupi, his native town. Times when he believed that renaming his security agency as Raagu's Detective Agency would make him rich and successful. Times when he learnt that dreams had to be dreamt anew.

But those times had just been that. Times that had not yet become events.

And then there were other times. When he left his old job as a security guard to set up the detective agency with Nagaraj as his partner. Times when he and his wife planned on renting out two rooms in their house to two young students. Times when they discussed Raghavendra's real ambition—of starting a grocery store. Those times had become events. But there was still something left to be done before Raagu's Detective Agency could become Raghavendra Grocery Store, or as he had lately been thinking, Poornima Stores. His wife, Poornima, had violently opposed this idea of having her name so brazenly exhibited to the public. 'Every time people read the board, they would be imagining me,' she had said animatedly.

Yes, there were some times that would soon become events. They awaited Raagu's last act of bravery.

So, perhaps it was Nagaraj who should have feared Raghavendra.

Marimuthu spoke ill of no one. When he made an exception with respect to Nagaraj, he had a reason. A few days earlier, Nagaraj had walked into the temple compound after nine in the night. Marimuthu slept in a small shed in the compound. He would make sure the lamps were lit and filled to the brim with oil before closing the door of the inner sanctum. The lamps burned till daybreak. 'For him,' he would say, nodding his head like the flickers of the flame, stimulating the listener to do the same. It was difficult to know whether 'him' referred to the snake god or to some other gods.

The temple with its ample courtyard had been a matter of dispute for many years. Even before real-estate prices had shot up artificially, the temple had potential landgrabbers who came in the guise of local leaders and rowdies (many times synonymous), traders, religious groups, mess owners and sundry 'entrepreneurs'. This was the new Bangalore, post-liberalisation, and everybody felt that they needed to start a business of transacting something or the other. It was the huge anthill and the majestic pipal tree that had saved the imminent takeover of the land. But before anybody could do that, Marimuthu had materialised.

He spread the story that he had been beckoned to this shrine, drawn from his abode 'down there' in Tamil Nadu. On discovering the empty land around the anthill, he started sleeping there. After a few days under the pipal tree, he discarded his trademark white shirt and chose a red towel to adorn his torso. It was also around this time that he began to call himself Mari Gowda, finding it useful to present himself as a local Gowda rather than as somebody from another state.

Marimuthu liked to say that 'everything is nothing but timing'. It was only the *right time* that made things happen, not people. The anthill had been on that land for a long time. Every Friday, married women came to offer milk there. Nobody had ever seen a snake come out of the mud structure to drink the milk, but the practice continued to flourish since it was seen as an important ritual for married women to protect their husbands and children.

One day, in September 1995, a sensational story was reported across the country that Ganesha idols were drinking milk. There was a Ganesha idol outside a hospital a little distance away from the anthill. There was a huge rush throughout the day in Mathikere Extension. Women, children and men (lagging behind casually as if they couldn't be bothered by such miracles) hurried to offer milk to the idol. Although that story died very soon, Marimuthu remembered it and used it well. He installed a small Ganesha idol near the anthill, not so subtly implying that both the snakes and Ganesha partook of the milk that devoted wives left every week.

But Marimuthu did not need dubious miracles to establish his authority over the temple. Instead, he did it most pragmatically by sleeping next to the anthill, when no one else dared to enter that place at night. He also began the practice of offering prayers. The locals adopted him as the priest of the temple, and one day he got a group of them to build a small brick room around the anthill. Offerings began trickling in, and he soon managed to raise enough funds to build a compound.

It was at this juncture, his prestige enhanced, his religiosity at its peak, that Nagaraj came to him with a suggestion. He envisioned a partnership between the two of them to construct a three-storey building in place of the anthill temple. He suggested that its rooms could be let out to the many students studying in the nearby engineering and medical colleges. When Marimuthu did not seem to respond with any interest, he tried to dangle the image of a shopping complex. The government-built shopping complex at Mathikere was an example of what not to do, and Nagaraj saw himself as a pioneer in creating modern shopping complexes. The possibilities seemed endless, and Nagaraj tried to enthuse Mari about the project.

A suggestion like this would not have been possible even a few years earlier. But this was 1999. It was as if the end of the century was also going to be the end of all that Bangalore once was. Even a place like Mathikere—on the outskirts of the city—had turned into a bustling residential and commercial area. It had become a place for immigrants from many states who came to Bangalore to set up paan stalls, grocery stores, sweet shops and anything else that would give them a living. It was not a place for the rich or the upper classes: the roads were narrow, cows clogged the traffic, there were places with open gutters on the sides of the roads, houses were spaced together tightly, one too close to another. In some of these buildings, one could lean from a bedroom into a neighbour's kitchen.

The area was filled with countless little shops of all kinds that seemed to crush each other, grabbing what little space the other had to offer. All this activity was a sign of things to come in Bangalore. That much Nagaraj was sure of. He told Mari that the future of Bangalore was going to be in the burgeoning 'compooter industries', as he called it.

Mari had little belief in what Nagaraj was saying but he had already anticipated how real estate was going to change Bangalore forever. The city would not remain the same in the next ten years. Why wait ten? He didn't think it would be the same in five years. Already, there were two real estate 'shops' in the serpentine lane next to his temple. Both were run by Telugu Reddys, who had suddenly landed in Mathikere with claims of land to sell and buy. Nagaraj had hinted something about the Reddys too, saying that this was all a plan of the people of Andhra Pradesh to take over Bangalore. It seemed as if Bangalore, the garden city meant for pensioners, had suddenly become the target of too many greedy eyes.

Marimuthu took Nagaraj's proposal as a personal insult. When he had ignored the meaningful gaze of the many women who flocked to him reverentially, Nagaraj dared to debase him by imagining that mere material desire could conquer him. He told him that he would think about the project, even as his anger threatened to strike and paralyse Nagaraj. But Nagaraj was a local, and Marimuthu was after all from another state. He knew his position in the temple was safe but he recognised that the mixture of politics and religion was getting increasingly combustible. The affable Vajpayee, who was the prime minister, was inspiring more strident voices in Mathikere, and Mari knew well that politics and religion would no longer be the same in Bangalore.

He had kept quiet when Nagaraj made his offering. But the time had come to speak; he hailed Raghavendra, and walked from the pipal tree to the gates of the temple. Raindrops lowered themselves along his forehead as unloading cargoes, and the saffron paste on his forehead slowly spread into his eyes, over his cheeks and flowed down his chin.

It was on 4th Street that Raghavendra finally lost his footprints in the thumb swirls of the rain. In Mathikere Extension, the roads were only streets, sometimes bylanes, and many times gullies. At the first sign of rain, it was these streets which hurriedly dissolved into little mud rivulets and tiny islands of mud, stone and tar.

Each step imprinted on that street could have been used later to reconstruct events, to collate together the whispers that rose from voices hidden behind doors. Each half-step could have spoken of the clues that made Raghavendra what he was. He tried to hurry through the dark street whose streetlights had vanished into the stars in the twinkle of a second, but his drowning footprints held his speed in check. He was too preoccupied to hear the distant thud. The transformer had blown, and light, imprisoned inside the houses, finally escaped into the darkness.

He walked with eyes on the ground, watching the flowing water. Streaks of mud produced mirages of squirming earthworms. He turned at the end of 4th Street, where it met 26th Main. The rain increased and every drop felt like a dollop of darkness, an inkjet that carried the weight of space downwards. The road was crammed with houses and shops, but they were all closed and silent. Only his footsteps made awkward sounds, as if it were they who led him on towards his house. Plachuk, plachuk . . . Follow me, they said, and Raghavendra, married to those sounds with a piece of rubber, went around and around the streets.

Suddenly, he saw a residue of light fall at his feet and rise again as a broken reflection on the water. He looked up, saw a flame at a doorway. He thought that the flame smiled, welcoming him into its abode. It stood tall and dignified at the end of a sickly looking candle, as if the candle was indebted to the flame.

Behind the smile was a face. Before Raghavendra could move his eyes away and leave the candle-smile frozen for the next stranger, he *saw* Shankar call out to him. Shankar's finger beckoned Raghavendra. The message came at the end of the flame that crooked its tip towards him. Raghavendra had no choice. In the darkness and rain, choice for him was just a dash to a sheltering roof.

Shankar stood next to the candle. His thin body with its own candle-like sheath made him look like a demure mistress next to the burning wax. His smile had moulded into the gaps in his teeth.

'Sir, why are you walking in the rain?' he asked, moving aside to let Raghavendra's soggy form enter his shop. Raghavendra stopped at the entrance, hesitant to leave puddles inside a tailor's shop. The workbench on which the candle was placed was covered with layers of cloth. A pair of big scissors with a green plastic handle held his attention. He let his hands hang loose, let the water drip down his fingertips, unable to find a spot to place his hand on. Shankar pulled out a plastic chair and asked Raghavendra to sit on it. As he sat down, his pants emptied more water that flowed through the capillaries of his slippers.

Shankar said, 'What is this rain? All the time raining. Horrible!' A cycle whizzed past with a young man bent over the handlebars. The tyres made a whirring noise, a centrifugal sound filled with whispers of parting, of leaving. As the sound died out in tiny spurts, Raghavendra thought he heard a girl scream. He looked at Shankar, who smiled back at him. The scream came and went, touching Raghavendra, passing him with a wave as if it was attached to that drowning whirr of the cycle tyre.

He got up suddenly, hesitantly nodded at Shankar and left, leaving Shankar to gaze at his back and the heels of his slippers as they went plachuk, plachuk.

When Raghavendra had agreed to a nameboard, he hadn't anticipated the scope of Nagaraj's imagination.

Nagaraj visited a numerologist, who told him that the lucky name for their firm should be Raagu's—Agency. The blank was left to be filled in with whatever word they desired. When he saw Nagaraj's sceptical look, he had this to say about the blank space: 'a place immune to the effect of numbers, the place where zero resides'. Raghavendra had become Raagu with the throw of a few little shells that had created a pattern, danced a song, which the numerologist listened to with closed eyes and quivering ears. Nagaraj was worried that the quivering ears were a trick to cheat the growing number of people who had started flocking to him. But when he saw the way the shells had fallen, when he noticed their pattern, and imagined them winking at him, he kept quiet. The numerologist told him that the mysteries of numbers were lost beneath mighty oceans, and only the shells that hid these secrets inside them knew the truth. Raagu's Detective Agency sounded sufficiently glamorous to Nagaraj. The name sounded halfway between a masala powder maker and a multinational computer firm. Detective in the blank space was an inspired addition, in keeping with the times. Prominent detective agencies had come up on MG Road, and big hoardings proclaiming 'Discreet Matters Handled' or 'Matters Handled Discreetly' had long made Nagaraj's roving eyes stand in attention.

Poornima, when she came to know of the name of their agency, asked Raghavendra: 'Why, for god's sake, why Raagu? What is this aaa in between? You are a sheep or what? And who is Nagaraj to decide all this? You are the owner, you are taking your house as the office. What has he done? What is he going to do for you? And what is this *dictactive*? You think you are the police? Why do you get caught in all this? I thought both of you are planning some business together. You said, Surprise, wait, surprise. Now I am surprised. Very surprised. I think you have forgotten that you are married, have two daughters to take care of.'

The way Poornima talked, every time she stopped, she created a monstrous pause. It was a pause that was clear and loud. It stayed around the ears, readying them for the next burst.

Ambition was an itch Raghavendra could have scratched away. But no, he had to nurture it, let it grow until it became unmanageable. How could he forget his responsibilities? Paul had even made him administrative-in-charge at Paul's Security Firm. He had twenty young men working under him. It was a challenging job to rotate his men in order to make sure nobody was missing on duty. Paul trusted him and look what he had done now: replaced gentle Paul with obnoxious Nagaraj.

Being a security guard had very little to do with being a detective. Where did such ideas come from? How did Nagaraj ferret out these visions? Raghavendra had been content, if not happy, walking around with a stick and a whistle. Night duties meant a shawl around his shoulders or a precautionary muffler, and a cup of tea every couple of hours. No robber dared to intrude when two or three guards were together. Only once had he caught anybody: an employee of a factory who was trying to steal some bathroom fittings, hidden underneath his shirt. At that time Paul, the ex-serviceman, stiff-chested and upright neck, had said of Raghavendra: 'This chap, full of brain, but no *prawns*.'

What pretensions! From a security guard whose main job was to drive away intruding dogs, cows and strangers on bicycles, to a detective who would . . . *do what?*

Nagaraj had been persuasive. He put his arms around Raghavendra's shoulders and said, 'Enough of being a failure. Be a man your sons-in-law can look up to.' Nagaraj's sweaty arms (*how did he manage to sweat in cool, dry Bangalore?*) irritated Raghavendra, but he was too caught up in a dream to complain. Enough of balancing incomes, enough of Paul's niceness—go on, move on, be a man his sons-in-law will look up to.

Dreams are made this way: Nagaraj would get clients. Raghavendra had only to supply the office, which would be a room in his house, and use his brains. He would work on the cases with help from Nagaraj. How simple it had sounded to him when he first heard it.

Dreams wake up this way: Raghavendra was already becoming suspicious that Nagaraj was running his own business using their office. Men, big and small, walked in and out, but no clients had been found yet. It had been over a month and only the rent paid by the two boys who occupied two rooms on the first floor of his house provided him with an income. Nagaraj had promised cases, had vanished into the evenings swearing that a client was around the next corner, but none had materialised so far.

But so far was becoming too late. Space and time had merged and only caused more anxiety for Raghavendra.

He decided that he would do what he should have done first. What he had played at when he was a little boy in Udupi. He decided to set up a grocery store. Thus, with one genius stroke, he would get rid of Nagaraj, become an entrepreneur, and not worry about stalking criminals in the dark, spotted lanes of Mathikere Extension.

Raghavendra hurried towards his house. Splashes of water crowded his ankles like pesky rats. Somewhere in the flow, real rats and cockroaches would be hidden, ready to do an alligator jump. The street lights had turned off, the rain increased, and Raghavendra felt a creeping fear. It trickled coldly through the soles of his feet and soon hammered at the back of his head. Poornima would have understood this. *Ever since you put up that board, ever since you joined hands with that Nagaraj, the evil eyes of our neighbours are on you, the cruel taunts of the criminals chase you. You think you have become a great man just by catching criminals? Why can't you stay out of their lives? It is not your problem; it is the worry of the police.*

To ward off evil eyes, once in a few months, Poornima would make Raghavendra and her two girls stand in a corner of their kitchen. She would light a bunch of broomsticks and wave it around the three of them, driving away negative spirits. Raghavendra would smile cynically through the smoke of the burning sticks, but deep down, he felt safer after she performed this act.

Raghavendra tripped over a piece of rock submerged in the water. It was his fault. He should have seen the unnatural glee of the water that swirled near the stone. His palms made a cylinder of the slush and brown mud made galactic patterns on his spectacles. He held his body up with his palms for a few seconds. Suddenly, his palms gave way and he collapsed on the road. Lying on the ground, his body covered in slush, he looked towards his house five doors away. He could see the outline of Nagaraj, another candlebeam man, sitting inside the office. The door was open, and Nagaraj's shadow, smoking a cigarette, waved impatiently.

What a mistake, Raghavendra thought, his cheeks feeling cold. What a mistake. What a mistake!

He rested his cheek on his forearm, giving in to a growing feeling of dread. His body refused to move, and his head drooped to one side. And then he heard it. Clearly. Heavy sounds, like furniture being moved. Or thrown about. Shouts and screams. The sounds came to him, liquefied, pushing through the veins and arteries of the earth, ready to burst inside his ears. He heard an anguished scream of pain. He jumped up, looked around him, and rushed towards his house.

The rain increased in intensity. On cue, as if to emphasise that his house was first and foremost a shelter. Or, perhaps, merely to drum some courage into him. But before he reached the office, a hand grabbed him and pulled him aside. At the bottom of the stairs stood Rajesh, one of his tenants. He was holding an umbrella, but his shoulders were wet. Come, he whispered. By the time the sound travelled to Raghavendra, it had become a sonic boom, an underwater explosion.

'First, come upstairs. Then you can jump down the wall to the back of your house. That . . . Nagaraj will leave soon.'

Raghavendra followed him, grateful but ashamed. He thought his guilt was surely going to give him a cold the next day. The first floor had two rooms that were rented by Rajesh and Bhaskar. Rajesh, who came from Bihar, was a student in the nearby engineering college. Bhaskar, from Madurai, had recently completed his engineering degree and was working in a computer firm. They shared the toilet upstairs, but little else. It was as if they were creatures from two different universes.

Bangalore was being inundated by students from all over the country, particularly from Bihar and Bengal. From Tamil Nadu and Kerala came young men in search of jobs. They had, in an instant, changed Bangalore, as a large number of small businesses came up to cater to their needs. Bakeries, restaurants where one ate standing, creaking houses that had suddenly transformed into PGs, paying guest accommodation for men and women, a deluge of two-wheelers on the road, each trying to outrace the others. And not to forget, hair-cutting saloons with glossy, airbrushed photographs of the latest Hindi film heroes. They had descended into this locality because it was still cheaper than other places. The locals who owned houses began to let out a room or two to these youngsters. Always viewing them with suspicion, especially if there were any girls at home. This is what Mathikere Extension was fast becoming: an area populated by young men from different parts of the country and local girls hiding their glances behind half-shuttered windows.

There were no steps connecting the first floor to the backyard of Raghavendra's house. Raghavendra looked down at the ground below him. The distance looked like a huge unending black well.

'Where is Bhaskar?' he asked.

'Working, what else? All these software *boys* are like this—working all the time.'

This was Rajesh's sly way of suggesting that what he was doing then—*helping my landlord*—was more important than office work. Particularly this new obsession with writing software. Bhaskar had finished his BSc from Madurai and had started working in an IT firm. Rajesh never missed a chance to tell Bhaskar that studying engineering was far more important than working in a software company. 'We engineers build the computers, you know,' he would say with a patronising smile. Bhaskar never responded to Rajesh's comments, and always deferred to him by addressing him as 'Sir'.

'You first go down to the perch above the windows,' Rajesh continued, pointing to the projecting windowsill. 'From there it is only seven feet down. You hang by your hands, that will be . . . six or so feet. Then you jump down. See? How easy!' Rajesh had measured Raghavendra with a careless look, his eyes a roving tape. Raghavendra felt like patting his young tenant, who had thrown aside his flimsy umbrella, as if by becoming wet he was exhibiting his camaraderie with Raghavendra.

To delay the inevitable, Raghavendra said, 'You are going to get a cold. You shouldn't have . . . '

'Cold! Me! Uncle, I swim in the Ganga in the winter. Everybody in our village does. What is this rain? What cold?'

His hand cupped a palmful of water, which he threw back to the skies. He might as well have said, 'Here, take it back, you puny fools, you won't get me so easily.'

Raghavendra tentatively put one leg over the parapet wall. He had wanted to smile bravely as if this was something he did every night, but the rain would only have distorted the smile. It was not worth the effort.

'Uncle, you be careful and slow. You can easily do it.'

Raghavendra saw the back door of his house. Remembered how Poornima had insisted on special Burma teak: 'There are too many thieves. I don't want to make it easy for them.' Every night they closed that door with two latches and one crossbar. Even a rat's tail couldn't get in.

A few yards behind the door lay the open well. They had covered it with a wire mesh. That way, they could prevent children falling into the well and yet hope that rainwater (when it came these days!) would sweeten the water in the well. A kind of marriage between Earth and Heaven, a metaphor for so many things in their lives. Now the mesh had seemingly dissolved, and it looked as if the water was flowing to the brim.

'Come on, Uncle, it's easy. Don't look down.' Rajesh, the cheerleader, amused and excited. 'Imagine doing all this at your age. Why did you have to go and open a detective shop?' As if Raghavendra was selling crime in coloured wrappers inside bottles. 'At your age, why do this? This is what will happen, Uncle. That Nagaraj is a rowdy. You can't beat him up. Neither can I. But if you tell me, I'll get some of my friends from Bihar and beat him so badly he won't come here again.'

Raghavendra pulled his leg up. He looked at Rajesh, squat and short, always with a smile that spoke a language of its own.

'Don't worry, Rajesh. I'll take care of Nagaraj. I will not enter my house like a thief.' He pushed past him and walked down the steps. Rajesh followed him down. The front door was still open. They could see Nagaraj dozing with his head falling towards his chest. The candle had eaten itself, its flame had a satiated look. Rajesh stopped at the doorstep while Raghavendra went into the veranda that served as their office.

'Raagu, you are finally here,' Nagaraj said, waking up. Spit sprayed from his mouth as he spoke, and his drooling thoughts left a stain on the table. Invisible in the darkness, but soon, in the morning light, the crystals of his desires would be seen.

'Nagaraj, I don't like you to come to my house so late. I don't want the office open at this time. There is no light, and anybody can enter. What will happen to my family? It is not good for them.'

Nagaraj was partly drunk. He came close to Raghavendra. 'Family. Always you use family as an excuse. How can you do business if you keep talking of family?'

He walked angrily to a corner of the room. Venkatappa, as promised, had delivered a sack of rice just that morning. Raghavendra wished he had sent it a few days later.

'What is this? Rice-aaa? What is rice doing in my office? We are a detective firm. What does rice do here then? You want to trap thieves by using rice?'

Raghavendra looked at the door leading to the inner rooms of his house. He knew, god, how he knew, Poornima sitting there, angrily twisting the ends of her sari as she listened to Nagaraj. I hope she doesn't come out, he prayed silently. Rajesh, as if on cue, moved to stand next to that door. A door meant to be guarded.

'Talk to me, Raagu. I do everything for you, but you are planning something behind my back.'

'No, Nagaraj. Nothing like that. You know we haven't had any clients for a month. What do I do for money? I have a . . . ' He paused. Family was not an excuse, it was an excusable reality. 'I have a family to take care of. I have decided that I want to set up a grocery shop here. I am too old for this job and . . . I like selling groceries.' The last few words spluttered, hid themselves in shame for having come out of his mouth. If these words could speak for themselves, they would have said: Does any self-respecting man say he likes to sell groceries? That, too, at the expense of being a detective?

'Groceries! You like to sell groceries? You are a weak man, Raghavendra. How you can be a father, I don't understand. What kind of a man you are to your wife, that also . . . You don't think about me. What am I going to do? I am your partner, you can't take decisions by yourself.'

From behind the door came Poornima's voice. It was a muted shout, but having escaped through the keyhole, her voice expanded and burst upon them.

'Shameless fellow! What kind of partner are you? You are sitting in our house. You only got the nameboard made, which we paid for. You sit here full day talking with your friends and doing what not. You are not any partner.' Her silence, as sudden, left behind a sucking vacuum that made Nagaraj furious. Words, angry little bees, were frothing near his lips and Raghavendra knew that when he spoke next, it would be . . .

'A woman dares speak for you. You are a man?' He spat in Raghavendra's direction, but the spit had long coagulated inside his mouth. It threatened to take off, but was held back in his throat. Two drops dripped down his chin. In a rage, he kicked at the sack of rice. Hundred kilos of rice stared back at him calmly.

But Raghavendra felt that kick, as if the insult to the sack of rice was a slap on his face.

His anger found a voice. 'Get out. Right now. Don't you dare come back again. I will call the police.' He went towards Nagaraj, pulled at his arms. Nagaraj tottered past, and Rajesh tripped him. Alcohol and anger did to Nagaraj what Raghavendra himself could not. He staggered out into the rain and shouted, 'Tomorrow I will be back. Then we will see.' He walked down the street shouting obscenities at Raghavendra, at the rain, the clouds, and even the street dogs that had all gone into hiding, crawling into leaking shelters.

2

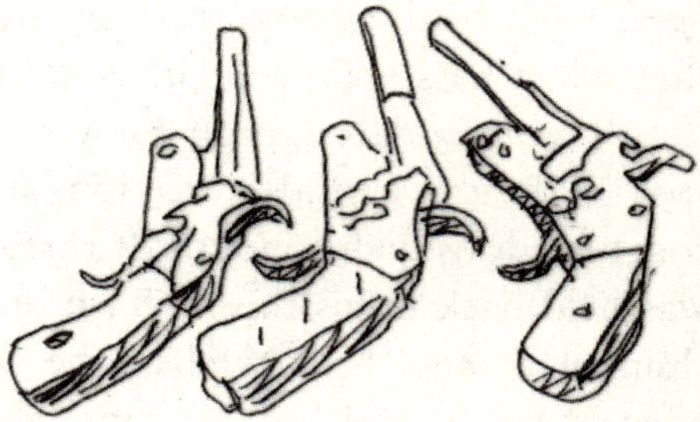

Forty-five years old. Creaking body and bored bones. A slump in the back. Spectacles that would make an owl look like a human. Can't run five steps before cracks begin to form on the body. Hands so weak that they need help to stay in place. On top of that, married and with, god help us, two girls fast growing into miniature thunderstorms. Had a job, not great. But not bad. At least we knew he would come home. Now he has thrown it out as if his life is free and for charity to others. Now he starts this . . . *this*. With Nagaraj.

How Poornima had washed, wrung and dried Raghavendra's pretensions before his eyes. His only answer had been to give her a hesitant smile, managing to magnify his weakness through his soldered eyes. Immediately,

Poornima had softened. 'It's only that everybody takes advantage of your niceness,' she said. He nodded gently into her earrings, and she could hear his voice tinkle inside her: *Yes, maybe, but I can handle all this.*

What a sight it was! Friday, a few weeks before, had auspiciously come to join the opening of Raagu's Detective Agency. The room, which had been used as a veranda, was covered with a glass panel. Nagaraj nailed the nameboard above the main door of the house, thereby establishing his position in the agency to all the onlookers. Raghavendra was dressed in a simple white dhoti and a cream cotton shirt. Poornima had pulled out one of her silk saris from the time of her marriage. It smelt of mothballs going stale.

Raghavendra's two daughters, aged thirteen and eleven, had ironed their salwars. The family had gone to a nearby temple (not Marimuthu's) and walked out with decorated foreheads and a basket full of half coconuts, fresh flowers and a crushed banana. The smells and tastes had combined to produce a colourful palette. Raghavendra's eldest daughter, Suhasini, tried to give the banana to a wandering cow, but Raghavendra stopped her in time.

'God's blessings are meant to be eaten by us and not by cows.' He plucked the pulpy pieces of the banana and gave one each to his family members. Suhasini swallowed the piece without letting her tongue taste it.

A priest had come at eight in the morning, ready with his prayers. By then, the nailing summons by Nagaraj had gathered a small crowd. The priest was very enthusiastic and his prayers rang loud and clear. When he was done blessing the nameboard, the main door and the office room by sprinkling water, Raghavendra and his family fell at his feet for his blessings. Nagaraj had wanted to be different, yet also be a part. He wore a shirt and pants, but had a sandalwood streak on his forehead. Instead of prostrating on the ground, he half-bent in front of the priest.

Rajesh made sure he was at the forefront of the event. It had been a good excuse not to go to college. 'Uncle,' he said, 'don't worry. I'll take care of everything.' There was little he could actually do, except run from one point to another. He stood near the door with an adultish smile, staking his proximity to Raghavendra. His presence reinforced the absence of Bhaskar, whose software job left him with no time for functions. When people rushed into the house, an excuse to take their curiosity for a stroll, they passed Rajesh. He exchanged hesitant smiles with the locals, as if smiles too had their regional languages.

Chandru had been among the first to peep and prod. He was a contemporary of Raghavendra, had grown up together in neighbouring streets long before the locality had got its name. They had gone to the same school, failed the same college, married at proximate times. All this sameness had alienated each other.

Chandru had a dominating face: thick lips, big nose and planar chin. His voice was as loud as his face. He had married a timid woman and had so bullied her with his mere presence that she slept most of the time, saying she was ill. He had a son (the same age as Suhasini) who looked and behaved like his father. Chandru worked as a clerk in Vidhana Soudha. His proximity to the political class only increased his pomposity. He had made enough money to buy a new scooter on easy instalments. His only problem now was Raghavendra's entry into the class of entrepreneurs and that too something as glamorous as the proprietorship of a detective agency. He was so irritated by this that he poked every corner of the office as if they hid dirty secrets that would expose Raghavendra. He was not looking for anything specific, just gathering all he could with bifocal eyes, a binocular vision that ate through the walls with their jealous intensity.

Nachappa, standing next to Rajesh, followed Chandru with his own misgivings. He told Rajesh in Hindi broken into Kannada bits: 'Look at Chandru! He is so full of envy. See him, like a rat. Why do you think he is envious?' Poornima passed in front of them, sheltering Nachappa's words under her silk pallu. 'That and also . . . because he got a dullard son instead of a bright girl like Suhasini.' Rajesh nodded, clearly happy that Nachappa had shared such a *local* and *adult* conversation with him.

It was also Chandru who, when he left, said, 'Who made this coffee? This is what happens if you buy cheap coffee powder.' He spoke to passing neighbours, but they had all, long ago, learnt to ignore him. The inquisitive crowd soon dispersed after having coffee and a piece of coconut burfi that the two girls dutifully distributed to all who had gathered. They left behind mud prints on the floor, fingerprints on the wall, oil stains on the back of the chairs, pieces of burfi near the door, and everywhere, cobwebs of their curiosity.

Paul, the ex-serviceman, who held the virtue of dignity upright in his body, could have been curious about Raghavendra's new venture, but he remained merely polite. 'You will be a loss to us, Mister Raghavendra,' he had said, the Mister a rite of honour which Paul bestowed on his employees only when he was not happy with them. Fifty-eight years old, hard and bald as a rock, the dark black colour of his skin betraying his southern Tamil Nadu ancestry, Paul had been courteous even at war. War, he remembers, frontline and beyond into Bangladesh in 1971, the very memory of it shutting his eyes, placing a board—Danger, Enemy Lines. War he forgets when he thinks of his son who, on another frontline, in Kashmir, had ended the stray trajectory of an insurgent bullet. As if to assert every moment that forgiveness is what forgetting is all about, he would smile each time he mentioned his lost son, as if his son had just stepped out to the corner shop.

Paul had started his business at the right time. Security agencies were the next big entrepreneurial venture waiting to happen in Bangalore. The nineties were still a time when houses were left open and people would sit out on the veranda, letting in not just the breeze, but also people who might be walking by. Already, by the end of the millennium, this was beginning to change. Knocks on doors now were not a welcome message but one to be met with suspicion. There were new definitions of outsiders now categorised in terms of the language they spoke, the place they came from and, increasingly, the religion they belonged to. The city was absorbing the anxieties of becoming middle-aged and it was obvious to many that the security problem would only grow over time. Earlier, security guards were needed only for factories and some offices. But Paul knew that they would soon become essential for independent houses and apartment buildings. He guessed that this too was as the urban planners had intended, as they built for the nouveau rich, the class that surely but strangely was changing the very face of this city.

Raghavendra was let down by Paul's kindness. He wanted to leave in a blaze of entrepreneurial spirit, wanting the past to echo its challenges to him. But Paul's kindness was an embarrassment. When this kindness had exceeded itself in the form of two pieces of cake, white and slightly hard with green icing on them, which Paul had bought for his daughters from the bakery right opposite, Raghavendra was forced to tell him that he would not be a competitor to him. Paul refused to listen to his explanations. He had no use for them. Confessions alone were enough. He tried to stop Raghavendra's spluttering explanations with an easy smile.

Paul had misunderstood and indeed viewed Raghavendra's agency as a competitor to his. Raghavendra knew this for sure when Paul suddenly started talking about his son. It was Paul's way of atonement for feelings of anger and betrayal. Raghavendra found no words or gestures to convince him otherwise.

There is an interpretation of the half-wall in Raghavendra's house, the room that served as the veranda, and later as the office for his detective agency. If not a story, at least an interpretation.

Raghavendra's father, Haridas, had bought that piece of land when he decided on the move from Udupi to Bangalore. He had been a priest in a place where there were already one too many. One of his cousins, who had got him to Bangalore to perform the Satyanarayana pooja in a 'grand' style, had suggested to him that Bangalore might offer opportunities that had dried up in Udupi.

Mathikere Extension was then unofficially known as Sollepalya—the colony of mosquitoes. It was mostly agricultural land and thought to be far away from the city, although it was less than ten kilometres from the city railway station. Haridas bought a piece of land there after selling his house and share of land in Udupi. He also brought labourers from there to construct his new house.

It was said, each time with an added element of surprise, that he stood in line with the labourers and passed bricks and cement. It was then, as he was building his house with his own hands, fighting impatient mosquitoes and shooing them away with the bricks, that he decided to have a veranda which would not be completely open but also not completely closed. He built a wall three feet high, leaving an open space till the roof.

The room looked like it had been framed, frozen in time. Nobody really remembered why he had built it that way. Raghavendra claimed that his father had always wanted to open a provision store and that the space was meant for that. He remembered sitting there and talking to his friends beyond the wall. How lovely an illusion. A barrier, yet not one. And ideal to sit and sell fresh groceries.

Poornima debunked this myth. 'Your father wanting to open a grocery shop? Ha! That Brahmin becoming a shopkeeper?'

Raghavendra stared at her, angry that she was questioning him about his own father.

Poornima relented. 'Okay, maybe he wouldn't mind. But do you know the real reason why he built the veranda like that? It is because he was unhappy leaving Udupi. He left behind open lands and an old house with a courtyard. He left this space in this house so that he could sit inside and look out—a view of the city from his village inside!' Poornima's flourish ended with mental applause from Raghavendra. *She should have finished her degree.* When their eyes met, they said the same thing to each other.

So, if not a story, at least this interpretation.

Poornima exploded out of the door, her quivering flesh yearning to grab Raghavendra by his collar. *If only he was not her husband*! Before she could utter the words, she saw Rajesh standing near the door. His body posture, still as in a picture, ready for combat, a small-sized version of the giant film posters. Ajay Devgn, Suniel Shetty, Sunny Deol had all metamorphosed into ready-to-fight muscles in his body.

Rajesh's presence stopped Poornima. He smiled at her, pleased, looking like a grinning miniature waterfall.

Raghavendra took the opportunity to tell her urgently, 'Get two towels for us.' Poornima went inside and got two thin cotton towels. Her daughters had come to stand behind the door. Suhasini's nose peeped out, a freedom granted to her growing years.

Raghavendra towelled his hair and gave the wet towel to Suhasini, whose hand came creeping out of the darkness. He then went in to change his clothes. Poornima, in a burst of thanksgiving, told Rajesh, 'Stay and eat something.' Poornima spoke to Rajesh in Kannada. He, after three years of staying in Bangalore, had learnt about a dozen words of Kannada that included idli, vada and dosa. On the rare occasions when he had to speak or merely communicate with Poornima, he would splutter in chaste Hindi and broken English. His English sounded as if he wrote the words in the Devanagiri script.

He had eaten his dinner earlier, at Guptaji's mess. The dinner of roti and rice had not been bad, but he was getting tired of eating potatoes in every size, shape and form. Public food all over the country had become synonymous with potatoes. Vegetables, colourful and succulent, had been banished into high-priced menu cards. When Poornima asked Rajesh to eat, he promptly said yes, imagining a plateful of his favourite greens, dal that smelt of the motherly fragrance of the pods, and cabbage or lady's fingers cooked in a generous amount of oil. He threw the damp towel on the chair and ran up to change.

By the time he came back, she had lit a kerosene lamp. The passageway had become an ancient corridor where shadows fought enemies on the wall, and her comfortable kitchen, a temple. Poornima, the mother goddess at the platform-altar, pointed Rajesh to a plate on the ground.

'Today is special.' Raghavendra translated the remaining words as if Rajesh had understood the first few. 'For your bravery.' He tried to say it with a flourish, but it was sucked into his newly formed cavities.

Poornima served rice, ghee and then hot saaru. Suhasini served the special of the day: potato roast. Boiled, peeled, diced and roasted well. Rajesh smiled wryly at his plate and the potato pieces seemed to smile back.

'Uncle, you let me handle this fellow. My friends can take care of him.'

'What friends? You are all students. You can't speak to a rowdy like him.'

Suhasini and her sister—whose name should now come out from behind the door—Sanjeevani, as if sisters are rhyming words in a couplet, as if through their names one extends one body into the other, were both busy competing to serve Rajesh. *More rice? More saaru? More pot-ate-o?* The daily assembly in their Catholic school where they said prayers to an anonymous Lord in a singsong tune made them speak like that all the time. *Pot-ate-o? Thanku, no.*

'How can you say that, Uncle? My close friend is Commander Bindra. He brings guns from Bihar and sells them to autorickshaw drivers and others here. Another friend, actually from my neighbouring village, has not passed his degree in ten years. Ten years, Uncle.' Ten years back that friend had come to Bangalore to study engineering, and repeatedly failed exams so that he could stay on as a student. For him, nothing was as good as being a student, as it allowed him the freedom to be the local leader and protector of all North Indian (but only Hindi-speaking) students in Mathikere. He spoke a mixed dialect of north Bihar, and every word he uttered was coated with the bright red colour of paan. His speech most often floated on the fumes of 420 zarda, the potent tobacco mix that he and his friends adored.

Ten gleeful years! Rajesh's smile overflowed into the saaru, although he could never understand why these Southies (as he had come to call them) diluted dal to this extent. Even the kerosene lamplight paled in comparison to his smile. In between bites of food, he added, 'Commander Bindra's father is a well-known dacoit, also near my village. I can bring these friends tomorrow. And Nagaraj will never bother you again.'

This was Rajesh's way of offering his thanks for the hot rice and saaru. When Suhasini gave him a glass of buttermilk, he drank it in one gulp. Eating rice with buttermilk was a habit he happily left to the Southies.

Raghavendra was sorely tempted to take the law into his own hands. 'In a lawless society,' Poornima said often, 'you should take the law into your own hands.'

'What lawless society?' he had once asked after a judicious pause. 'We are a lawful country, we have a functioning police and courts.'

'What law?' Poornima countered. 'You really think the police will do anything for us?'

Poornima had very clear views on what the law meant for her. Law was never a matter of justice. Every time he uttered the word justice, she would ask, 'Where is justice to be found in the country?' When she was in a belligerent mood, she would drag the gods into it saying, 'Rama liberated Sita from Ravana, who then jumped into the fire to prove her chastity, and through this set the minimal definition of justice.' That sense of tragedy and inevitability eclipsed the idea of justice for her. Even now, her rare visits to a Rama temple would trigger guilt in her.

Poornima had only this to say. Quite often. One, her little finger at attention, we are not rich. Actually, poor. Two, the finger which quivered with the anticipation of a gold ring that had been pawned years before, we are Brahmins. Actually, Madhwa Brahmins. Orthodox (although Raghavendra's father stood in line with the labourers), traditional and far removed from the other castes. Actually, not really so, for once the move had been made to Bangalore, Haridas the priest had lost his orthodoxy in proportion to his sight. (Not surprising, since he was always considered a rebel by his own family.) Three, the finger which stood tall, which seemed like a miniature version of Poornima herself, since we are Brahmins, poor Brahmins, we will be treated like Shudras. Her emphasis ended at the tip of her finger, stiff and straight, as if asking: now, how do you like this reversal of roles? Four, the little finger trying to stand on tiptoe so as not to be dwarfed by its neighbours, the police and the politicians (and the rowdies, don't you think, she added coyly) are not Brahmins, they hate Brahmins, what have we done to them, and so they will never help us in anything. Thus leaving behind only the four of us to fend for ourselves. Justice and law are like this.

Oh, and wait, yes, the thumb, squealing and running to catch up, the upright thumb: five (the thumb a fist now, a caricature of a bent nose soon after), we live in Mathikere Extension. We live at a time when Bangalore is changing rapidly. At a time when its gardens are becoming garbage mounds and its casual life is being replaced by impatient, angry, exhaust-spewing vehicles in their hundreds, soon to be in thousands. At a time when all of us living in Bangalore with jobs or small businesses will have to find other places to live because it will no longer be affordable. All these times. And more. All these reasons enough to guarantee that no law exists, no justice can be expected. Reason enough to think of Rajesh and his friends from Bihar who smuggle guns. Reason enough to give in to the temptation of taking the law into one's own hands.

'This is not Bihar,' Raghavendra tried to explain, after they had washed their hands and moved to the office room. The girls stood near the door, waiting for their mother to send them back to sleep. The rain fell steadily, evoking kerosene-lit images of bullock cart rides through the streets of Udupi. *How long ago that was*!

'Because it is not Bihar, we cannot go around getting our friends to beat up Nagaraj. He will then get the police or his own goondas, and then what do I do? I have a wife, two children . . . '

'Wife and children!' Poornima was irritated. 'If we are so important, you shouldn't have allowed Nagaraj into the house, and not started whatever you have started now. Not a single rupee the last month!'

As if on cue, Raghavendra looked at his children. Suhasini knew it was coming. She had turned her face away to look at the rivulets of brown water which flowed, swirled and caressed the little pebbles on the street.

'This is the only way, Uncle,' said Rajesh. He tried speaking in Hindi and English with happy smiles at Poornima in between. Reassuring her, not through language but through these smiles. And when he smiled, his muscles tightened under his T-shirt. 'I will make sure Nagaraj doesn't do anything else. We will threaten him so badly . . . '

Raghavendra was suddenly afraid that Rajesh would do what he was offering to. He immediately said, 'No, no, Rajesh. Don't do anything unless I tell you to.'

Poornima took the girls inside. To their beds, to lie under snuggling, companionable covers. She lit a new candle and led the way. The girls followed, in line, one step behind another. Left, right, left, right. Left turn. The beds were in a corner of the hall, next to the puja room. The two girls slept with the snoring smells of the incense sticks and the flickering flame from the lamp in the puja room that vainly tried to stay awake through the night.

Poornima walked back, her palms scraping the walls for support. Rajesh was standing at the main door. Seeing her, he said, 'Auntie, lock your door tight.' Establishing an adult relationship with her, saying we can't trust your husband, nice husband, to do these things. The rain had finally died down, had become a sound wrapped into a whisper. Rajesh peeped out of the door, looked up and down the street. There was nothing to be seen. The dark clouds were breaking up. The road had dissolved into more holes. Suddenly, some birds twittered in the night. The lights still lay silent.

Rajesh skipped up the stairs, peered into Bhaskar's room through the open window. Bhaskar was hard at work in front of his laptop, as always. Trying to save the world from the impending Y2K disaster, a disaster apparently just a few months away. For Bhaskar, the whole world was moving into a disaster zone. He had been drawn deeply into the world of cryptography and coding, and was beginning to look at everything suspiciously. He felt that the Y2K problem was only a foreboding of things to come, not just in Bangalore but in the whole world. He was convinced of this, and had even told his parents that he would only think of marriage after a year—if the world survived! These stories of forthcoming disasters were the only distractions from the common obsession of all his co-workers: buying a flat in Bangalore before the prices shot up. Everybody who was working in software seemed to be driven by two goals, one to go to the US and the other to buy a flat in Bangalore. Bhaskar's father, when he heard about these goals, had only this to say to him: 'I bought a flat in Madurai from my retirement money. What is the hurry for all of you?'

But Rajesh had none of these worries. Not for somebody who had grown up on the banks of the Ganga, and who dealt with dacoits as an everyday pastime. Rajesh, the daring saviour of the Indian Empire, got ready for bed with a couple of pull-ups and exercises. This is the way we are, his body would have said if it could speak, if it had not mortgaged his mouth to his mind.

It was close to twelve when Raghavendra went to bed. Poornima had come to lie down, but then suddenly got up and went around with the candle to make sure that all the doors had been locked. He heard her shuffling footsteps. He heard them through the ground, the bed and the pillow. The muffled sound gave a different message to him. *I am coming to you . . .*

She came back, extinguished the flame of the candle with a swish of her palm and lay down. She smelt of cooking, of the stone smell of the kitchen. The flowers in her hair drooped, and their smell wafted limply to him.

Raghavendra's hands itched to reach out and cover her. Without his spectacles, she was a haze, a bundle of cotton piled close to him. He could feel the ends of her irritated hair and stayed silent.

'Listen to me. If Nagaraj doesn't leave, I am going to move the kitchen to that office. I'll cook there, wash my vessels, and eat on the floor there. If you can't throw him out, I will.'

Suddenly perturbed, Raghavendra said, 'I'll do it, Poorni. I told you. I will do it my way.'

'And what is that way? You'll smile at him, remove your glasses and twiddle them in your hands, embarrassed as if you are in the wrong. You will be apologetic and . . . '

'Enough, Poornima. I told you I will handle it.' *But this is the way I am, I can't bring myself to start a confrontation.*

'I have seen your handling.' Poornima was brusque. 'I heard him tonight. Remember what he said when you told him about your grocery store?'

'We can't go down to his level.' His hand gently fell across her chest. 'We will do what we want.'

She moved, making his palm fit more snugly. 'What we want is a grocery store. You know Venkatappa has already promised to send you groceries that he gets from the village. Look at the rice he has sent. One whole bag. He says it's the best rice he has eaten in years. And what about that toor dal he gave us last year? Even you, even with your indifference to taste, even you said that it was the best you'd had in years. Think of it. We can have a special shop. Our groceries will be the tastiest.' She turned on her side, letting his palm slide down her back. A thin layer of sweat lubricated his palm as it moved. *What a woman!*

'You are right, Poorni.' His breath, in a fit of passion, rushed towards the curve of her neck. The words, in an embrace, gathered around her neck, formed a necklace that dipped into her bosom. Tickled, she giggled. The laugh of an older woman, which lit the dark room in flashes.

He said, 'You are . . . right. We will start our store tomorrow itself. We can call it Poornima Grocery Store.'

Poornima turned away. His hand got entangled in her blouse, his fingers fleshy hooks holding it together. 'I told you before and I will tell you again, I don't want you to name the shop after me. After I am dead, you do what you want.'

The desired effect was quick in coming. Raghavendra's fingers closed on themselves. 'Don't be a fool. Why talk of death? Okay. We will call it something else.'

All forgiven and forgotten, she slid up to him and lay close in an embrace. How much of a woman she had to be! Part lost as a mother, part as a wife in charge of the house, leaving just that little bit for a tiny hug. *But when you are this old, what does it matter?*

Still . . . Raghavendra's hand got lost inside her blouse as she said, 'Remove that board tomorrow. Give it back to him. Break it on his head.' He moved his fingers, and her giggle suddenly splattered into an idea. She removed his hand and said, 'I know what we should do. Let's name the shop Sri Krishna Provision Stores.'

Raghavendra, in his urgency, agreed immediately. Why not? It was after all apt that they should name the shop after the presiding deity of Udupi. His father would have been happy. It was far better than Raagu Detective Agency. And surely his favourite god Krishna would help them against the competition from the many small grocery shops all around them!

How much easier life would have been if Archana had not died that night. Raghavendra would have inaugurated his provision store. Poornima would have taken care of the accounts, the two girls would have sat in the shop with books in their hands and eyes perked up to listen to the customers. Rajesh would have strutted around, made all his friends buy their groceries from this shop, though he himself would never buy anything on credit—his father had firmly advised him that credit was not for dignified people. Nagaraj would have been banished to the Mathikere underworld where he would spend his days sleeping and nights in roving autorickshaws.

Instead.

3

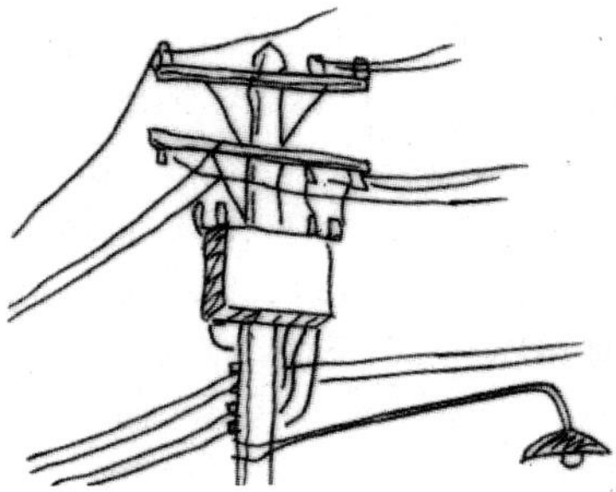

THE NEXT DAY WAS A 'WATER DAY'. DRINKING WATER IN that area was supposed to be supplied every day from public taps that were distributed across the locality. But there would be water flow in the taps only early in the morning. Most times, water would be sent on alternate days, although that never stopped expectant queues forming in front of the taps every day. At 3 a.m., the streets of Mathikere Extension were transformed into ghostly lines of sleepy, drooping bodies around every public tap. Sometimes the water came at four, and people would wait patiently, twisting and untwisting the taps periodically, in the hope of getting a faint stream of water.

Bangalore had grown chaotically. The urban chaos above the ground had transformed into dry lands underground, with the groundwater becoming lesss day by day. Almost every bit of land had a borewell drilled into it. Initially, water could be found after a few hundred metres of drilling but not anymore. In some places, it had gone past 1,000 feet. A new set of entrepreneurs arose around these taps: water diviners, those who rented borewell trucks, mechanics' shops to repair and sell parts, hardware stores that suddenly had a supply of fancy taps (ironic, these fancy taps for pipes that carried little or no water) from Ghaziabad and plastic taps from Gujarat.

Water for Bangalore came from the Cauvery River, and Bangaloreans spoke with pride about this relationship. The Cauvery was a holy river in its own way, although minor in comparison to the holiness of the Ganga. The river was quite far away from Bangalore, and water had to be pumped through huge pipes from a dam near Mysore. Localities in Mysore close to the dam did not get water, but the powers in Bangalore never seemed to be concerned about this anomaly. It was the same with electricity, which came from a hydroelectric plant far away. It supplied electricity to the city while villages and towns near the power plant went without electricity for several hours each day. Bangalore was already becoming alienated from every other place in Karnataka. It was fast becoming the place that sucked water and power from other parts of the state. As the capital, political power had become centralised within the city, exemplified by the majestic legislative house, Vidhana Soudha. The city was fast growing out of its perceived traditional boundaries. It was already becoming famous as the booze capital of the country, with claims of making the best beer. Now, it had become the face of the country with its own version of the gold rush: the IT industry, which would soon transform the city into a shadow of what it had once been.

Mari seemed to be the only one in Mathikere Extension who had anticipated all this and more. He had begun asking anybody who bothered to listen to him: 'Where is your water going to come from? What is going to happen when the apartments come?' And the apartments would come, even in the crowded lanes of this locality. The Reddy Brothers used two garages for their office, and their tables had a scattering of models of high-rise apartments. Some of them looked like they were made of plastic and bought off the pavements outside the railway station. They symbolised the vision of these ever-warring brothers, who seemed confident that Bangalore was going to grow like Mumbai. There were already calls for changing the name of Bangalore to Bengaluru, just as Bombay had become Mumbai earlier. The brothers knew that even small-sized plots would be converted into multi-storey apartments with flats that squeezed light and space out of one another. The Reddy Brothers promised to transform Mathikere Extension into a network of apartment buildings. All they had to do was convince the owners of those plots of land to sell their land to them.

Pumping water to Bangalore through huge pipes was not an efficient way to distribute it. Some of the water was lost through leakage in the pipes; some of it was pilfered by villagers who found ways to tap into the flow. Water reached the southern part of Bangalore first, and then worked its way up north. Mathikere Extension was in the northern part, and once upon a recent time, was the northernmost part of the city. By the time the water reached there, the flow would have normally reduced to a trickle. The best time to 'catch' water at Mathikere Extension was around three in the morning. Poornima had once observed that any calendar originating in Bangalore would have to be based not on the solar or lunar cycle but on the water cycle of the Bangalore Water, Sanitary and Sewage Board. The acronym BWSSB was enough to raise the blood pressure of people in Bangalore.

The need to store drinking water meant that somebody in the family had to get up that early. Poornima used to do it earlier, when Raghavendra was working at Paul's Security Firm. But after he left the job, he had offered to take on this responsibility. 'What if I lose sleep?' he said with a flourish. 'I can afford to sleep in the afternoons.' As if being an entrepreneur *necessarily* implied having the freedom to have an afternoon snooze.

It had not always been that way. Five or six years before, they used to get water all through the day. On the days it didn't come, the well water was a sweet substitute. But with more buildings and borewells, the level in the wells had fallen. Now it would fill up only when the rains came in plenty, but the water always looked suspiciously green. Down in the bowels of the land, sewage and water had mixed together into one common government department—BWSSB.

Inevitably, the change in the water timings also introduced changes in lifestyle. The foremost being the introduction of the alarm clock, which Raghavendra bought on BVK Iyengar Road. Never before had Poornima got up to the sound of a machine, however small. Her waking moment was an alarm in itself—suddenly she would pop up, invariably at half past five in the morning. But after three years of waking to the sound of the new clock, she had lost her internal rhythm. Her time had coiled into the eighty-rupee clock. The clock soon found its own rhythm: irrespective of the time the alarm was set for, it would, of its own accord, ring at 3 a.m.

The alarm had also been the initiator of technological change in their home. Their old wall clock from Udupi, so lovingly polished by Raghavendra's father, had needed an overhaul. When it stopped ticking, Raghavendra took it as an excuse to make a trip to BVK Iyengar Road, where time could still be bought and sold at wholesale prices. He found no one who dared to repair that old clock, so he bought the alarm clock instead. The battery price was extra but his persistent bargaining got him the batteries for free. He never said it aloud, but he knew that the alarm itself was a free bargain for time.

Now Poornima wanted to buy a washing machine. She told her husband, 'Once you have an alarm clock in the house, why not a washing machine?'

That night, Raghavendra was up before the alarm, woken by the sound of water flowing in his neighbour's house. Swiftly he got up and went to the kitchen. He took a big steel vessel and tiptoed his way to the door. As he opened it, the first of the dogs stirred and ran past the house. The rain had vaporised into a cool mist that formed shapes around the tube lights on the road. The road itself looked as if bathed in a fine spray of milk.

The tap was at the side of the house, the side that adjoined Baale Gowda's. There was a barbed wire mesh separating the two houses. Baale Gowda had bought his house a few years after Haridas had built his. He was a schoolteacher, and his wealth came from his father's banana and paddy farms near Shimoga. This was the story he told people whenever he wanted to make himself interesting: I was born in the shade of a plantain tree and so my mother called me Chikka Baale—little plantain. Chikka had dropped off after marriage, and Gowda, the caste name, had taken its rightful place.

Baale Gowda had no corporation tap in his house. When he had seen the tap in Raghavendra's house, he had decided that one tap would do for both of them. There had been no barbed wire between the two houses initially. Gowda had told Raghavendra that he would collect water, 'a little drinking only', for a few days till his own tap was fixed. The few days had become many years. Early on, he had connected a water pipe from the tap to his house to catch water at his leisure. Poornima put a stop to that. She removed the pipe and threw it back on Gowda's land. She then got the local hardware boy to fix a length of barbed wire between the two houses.

The tap still did not materialise in Gowda's house. Gowda talked to Raghavendra, man to man, and confessed that the corporation refused to give him a tap. He offered no reasons, but added that denying water to a family was the most inconceivable sin a man could commit. Raghavendra responded immediately, not because of the reference to sin. He cut a piece of the fence. Gowda had to contort himself to enter, while his wife just about made it through. Poornima was irritated, but Raghavendra said, 'After all, we don't pay the corporation for water, so why be selfish?'

And now: the corporation was threatening to fix metres in all the houses in the locality (as they had been threatening to do all these years), dried red bougainvillaea covered the fence, and Gowda's wife shared the water-collecting chores along with Poornima. They were barely civil to each other and on festival days, only a touch friendly.

That morning, when Raghavendra went to the tap, he saw Gowda's wife filling water. The few times he had collected water, it had always been before her. The moment she realised it was Raghavendra, she covered her head with her sari, as if it was through the head that a man spies on a woman. She ignored him and stood sullenly staring at the flowing water. The water pressure was low, and it took an inordinate time for her vessel to be filled. Raghavendra looked at the stars lying at rest on a few cloud-beds as the water trickled in leisurely. After her vessel was filled, she tightened the tap more than required and hurried through the gap in the fence. A thorn in the barbed wire caught and pulled her sari off her head. It fell across her shoulders and came to rest on her oscillating chest. She walked faster, the water spilling on her blouse, but all that Raghavendra could see, even as he tried to open the tap, was her broad back, shaped by a pot of water on her hips going slosh, slosh.

As the water began collecting in his vessel, the alarm went off inside the house. As soon as it began, it stopped, slapped into silence. He knew Poornima would be angry. 'What is the point,' she would ask, 'if you are going to wake me up also? I may as well get the water.'

The light in Gowda's house suddenly vanished with a speed that told him Gowda's wife had transferred her irritation to the light switch.

As he bent down to peer at the level of water in the vessel, another dog swiftly ran by. He looked up, following its footsteps in the milky mist. Through the mist he could see, clearly now, with no ambiguity, two silhouettes rushing along the main street. They turned and vanished onto a side road. Two dog shapes followed them. Raghavendra stood staring, wondering about people who hurried in the early dawn. They could not be thieves, for no thief dared break in after 3 a.m., thanks to the timing of the water supply. He suddenly saw the water overflowing and running towards his feet, a horde of little child-drops rushing to embrace him. As he shut off the tap, he thought he heard voices, a shout, a wailing cry. He lifted the vessel with both his hands, the fingers bearing the weight, and shuffled towards his house.

Mrs Gowda, for this was the name she preferred to be called by, not Malini, not Gowri, not any of those many names whispered into her ears during her naming ceremony, woke her husband. Her blouse was wet and she was sweating a little, hesitant droplets forming on her forehead. At the right angle, Baale could imagine seeing rainbows in them.

'This is the last time I am getting water in the morning.' Baale heard one in three words, the other two lost in the rhythm of his sleep. When he didn't respond positively, she poked him in the ribs. He swotted her hand away and turned on his side. Furious, she pinched his inner thigh. His dhoti had come loose in the night, and he was sleeping in his underwear.

Baale jerked awake, her words crowding him. 'No, never again. Not while that man comes and stands there looking at me as if I am a beggar begging for his water. And how is it *his* water? It's ours, all of ours. Imagine! Three in the morning and I have to see his owl's eyes, the blind old fool, staring at me with a smirk, thinking god only knows what!'

Baale was astounded. 'What? Raghavendra you are talking about? Did he say or do anything to you? Wait, doesn't his wife collect the water?'

'Used to. Now it's all modern, I think. He is a man who listens and cares for his wife. I will not collect water anymore. You go the next time. Oh! What a terrible fellow he is!'

'I can't get up, Malini, every day at three. I have to go to work full day.'

'I take care of your house, your son—that fellow never listens to me—and this also? No.' She waded into the bathroom to change her blouse, and in the sound of a bolt, Baale had gone back to sleep.

The whistle of the pressure cooker woke Poornima. The sound entered her kitchen and then her bedroom—hesitantly, as if sounds had their own unique places. She got up, looking at the dark room through the strands of her hair. Another whistle shot out, bouncing from one room to another. The houses here were bound into a locality by the sounds intruding from one kitchen into another. The sound came from Bhat's place. Bhat left for work at seven in the morning but wanted a proper meal to be cooked before he left.

Raghavendra was on his stomach, his body collapsed into a plastic amoeba. She saw the holes in his banian, and was reminded that she had planned to buy a few banians and underwear for him. *How easily banians get holes these days!*

She picked up the milk coupons and opened the door of her house. The promise of yet another dawn had arrived; there was already a small queue outside the milkman's house. George was not strictly a milkman, merely a vendor for the Karnataka Milk Federation, which sold milk and milk products. Milk packets would be offloaded near his house around four in the morning, and at five he was ready for business.

Poornima stepped out into a puddle of water. The rainwater had flowed past their house into the low-lying areas, leaving little islands of mud in front of the houses like an offering. As she opened the gates, she heard someone calling her name. She turned towards the voice, and her foot strayed into a puddle. Mud in the guise of liquid massaged her ankles, and she hurriedly lifted her leg. Suddenly, unaccountably, she remembered Nagaraj and the drama the night before. *Just last night!*

The voice that had hailed her was already lost amidst a small group that had gathered around. *Gossip at this time of the day?* Poornima would have not a syllable of it. She crossed the road to George's house. It was his wife, Josephine, who was handing out the milk packets. Raghavendra had expressed shock (so predictable and routine these days) that milk cost ten rupees a litre. Before he could go on further, Poornima had snapped, 'Now don't start on how much it cost fifty years before. Anyway, milk is so much cheaper than vegetables now. Your father should never have left Udupi.'

How far off the mark she was! Udupi was no longer the rustic town she imagined it to be. Vegetables were costlier; the weather had become drier. Udupi was now another bustling memory of a village.

She handed her coupons to Josephine, big and matronly, who sat on a stool in her nightdress. She had a smile for those whom she considered worthy of it. Others received a frown, especially when the rupee notes they gave her were torn or soiled beyond recognition. 'What is this,' she would say, waving a crumpled two-rupee note, the colour having become an oily blackish red. 'What is this, I say, is this money, is this a note you expect me to take?' Her Kannada would lilt, would dance with the accent of

Malayalam, and the high notes in her voice would be held by her two fingernails.

Everybody in the locality accepted Josephine's hold over them. It was far easier to be acquiescent than respond to her comments. A smart retort had often found its owner going back without milk.

But that day, Josephine beckoned Poornima closer. She took her coupons, gave her the milk and said, 'You know what happened last night? No, no, early morning today?'

Poornima shook her head, the chill of the packet numbing her thoughts.

'Archana, you know, the carpenter's daughter, died this morning.'

Poornima was generally of a calm disposition and shocks were but little tremors smoothed out with calm thoughts. But this early morning message shook her.

'What did you say?'

'That girl, the carpenter's daughter, you know . . . '

Poornima turned back, her thoughts still lethargic, unable to go beyond the lilt (*was it too gleeful?*) in Josephine's voice. Had she heard right? Archana, sixteen, magic teenage sixteen, healthy and vibrant, gone in the wake of a confused accent and stumbling words in Kannada. Even as the words tripped one over the other, they seemed to say: wish we were all words in Malayalam instead.

Poornima turned back to Josephine, pushed her way past two little girls who had elbowed their way forward in the meantime, clutching their coupons tightly in their hands, palms spread out in hope, waiting for Josephine to snatch them, and asked her, 'How did she go?' As if death was yet another journey that Archana had gone on.

Josephine was happy to have caught Poornima's attention. She embraced her curiosity with an all-knowing smile. She leaned close to Poornima, sheltered her words with the cup of her palm and whispered, 'Girls these days. Come with a wail and gone in a puff.' Her gaze swept past the little girls with coupons in their hands and knocked on Poornima's door knowing that there were two girls sleeping inside. 'You should be careful of girls growing up these days.'

'How?' Poornima asked, sheltering the two girls from malice.

'How? Accident, it seems. Or so they say.'

Poornima turned to leave. But Josephine was not done as yet.

'So they say. But if you ask me, and the others too, they would say it was suicide.'

Josephine's fat cat came out and purred at the two girls. A queue had already formed, not in a single file, but horizontally. Hands jutted out into any space available, some with coupons, some with soiled notes, some just stretched out in vain. At the mention of suicide, the word clearly enunciated, the fingers twitched and glanced at one another: Suicide! Where?

Poornima hurried back home. Before she opened the gate, she glanced towards the street where Archana lived. The streetlights had just gone off, leaving the early morning light in diffused patches. She thought she saw a group of people standing at the junction of the street. A few dogs lay there, waiting for titbits of attention. Or at least a kick, if not a stone.

Raghavendra stirred in his sleep, his early morning dreams leaking out through the many holes in his banian. Poornima placed the milk on the stove, went to Raghavendra and nudged him. He was up in an instant, his right hand grabbing a fistful of air, ready to defend his family at a moment's notice.

'What?' he asked, seeing Poornima. 'What is the time?' His hand groped towards the alarm clock, squinted eyes showing the way.

'Get up. It's already late.' Poornima would wait for him to have his coffee before telling him about Archana. *You cannot wake somebody up with bad news.*

Raghavendra should have known something was wrong the moment she hurriedly gave him his spectacles. She pushed him towards the bathroom while she went to make some coffee. Coffee had become so expensive that the two of them had it only in the morning. They had switched to tea in the afternoon and to anyone who asked they would both say, 'Tea is good for the body. We drink coffee only once.' Making a virtue out of an economic molehill. But tea too had risen in price, even as the daily papers showed a percentage fall in inflation. Poornima's strongest political comment thus far had been: 'We even had our own prime minister, a Gowda who should have known the importance of coffee for us, but did the coffee prices come down? No. Now we have a North Indian fellow, and does the tea get cheaper? No.'

By the time Raghavendra came out of the bathroom, the coffee had filtered in tiny drops into the brass filter, one of the few remnants of Haridas and Udupi. She waited for him to finish his coffee. The Kannada newspaper would be delivered close to seven, so she had his attention till then.

'Are the girls up?' he asked, looking around, as if they slept and woke to his questions.

'Time is there. You know what I heard this morning? It seems that the carpenter's daughter, the second one, Archana . . . '

He stared at her, trying to remember if he knew the girl.

'It seems she had an accident last night.'

'Accident? Scooter? Or is it the autos? How many times I have . . . '

'No. At home. Something happened. She is dead.'

'Dead?'

'It seems.'

'What do you mean, it seems? Is she really dead?'

'That is why I woke you up. Why don't you go and find out?'

'Go there? How can I?' He didn't say it, but Poornima knew what he was thinking: early mornings are for life, not death.

Suddenly awake, he added, 'Accident, you said. What accident?'

'I don't know.' He had rarely seen Poornima so anguished.

He decided to go and find out about the girl. He tightened his dhoti, cleaned his spectacles, and put on a shirt. *Not that shirt again.* But Poornima kept quiet.

The news spread rapidly. Hesitant men walked softly to the end of 6th Cross. They had been woken and dispatched. More assertive women joined the shuffling horde, but they walked faster and with purpose. They were going to share in the grief, while the men looked on from the edges of a newsworthy event.

There was a hunchbacked crowd in front of Prasanna's house. Prasanna had flourished as a carpenter. His gate, made of pure teak, first grade, and carved to look like it, bore testimony to this. Raghavendra stopped at the end of the street and stared at the little water rivulets under his feet. The clouds had filled up again, and in their darkness flashed a message. *Not more rain, please.* Raghavendra hated flooded roads the most.

A shadow of a cry suddenly fell at his feet. He looked up, and the crowd near the gate moved. He turned around, his feet striking his neighbour's. Chandru was standing close by with a toothbrush in his mouth. The foam from the toothpaste made his mouth bulge unnaturally. They were both standing near the open garbage bin. The rain had uprooted the garbage and left it open to the skies. Chandru aimed his spit at the bin. A streak of his foamy spit hit the rim and flowed down the sides of the concrete bin.

'What is this?' he addressed Raghavendra. 'Early morning and everybody is out. Can't even let a little girl die in peace?' When he saw Raghavendra, Chandru was inspired to aggression.

Prasanna's assistant, a thin boy from Calicut, walked past them. Chandru caught his hand, removed the brush from his mouth with the other, spat again and said, 'Hey, so what happened?'

The boy would have pushed Chandru's hands away and walked on. But he knew that with the locals, it paid to be polite.

'Master's daughter, sir, younger one, she died.' His voice reflected his genuine sorrow.

'How did that happen?' A few more middle-aged men had gathered around. Raghavendra moved to the periphery, away from that circle but within listening distance.

'By accident. She drank something.'

'What something?'

'Rat poison, sir. I have to go now.'

'How can anybody drink rat poison by mistake?' Chandru bit down more firmly on the toothbrush. *These brushes are not worth the 4.50 you pay for them.*

'How do I know? By accident she drank it.' The boy found a gap in Chandru's thoughts and hurried away.

Chandru turned to Raghavendra. 'How can you drink rat poison by accident? Unless you are a rat, of course.'

Raghavendra walked away. He wanted no part of the Q&A session. His thoughts were on that poor girl. *How she must have suffered.*

Chandru was not done. He caught up with Raghavendra, and said in a tone that made it clear that this was all he had wanted to say, right from the beginning, 'Girls. This is what happens if you have girls, teenage girls, growing up girls. These days, I pity any man who has a girl.' He paused, turned Raghavendra so that they were face to face and continued, 'Pity if a man has two girls.' He released him, half pushing him away, and went back to chewing his brush near the open dustbin. Even the dogs stayed away from the wet bin that morning.

By nine, stray thoughts of sunlight escaped through the clouds. Almost all the shops were open. The noise level on the main road had reached its usual constant hum. Cart vendors selling vegetables, flowers and tender coconuts were already at the end of their early morning routes. In an hour or so most of them would go back to other occupations, hopefully having sold most of their produce.

Rajesh left for college at eight with rolled-up sleeves and in a blue lab uniform, blissfully unaware of Archana's death. Bhaskar had gone quietly, his departure a gentle purr of his new motorbike. Raghavendra had watched him leave from the window, reminded once again that he should ask him to use a helmet. Poornima heated a vessel of water for his bath on the kerosene stove. Their old geyser, she was convinced, had increased their electricity costs. Poornima had her bath with cold water and used to tell Raghavendra often, 'Why you can't bathe in cold water, I don't know.' But Raghavendra knew; the very possibility of a head cold made him boil the water and have a hot bath. Only once had Poornima said, 'You think kerosene is cheap? Get rid of that old geyser and buy a new one.' Thus, a geyser had been added to the list of things to be bought. *It started with that little alarm clock and who knows where it will end*!

That day was special for one more reason: Poornima refused to make breakfast for Raghavendra. 'You want breakfast? When that girl lies cold and dead?'

Raghavendra answered, his usual unruffled self, 'I too feel bad, no, very bad, that she is dead. But we cannot stop living because of that.'

'Who is asking you to stop living? I am just telling you that I cannot cook any tiffin for you this morning.'

What had got into her that she was so upset? Had the asthma of death entered her spirit?

She added, 'Even for my children, I am not making tiffin.'

The two girls had been woken, bundled into the bathroom, and one after the other they had come out with smiles of powder and stick-on bindis on their foreheads. They wore their ironed uniforms, green skirt and white blouse, and sat in the office room, dutifully staring at their books before they left for school.

'Poorni, you are making something big out of nothing.' His voice was a whisper. 'Do they know?'

'No, they don't. They will find out soon. Why disturb their studies?'

'You think they are studying?' he asked, just a moment before two sudden giggles, intertwined and echoing each other, raced past their ears.

'Anyway, you can eat bread if you want.'

'Bread!' Raghavendra was horrified, his tongue morphing into a malleable plastic spoon as he said, 'Bread? Not for me. Who eats bread in the morning? You are also becoming one of these fashionable people?'

'Fashion, what fashion? The children love it. You can have the bread with pickle.'

'I can eat idli at Ganesh Darshini,' he replied, provoked into finding an excuse to visit the new restaurant.

'You can. You can waste your money there. But remember when you eat, that little girl, dead and cold.'

Raghavendra, suddenly furious, walked out to the office room. The girls sat in the midst of their own tossing thoughts. He looked at them and went back. Poornima was in the kitchen opening a packet of bread.

'I'll take the girls to school today,' he said, looking at the bread, dull brown and like pieces of cardboard.

Poornima was noncommittal. 'Do you want this?' she asked, her hand moving towards the bottle of lemon pickle.

He gave in with a cynical murmur, 'You don't even make pickles at home.' The complaint was spread ferociously by Poornima on the slice of bread before she thrust it at him.

Raghavendra changed into a pair of pants—*oh no, not those pants again*—and a newly washed shirt that hung over his hips like a cylindrical veil, and took the two girls to school. The girls walked on either side of him, one hand holding Raghavendra's and the other carrying a small lunch basket (identical, plastic and blue in colour) with a bottle of water. He carried the two school bags on his shoulders and they walked, occupying the middle of the road. The school was merely 200 metres away, and within a few metres they saw other children walking along. Raghavendra's two girls grinned, although they were embarrassed that their father was herding them along. At the gates, he nudged them inside and turned away. Suhasini shouted, 'Appa, our bags!' The watchman looked at him with a smile, a few children laughed, and his own daughters joined them. Awkward Raghavendra, always forgetful—that is what they would have said, if they had learnt by then to pass such judgements on fathers.

He went to the market from the school. As he was walking back to his house, he passed Durga Tea Stall where Soumitro called out to him. Raghavendra, a revolt rising from the embers of his rebellion, of his threat to eat idlis at Ganesh Darshini, converted that wish into a command. He entered the small teashop, saw the tea boiling on the kerosene stove and said, 'I will have one tea.' After a pause, he added, 'Today.' Each word was important. For they conveyed to Soumitro that 'today' was an exception; it was not good for a married man like Raghavendra to have tea outside his house. It meant his wife was sleeping late or had refused to make him tea. Or worse, was 'out of house'.

Soumitro knew best. He knew why every single local resident came to have tea in his place. Depending on the time they came or the first words they uttered, he could guess at the marital situation. A litmus test through the tea filter.

'Do you want mixture also? Very good, very fresh.'

Raghavendra stared at the spicy mixture, a collection of round and oval bits. The oil they sweated coated the big aluminium vessel. Stray pieces of groundnut winked like drunken eyes. No mixture, he wanted to say, but a sudden flow of saliva silenced the words. He nodded vaguely, looking at the tea which continued to boil. It had become mud red in colour, seeing which Soumitro added some more milk and heaps of sugar.

Raghavendra knew he would be drinking not tea but sugar water. But nobody dared complain: Soumitro was originally from Bengal!

'We invented tea, we know best how to make tea,' he had said many times before. Even though anybody with working taste buds would know never to boil tea, that too for hours. Being from Bengal also meant that he spoke with an accent which made it very difficult to have a conversation. Soumitro had learnt to speak Kannada, but it was recognisable as such only once in a few lines. His smile below the pencil-thin moustache filled in the rest.

The mixture was quite tasty. *How did a Bengali learn to make spicy food?*

'You bought it where?' Raghavendra dared to ask.

'Bought? I make it. All by myself. I never buy. Good quality oil, good quality provisions.'

The mention of provisions reminded Raghavendra of Venkatappa. He would have to meet him soon to order groceries.

'For a Bengali, you make a good mixture.'

'I also make good sweets. But you Kannadigas don't know how to enjoy them.'

How true. Soumitro the Bengali, an alien in Mathikere Extension. Who got wild when people called him Mitra or even Soumitra. It had to be Soumitro, he would say, Soumitro, see, O at the end? His whole face would look like an O when he was done saying that. Raghavendra was tempted to tell him about the sweets his family used to make in Udupi. But he was becoming a little self-conscious about invoking Udupi too often. After all, his father had left the place so long ago. He also realised that Bangalore was changing rapidly. It was becoming more difficult to speak in Kannada. The vegetable vendors were Tamilians, the bakeries were run by Malayalis, the cooks were Bengalis and Odiyas, and many shopkeepers were Telugu. It was as if each day foisted a new linguistic community on Bangalore. His own daughters now preferred to have samosas and masala puri from the roadside carts. He tried to tell them that 'our' food was more healthy and tastier than these dishes that his daughters craved. Poornima had not only sided with her daughters, but would also get samosas home for them once in a while. She too was finding a new sense of freedom through these new tastes.

Like the country, the city itself had become demarcated into colonies of people who spoke and ate alike. He had never been to Indira Nagar, but had been told by Paul that Bengalis and Malayalis had taken over that locality. The Bengalis there were richer and more sophisticated, he was told. One of his colleagues in Paul's office had added: 'It is dangerous to speak in Kannada there, can you imagine!' Yes, Raghavendra could imagine that and more. He knew it was just a matter of time before hordes of people from all over India entered Bangalore. Soumitro had once hinted at a secret revolution where Bangalore would be inundated with Bengalis and Biharis. Soumitro had no hesitation in adding, 'Perhaps then these Kannadigas will finally learn to appreciate the great sweets of Bengal.' He had already begun to think of a board in red and white, like the famous K.C. Das sweet shop near MG Road, which even people in Mathikere Extension seemed to know.

Poornima decided to make a hot lunch. Rice, saaru and vegetable. The curd had set, and sat patiently now under a blanket of thin cream. Seeing the curd, she was reminded of pickles, and of Raghavendra's comment on buying pickles. *With the cost of things nowadays, does he think it is cheaper to make pickles at home? He can talk of taste, but he should think he is lucky to get what he does.*

She walked to the grocery store a few houses away. It was generically called the Malayali Shop. It seemed as if there were four owners and at least six assistants even though the shop was small. When there were no customers, the assistants would all choose a sack to sit on. Ahmed on the toor dal, Basha on chana dal, Imran on ragi. The assistant who sat on the sack containing the costliest rice was the favoured helper of the day.

Poornima wanted to buy mustard, red chillies and sugar. Even as she made her way to the shop, her steps had become a larger list, starting with mustard and ending with oil.

By the time she began listing out her needs to Ahmed, she had added onions to it. Small onions with shoots, amassed behind a metal mesh. Space enough to breathe but not to roll.

'How much is it?' she asked.

'Twenty rupees.'

'Twenty? What do you mean twenty?'

'For you it is twenty. Outside it is twenty-five, do you know that?'

Ahmed and his selling ways. He continued, 'Rains have spoiled the crop in Maharashtra.' Pause. 'It seems.'

It seems. Everything, always: it seems. Reality mortgaged, not into illusions, but into endless seemingness.

'How much is that Flora packet?'

Ahmed made a show of reading the MRP printed on the back of the oil sachet. He knew the price well.

'Says here it is forty-eight rupees. For you, fifty paise less.'

'And the mustard? It is clean?'

'Clean? It is cleaner than . . . ' Ahmed was lost. Nothing was clean these days. 'We only sell clean stuff, you know that.'

Basha started measuring out sugar from the sack. The dampness in the air had entered the granules.

'What kind of sugar do you people give?'

Ahmed grinned, his sweet smile shading her annoyance. *These Malayalis, they can sell a cockroach to a vegetarian housewife.*

'See how much I am buying from you. Don't give me the usual price. Give some discount.'

Ahmed made a big show of totalling the costs. Showed her a figure. 'Now I cut three rupees from this.' His flourish could have done with applause, but Poornima was watching the scales on which Basha was measuring red chillies.

Ahmed suddenly leaned closer and said, 'You heard about the girl?' A line that involuted on itself and came out as a dramatic whisper. His eyes, youthfully sad, remembered Archana and her constant visits to his shop. How often she had leaned over the bottles of chocolates and biscuits, her little breasts crushing their covers, sucking the sweetness from them. How she would smile and how she would flirt! So harmless, so innocent, so much a creature of her age. Ahmed, with his sweet smile and twitching strands of hair on his face, how he had dreamt!

'Such a tragedy,' he said, drawing Poornima's eyes away from the scale. She stared back at him, felt his sorrow entering her throat, and swallowed. As Basha poured the red chillies with a flourish into a newspaper cone he had made, its dust rose and they all sneezed. Ahmed had tears in his eyes, tears that seemed to have been waiting for an excuse to escape.

'Yes, such a . . . ' She stopped. Such a what? 'These are god's ways.'

'Which god's ways that a little girl is killed for no fault of her own?' Ahmed moved to a corner, hiding his body behind the counter of glass jars. She followed him, moving parallel and staying outside the shop.

'Killed! She was killed?'

'Of course.' What a funny lilt he too had. A Malayali who spoke both Malayalam and Urdu, and who spoke in Kannada to Poornima. The final syllables of his words trailed off in a coastal vapour, making it seem as if the whole country had been partitioned into a thousand accents.

'Of course. A young girl, full of life (*and with so much interest in me*) would not just die. She was killed.'

'You watch too many movies.'

'No. Where is the time for movies?' The shop opened at six in the morning and closed after ten in the night. Only time for this and that. This lunch and that toilet.

'Nobody can kill a girl inside her own house.'

'Ah, that is what you think. There are a hundred ways.' His eyes strayed, took in a customer walking slowly towards the shop. 'Yes, hundred ways and you need only one. Think about that.'

Poornima thought about that. The tired shadow of the customer fell on her and asked for two kilograms of rice. The thirteen-rupee one, it added. Ahmed looked at Basha.

'What really happened?' Poornima turned her body to hide her question, her hands gesturing at the streams of little sachets that hung above Ahmed's head. Little packets of tea, instant coffee, shampoo, herbal mixtures for indigestion and cough, soap, supari. Poornima was struck by this new commerce built entirely out of little, colourful addictive packets.

Without any volition, she said, 'Give me two packets of that sheekakai shampoo.'

Ahmed pulled them out, laid them on his palms and gave them to her. 'This I won't charge. You know why? The girl was killed with poison. Remember that. And I also remember your husband's new shop, maybe he can find out something about this. For that girl, I am giving you this as a fee.'

It is not a shop, she wanted to tell him, it is an agency. She felt suddenly guilty. Their planned grocery store would be in direct competition with his, and knowing the quality of her rice and dal, she knew it would really be no competition.

'I'll tell him,' she said, eager to postpone the inevitable moment of shock when he saw the new nameboard on their house. As she paid, she leaned across the counter, her breasts massaging the many bottles on it. Ahmed's eyes strayed into his memory of Archana. He thought of the time when she would have (should have) been as old as Poornima, giving Ahmed a womanly smile. That thought brought tears to his dreamy teenaged eyes. So unfair! He hurriedly turned to the next customer and said, 'For you, I will give twenty-five paise discount per kilo of rice. This is Sona Masoori, the best.'

Poornima hung the bag of groceries on her forearm like a purse. The street was full of life, the shops continued their monotonic business, scooters and bikes raced up and down, leaving behind puffs of smoke which gathered into mini clouds at eye level. She was sure that if she sneezed into one of them, a cloudburst of germs would be showered at her feet. Her eyes automatically went towards Archana's street. (From now on, till the next disaster, that street would be referred to as Archana's street and not 6th Cross.) There were no crowds to be seen near the dustbin. Curiosity had dispersed and only grief stood in its place, right outside the gates of Archana's house. Depressed beyond her own expectations, she stepped into more puddles on the way. She opened the door of her house, washed the feet in the bathroom, and allowed a few unformed tears to mingle with the soap water. What she cried for, she herself did not know. It was clear, even at that time, that the lunch she prepared would be as listless as she felt.

4

POORNIMA DID NOT HAVE LUNCH. SHE HAD EATEN A banana before serving rice and saaru to Raghavendra. He tried to tell her that she should also eat, his mouth full of food. After the third time, she was irritated—both at his insistence, and for speaking with food in his mouth. She said, 'That was a girl who died. She was just a few years older than our daughter.'

What does that have to do with my lunch? He pulled the plate closer to him. 'What is this rice? Not properly cooked!'

Poornima ignored him.

'Ey, even the saaru is not hot. Look, why do you want to take it out on me? And on yourself? Why are you fasting?'

'I am not fasting, not for any reason. I don't feel like eating, that's all.' *And if you had a drop of sensitivity, you too would fast.*

She served him buttermilk, tossed a spoon of pickles onto his plate, and went to sit in the office. The table was clean, not a paper scratch on it. The room smelt of the mixed aromas of a dusty gunnysack and unwashed rice. She swallowed her saliva. *What has Nagaraj done to our lives!*

Raghavendra went to lie down after lunch. He piled three pillows, one over the other, and leaned back on them. When he began to doze, he would slowly slide down till, finally, he slept on one pillow, with the other two as guards on either side. He cleaned a betel leaf, spread sunna on it and placed it carefully in his mouth. Masticating the leaf slowly was the rhythm, the counting machine, that carried him to an afternoon nap. He opened the newspaper and peered at it. Such small pleasures created the architecture of his time. Ticking slowly, steadily and comfortably. *But now, with the alarm clock . . .*

Poornima came in, more at peace with herself because of her hunger pangs. The sacrifice was well worth it. She rolled out a mat and lay down.

'If you take all the pillows, how do you expect me to . . . ?'

'But you never sleep, Poornima. You always say that afternoon sleep is the sign of a lazy mind.'

'Well, I want to sleep today.' She grabbed a pillow and his shoulder slid down. One loose sheet from the newspaper fluttered down over his stomach and covered his crotch.

'I'll also sleep.' He looked at her guiltily. 'I got up at three today!'

She turned over, murmuring, 'One little job you do, and that is an excuse to sleep all day.' She closed her eyes, turned her mind to the rhythm of the fan, and waited to fall sleep.

She woke to the sound of her name with a sense of heaviness enveloping her face. She turned her head towards the sound, and saw Mrs Bhat peering through the window. Mrs Bhat was on her toes, the tip of her nose resting just above the window. The two bottom windows, originally green in colour but steadily paling into streaks of grey, were closed. The hinges had stuck, as if in a bid for more privacy. Mrs Bhat's eyes dropped to Raghavendra's stomach, that part of the body which she thought betrayed a man's age more than any other. Poornima got up, adjusted her sari around her shoulders, and caught Mrs Bhat's glance in the palm of her hand. She opened it and a mosquito lay half-squashed.

Impressed, Mrs Bhat said, 'Poornima, come to the kitchen.'

They had both conversed so often across their kitchen windows that they found it awkward to talk face to face, body to body. Face to face: one, white and round with a big circle of red kumkum powder and the other—Poornima's—soil brown, angular, with a small circle of naughty red.

'It seems,' Mrs Bhat began, 'the body will be taken away now.'

'The van has come?'

'Just now. My boy said they are removing the body soon.' She moved away from the window. 'Shouldn't we go?'

'Of course not.' Poornima suddenly felt awash with shame that Archana had been forgotten in the space of a few winks. The afternoon nap had exaggerated the effect of her morning fast and her face looked puffed up.

'Why should we go?' she added.

'I am not going alone. I don't know their family. But we can go to your terrace and see.'

Poornima, giving in to the inevitable, told her to wait. She went into the bathroom and washed her face. She poured a mug of water on her neck. Drops of cold water flowed into the ample, welcoming planes of her breasts. She pulled her sari around her chest more tightly, and told Mrs Bhat through the window, 'I'll come up in ten minutes. I'll make some tea for *him*.' Raghavendra had become *him*, a sleeping man tied to the last syllables of a dismissive nod.

He should not have been doing this—getting up with angry thoughts sticking to his eyes, with a feeling that it was morning (*which morning?*), then smelling tea and knowing that the dawn was an afternoon illusion. This sense of displacement irritated him, upset his balance, and even a few extra-hard scrubs with Mysore Sandal soap on his face did not help to clean it away. Poornima made a large cup of tea for him. Raghavendra drew patterns on the froth, indulgently licked his finger and drank the tea. She stared at that finger, thinking how times had changed that he so brazenly licked his finger—*if only his father could see him now*!

Poornima looked (even after he had adjusted his thick spectacles) as if she was drenched.

'What's happening? Rain?'

'No rain. I was hot, that's all. I am going to the terrace. It seems they are removing the body.'

'What body?'

'Ho! You have forgotten. Not even a day since that poor girl died . . . '

Raghavendra shook his head as if he could dislodge forgotten memories. Was it just that morning, or the previous night, that Archana had died?

'Don't you remember? You collected water today. This is why I tell you, don't sleep in the afternoons. Especially at your age.'

Yes, he remembered. Hadn't Nagaraj created a scene just the previous night?

To get back at her, he said, 'Why do you want to go to the terrace? You think that girl's death is a circus for you to watch? And anyway, I don't think that the police would have released the body so soon.' He spoke confidently about the police, suggesting slyly to Poornima that being in the business of security, he had special knowledge about the way the police worked.

Poornima countered quickly, before he could even finish, 'You have no idea about the police. They will do anything for money. And you think Prasanna is like you? I am sure he knows enough influential people. He would have paid a lot of money to get the body released. What impatience! What is he so scared of? Or ashamed of?'

She paused, and before he could summon up the words, as if they were patiently waiting in a queue to respond, she added cuttingly, 'If I were a man, I would go and lift her body on my shoulders.'

'Oy! What is this drama? Why should I lift her on my shoulder? You go, go up and gossip across the terrace.' As she left, he murmured, 'Like crows.'

Like crows indeed. She and Mrs Bhat flew to the terrace and found almost every other terrace also occupied. Women and children stood chatting under the darkening clouds. Bolts of lightning occasionally lit the sky; Mari would have said that the gods too had come to watch. Poornima hesitated, felt a tremor of shame, but Mrs Bhat and her voluble voice submerged it in a moment. Even as Poornima thought of going back inside and hiding herself in the bedroom, she saw Raghavendra leave the house. His shirt looked like it had been worn hurriedly, suggesting that he had acted on an instant's decision.

Raghavendra had peeped out of the window and seen people hurrying past the house. He knew the whispered message had gathered into a huge round jaggery ball in which rumours had stuck like roasted sesame seeds.

Children too joined in the hop and skip of the elders. In between came a few dogs, tails wagging—*do they think it's festival time?*—and a couple of cows managed to produce a few moos.

Knowing that no man alive could resist the coronation of death, especially a tragic one like Archana's, he fumbled for his shirt, which hung from the top corner of the bedroom door. He put it on, in awkward twists of the buttons, cleaned his spectacles, tightened his dhoti, and walked out of the house without closing the door.

He left it wide open on purpose, testing his belief that no one would rob a house while a body was being given a farewell. It was also his way of atonement, a gesture that offered a sacrifice of material wealth so that he and his family could appease the finicky god of death.

It was that kind of a time then, approaching 4 p.m., with unruly dark clouds above. It was the kind of time when every man, woman or child walking on that street clutched their fears to their constricted chest. The silence, sudden now, was similar to the eeriness of eclipse days when night suddenly invades the day, puzzled birds stutter and animals whimper, and pregnant women are locked inside rooms. It was suddenly that kind of time.

Close to Archana's house, there was a growing crowd. Near the dustbin stood middle-aged men, those who knew Prasanna only in passing. Closer to his house were old customers of his. At the gate of the house was a crowd of women, teenaged girls and children. The Corporation mortuary van stood outside the gates, its worn paint conveying a sense of tiredness. The sides of the van were made of glass, as if the final journey of the body was a flowery parade, gathering the curious and frightened sights of the living into the shroud of the dead. The body would be accompanied by a few men sitting around it. The van had come straight from the cremation grounds after delivering another body an hour earlier. The glass on the sides of the van had marks of oil and colour from the flowers and kumkum that had covered that body. The marks looked like giant fingerprints left behind by the grieving men when they leaned against the glass, like a seal of entry into the land of the dead.

The van driver was a young man, not more than twenty-five years old. He was standing by the van, waiting for the body to be brought out of the house. He caught a boy running past and asked, 'Who is dead?'

'A girl.'

A girl! His eyebrows shot up. *Hope there won't be too much crying*. He hated scenes at times like this.

Near the dustbin stood Chandru, Baale, Shankar, George and a host of others whose names Raghavendra had never bothered to learn.

He could hear the sound of crying from inside the house. He saw Marimuthu standing near the van, beckoning him with a glance. Raghavendra followed the hint in his face.

'How are you?' Marimuthu asked, forcing a ritual of normalcy upon him.

'I am,' Raghavendra replied, telling him that it was enough to be. Here, there or around. Especially when someone had just ceased to be.

'Poor girl,' Marimuthu said, chewing at the trailing ends of his moustache and indicating the metal plank inside the van. Empty and waiting for a body to occupy it. He pointed at the emptiness inside the van. Raghavendra looked at the plank and thought he was pointing to that. But Mari said, 'See, space is like this—this emptiness—perpetually waiting for a body to possess it. Living or dead, what does it matter?'

Raghavendra leaned against the van and immediately recoiled. He would have to take a bath after that contact. The sounds from the house were becoming louder. The body was being lifted. The gates opened. A sudden rush of people caught Raghavendra's attention. He stared at them with an angst that threatened to bring tears to his eyes.

Prasanna led the way bravely, hiding his feelings well with his steady walk. Behind him, four men carried the body of Archana on a pier made of wooden sticks and coconut leaves. The mother stood at the door, held up by a group of women. Her wails flowed forth, as if they were parting gifts to go along with her daughter.

Archana was at peace. The cotton stuffed in her nostrils mocked the illusion of breathing. 'She lives somewhere else,' Marimuthu said, and suddenly walked away. Eyes swept the van from all the terrace tops. The shopkeepers who had stayed back rather than leave their shops unattended stood at the entrances. It was a guard of honour, a symbolic acknowledgement: We too will follow, but you go in peace now.

A few drops of rain fell as if on cue. It soon became a downpour, the drops a sheet of cold thorns. The driver of the van was ready to leave, but the engine refused to start. He asked people to push the vehicle. Eager hands pushed and shoved. The van began to move jerkily, then suddenly spluttered to life, and in one smooth move had turned into the main street and was gone.

Chandru put his wet palms on Raghavendra's shoulder. 'I couldn't go to the office today. How could I?' Raghavendra knew what he meant. *I am a man of the community*. Archana's death is a death within this (sweeping, expansive gesture at the people around them) extended family.

Baale and Shankar joined them. Chandru asked Baale, 'Arre, what are you doing at this time? No school?'

'I am not well,' Baale replied, summoning a sneeze.

Chandru sneezed back, turned to Baale and said, 'Now you have made me sick.' He managed a deep cough and spat on the road.

Raghavendra looked for Rajesh in the crowd, but he was not to be seen. He walked with Shankar to his tailoring shop, Baale and Chandru following them lazily. They stepped into slush, leaving behind patterns of grief that swiftly flowed down the street, depositing its residue at many doorsteps. Shankar spoke not a word. He walked into his shop, wet and dripping. Raghavendra saw him put his hands on the table, and water flowed down his arm and onto a new piece of cloth waiting to be cut.

As they neared his house, Raghavendra looked up. Poornima was not on the terrace, and the door was closed. He passed Mrs Gowda at the entrance of her door. A pool of water, still and stagnant at her feet, attested to her participation in the spectacle. Baale looked at it, then turned to Raghavendra.

Baale said, 'So much water and yet . . . ' Chandru walked on, turned the corner towards his house, sneezing all the while. Raghavendra made to move on, but Baale held on to his elbow.

'I hear that you *pick* the water in the morning.'

'When?' Raghavendra was confused. He had already napped twice after that early morning trip to the tap.

'Today also you collected, yes?'

'Today? Yes, I suppose so.' He looked at the mud flowing past him, carrying the smells of the hospital at the end of that main road. He continued to look at it suspiciously, as if germs would jump up like toads.

'My wife told me.'

'Your wife?' His glasses, swept clean by the water, fogged up suddenly. He tried to clear it with his shirt but only succeeded in leaving streaks of water drops on it, spread flat in dosa patterns.

'Don't you find it difficult at your age to carry water? I suggest you hire a boy, or maybe your missus, like mine, can do it.'

Raghavendra remembered. How Poornima had insisted on buying a long pipe so they didn't have to carry the water in. It was taken away the next day, and Poornima said she knew it was Baale's wife who had done the deed. Raghavendra refused to fight over a piece of plastic. Poornima had then said, 'If so, you go fill the water every time.' But he hadn't, and Poornima had forgotten and forgiven. She had continued to fill the calendar days of water, at least till he worked for Paul.

Inspired, Raghavendra replied, 'I am thinking of putting the tap inside my house.' Baale clutched Raghavendra's palms tightly. Both Mrs Gowda and Poornima were visible, one continuing to stand outside her door and the other staring through the window.

'No, no. That is not fair. I will be getting the Corporation connection soon. Very soon. Till then, think of my wife, my son . . . '

Poornima saw Raghavendra's shoulders slump, weighed down by his eternal forgiving silence. But she had not reckoned with the anger driven into him that morning. *So much he did for the living, and so little one can do for the dead.*

'No, Baale. This is the final warning. I will give you two weeks and then I am putting the tap inside my house. If you can't get your connection in two weeks, you take water from a tap on one of the other streets.'

'But that is impossible. Carrying water from here to my house is itself so difficult.'

'So what? It's not my problem.' Raghavendra paused, feeling that he had been too harsh. 'As it is, I have so many problems of my own.' He looked towards his house guiltily and added, 'Two weeks. Remember, Baale, just two weeks.'

Poornima saw him, imagined his harsh words and wondered what he had said. She hurried to the door, opened it and stood with a face whose nose was a question mark.

Baale entered his house and Mrs Gowda slammed the door behind his back. He walked towards the bathroom, artificially stimulating sneezes which he thought would shelter him from her questions. He dried himself, demanded a hot cup of coffee and said, 'Don't worry. Everything is taken care of.'

She was about to raise her voice when he went into another bout of sneezing. Two weeks indeed! Baale knew he had to think hard and quickly.

'I had a bath,' Poornima said, staring at the dripping form of her husband.

'I have had mine,' he replied. 'I have been cleansed by the gods themselves.' He went into the bathroom and came out towelling his hair. The towel smelt of sandal soap. 'Anyway, why should we clean ourselves? Is death so dirty, does it stick to our bodies?'

Poornima looked fresh, and her hair, still not dry, glistened. Her face sparkled and her sari filled Raghavendra's mind with imagined possibilities. Such a sheath, covering so much flesh underneath. He had a moment's desire, the desire a fleeting thought. Poornima's brisk voice intruded into his thoughts.

'I am going to the temple this evening. I am taking the girls along.'

'Yes, you do that. I'll go get the girls from school.'

'No need for that. Don't start new habits for them.'

'Times are bad. Look at that girl. In the morning you say it is an accident, in the afternoon it is murder, and you also say it is suicide. This is all because of what has happened to our society.'

'Society, society! What does society have to do with this tragedy? If Archana is dead, Meghalatha is still there. Did you see her?'

'Who? Archana's sister?' He had seen her, a ghostly scrawl, one among the women holding Archana's mother. Megha was two years older than Archana, reaching the last giggle of her teen years.

'What a pretty girl she is!'

Raghavendra had barely noticed Megha, except for those few times when she had passed their house with eyes fixed on some secret path that she walked on. So unlike Archana, who spent her time walking from one shop to another, from one dimple to another smile, talking to the milkman, then Ahmed, the vegetable man, and so on. Her life had been one joyous, tipsy walk. Megha was not like that. Like her name, she was a cloud. Silent, with grave looks that only parted occasionally to let some light through.

Suddenly remembering, Poornima added, 'What wonderful skin she has!'

'You look at people's skin?' For Raghavendra, faces were mere outlines.

'Not people's skin. You think I have no other work? I mean Megha's skin. It glows. It's smooth, like, like . . . '

She found other words instead of an image. 'I am sure she never uses those fancy creams. Look at Suhasini. She wants to try lipstick, it seems.'

'This is what happens if . . . ' Raghavendra stopped. But Poornima knew what he refused to say.

This is what happens if you let girls go to college, go to work, and nobody to care for the kids and all the time watching fat girls dancing in film songs and going out to restaurants and movies, dressing up for them with colour and lipstick . . .

Poornima had responded angrily each time he started with this message. The times are different, she would say, and I don't want my daughters growing up like me.

And what is wrong with you, Raghavendra would counter. Poornima would remain silent.

'Anyway,' Raghavendra continued, leaving his unsaid thoughts on a dusty shelf, 'if you see Megha next time, call her in and talk to her. Poor thing.'

'I don't think she will come out of her house now.' Poornima, unaccountably reminded of the tailoring shop, continued, 'I have to get my blouses from Shankar tomorrow. He will know more about what happened, I think.'

Raghavendra heard her from inside the bedroom, where he was changing into a fresh dhoti and banian. He shouted, 'You give your blouses to Shankar! You don't have a ladies' tailor? God! But who am I to say anything? If I begin, you will say, times are different. But what times have changed a man to a woman? What times makes a man stitch a woman's blouse?'

The main door crashed open. Suhasini and Sanjeevani came in. Suhasini ran to Poornima, held her hand and said, 'Do you know what happened? It seems one girl died today!'

Her sister jumped in, a little balloon among hundred floating words. 'She was kidnapped and then the kidnappers killed her.'

Raghavendra came out of the bedroom. Powder had spotted his face with white uneven patches. His neck looked like a white cylinder with black ridges.

He looked at Poornima and said, 'When you want your blouse, tell me and I'll get it from Shankar.'

Poornima, still dressed in grief, sat in the outer office. Raghavendra gave a few pieces of bread to the girls and made tea to go with it. The tea tasted of vacuum-sealed cardboard. All the flavour had been exported, and now the shops were only left with CTC residue and dust bits in multicoloured packages.

The evening had silently slunk into the dark clouds as lights came on, one by one, in plastic clicks. The doorbell rang. Poornima left the office room and went into the house. *It has to be Nagaraj, that bastard.* Raghavendra hurried out, a towel over his shoulders, drying his palms on his dhoti.

It was not Nagaraj. Rajesh walked in, animated, still in his lab uniform. In his excitement, he had forgotten to remove his shoes, black always, but now wet with muddy patches. Poornima, peeping out from the inner room, saw him and came out. She ignored his shoes.

'Auntie, I missed it all, it seems.'

Poornima smiled. Once again, it seemed as if nothing ever happened without first seemingly happening. 'Yes,' she said.

Raghavendra interrupted, 'What is there to miss? Is it a show?'

Rajesh's face reflected the shock he felt. There was no smile, not even that pencil-layer of a grin on his neatly shaved face.

'Not a show, Uncle. But that girl! What a bad thing to happen!'

'I expected to see you earlier. You and all your college friends. When she was alive, they stood around on the road looking at her and all the other girls. When she is dead, nobody . . . nobody comes.' Raghavendra's irritation, partly at having to make the tea, partly at the tastelessness of it, erupted as angry barks at Rajesh. But mostly it was his anger that his home had been turned into a house of death, as if Archana was related to them!

Rajesh accepted this uncharacteristic reaction as part of the atmosphere of grief. In times of trouble, he knew that people came together and overlooked anger. Grief was best handled by embracing it along with other emotions. How well his father had taught him all this, especially at the mouth of a coal mine in Dhanbad, after a sudden flood had killed sixty-three people, including his father's colleagues, relatives and friends.

He might as well have said: From Dhanbad to Mathikere Extension, the space of grief is just a dimensionless point.

'I would have come before. I only heard about it after they took the body away. If I was here, I would have gone and lifted the body on my shoulders.' His shoulder tensed as he said it, and Poornima looked at Raghavendra. *See how he thinks, and you!*

'What a shame,' he continued, 'that she should die this way.'

'Which way?' Poornima asked, rhetorically.

'You know she took rat poison, right? So many people take rat poison. These poisons kill more people than rats.'

There had been an attempt to stop selling rat poison around the time when the Tenth Board exam results were to be released. They had also posted more policemen at Sankey Tank to stop kids from jumping into it. That hadn't stopped the suicides.

Poornima closed the office door. Her daughters would be sheltered for as long as possible.

Rajesh sat on the table, and Raghavendra looked at his shoes.

To distract Rajesh, and as an apology for her husband's irritation, Poornima said, 'Who told you this? You are now saying it is suicide, as if you were there to see it.'

'Of course it was suicide. All my friends know it. They also know why.'

Raghavendra moved to stand near the window, but was too late to stop Rajesh's words from fleeing outside. Rajesh stared at both of them.

'You don't know? She was pregnant.'

Poornima's stomach contracted. Not that kind of a curse on a young, unmarried girl. She felt the grief as though it was her own, as if it was she who had become pregnant.

'She was not that kind of a girl.' Her words flowed from the edges of her mouth, up her cheeks and into her eyes. She blinked rapidly.

'What do you know, Auntie? She was a friendly girl. A very friendly girl. And these days, what can you say about girls?'

'Oh, keep quiet, Rajesh. What do you know of girls?' Raghavendra was visibly angry. He had had enough of men who had no daughters telling him about girls.

'Enough to know she had boyfriends. All my friends knew.'

Poornima stopped Raghavendra's outburst. She knew the signs: flickering eyes, reddening ears.

'Who was the boy?' she asked.

Rajesh wanted to shock them by saying it could have been anybody, but he kept quiet.

Poornima had rarely seen Raghavendra so upset. He stood staring out of the window. Suddenly, he turned and said, 'What does it matter?'

Poornima stared at him, and in her eyes he saw the answer. Of course it mattered, it mattered terribly.

'Her father found out about it yesterday evening. He beat her up, then locked her in a room.' Rajesh had heard the story in various iterations in the canteen, while eating an oily samosa and drinking hot tea. There were six of them around the table, from Bihar and UP, six young boys who had spoken animatedly about Archana. There was a heaviness in their comments. Even her pregnancy had not elicited a comment about girls or sex.

Raghavendra was surprised. 'Her father is such a mild . . . '

Poornima jumped in. 'Mild? He? And anyway, which mild father would remain mild after hearing that his sixteen-year-old daughter is pregnant?'

She stared at him, challenging him to respond. Raghavendra had had enough of her anger. 'Enough of all this gossip. Didn't you say you are going to the temple? Go then and take your daughters with you.'

'Yes, I'll go when I want.' She turned to Rajesh. 'So, she was locked in the room, and then?'

'Then what? Early morning, she took the poison. She hadn't eaten at night, kept arguing all the time. Late night or in the early morning . . . '

Raghavendra remembered seeing running shapes in the early morning–late night as he stood bleary-eyed at the tap.

'She started screaming, but her parents didn't open the door because they thought she was just making a fuss. By the time they realised she was screaming in pain, it was too late. When they opened the door, she was lying on the ground with vomit all around.'

'Heartless bastards.'

'The father didn't know . . . '

'What didn't he know? I shall spit at him when I see him next.'

Poornima had nothing more to say. Unashamedly, she cried for the pain of a girl who was almost a stranger to her. When she got up and went inside, Rajesh said, 'I am sorry, Uncle. I didn't know she would get so upset.'

Raghavendra had turned his back to him.

'Anyway, why does Auntie let herself get upset like this? After all, it is some girl, somewhere . . .'

Raghavendra walked past him without a word. Rajesh looked at his shoes, surreptitiously scraped a bit of mud on the bottom of the sack of rice, and went upstairs to his room.

As soon as Poornima left with her daughters that evening for the temple, Baale came over to the house. Raghavendra was sitting in the office room trying to plan his future on sheets of paper. He had absently tried to open one of the drawers of the table and found it locked. Poornima was leaving when he asked her if she had locked the drawer. She hadn't. Did she know where the key was? Poornima had walked out in a hurry, dragging the girls with her. The youngest one waved her unsaid answer away.

Baale walked into the room, tapped the table and looked at the sack of rice. 'Good office you have,' he said.

Raghavendra was worried about the locked drawer. He had begun to fear Nagaraj, imagining dark secrets.

'Your wife left in a hurry,' Baale said, 'as if she wanted to get away from here. I don't blame her.'

Raghavendra was worried that Baale had come to talk about the tap. He had no time to regret his impetuous threat to put the tap inside his house. It was not that easy to fix a tap. He had to find a plumber and, more importantly, get him to come. Was it worth all the trouble?

Baale sat in a chair next to Raghavendra. 'You have become a big man, Raghavendra. Everybody talks about your shop with a lot of respect.'

'What shop?' Raghavendra was suddenly worried that Baale had heard about the provision store.

'This . . . this.' Baale's sweeping hands spelt out the mysteries associated with a detective agency. 'You are a man to be feared.'

'By whom?' Raghavendra's irritation had still not left him in full, and with this discovery of the locked drawer, it was threatening to become a headache.

'By whom?' Baale laughed. *The whole world fears you*, he meant to say. 'Even I fear you!'

'For what?' Raghavendra tried nudging the drawer with his feet. Only the table shifted, and Baale's elbow, which was resting on the table, slipped.

'See?' Baale showed him the tip of his elbow, the dried patches of skin due to the dry weather in Bangalore. 'If you want, you can put me down in a second. What am I after all? Just a government school principal. What are we teachers in front of people like you?'

Raghavendra was relieved. As long as Baale was not going to talk about the tap! His spirits lifted, and in a gesture of goodwill, he said, 'Just a teacher! They are the most important people in the world.' Baale was silent. 'Especially in our locality. You are the hope for all the kids here. Without you, how would they get an education?'

Baale smiled. He wanted to reciprocate Raghavendra's gesture. 'It's tough being in a government school. Everybody sends their children to private schools.' He paused, and added: 'Including you. What do we have?' He got up and sat on the sack of rice, ignoring Raghavendra's worried look. 'All we have is a dirty, leaking building. A few blackboards. To get chalk pieces, I have to fill up a form. Forget getting good teachers! What use are we? Only on election days do we get any prominence. It's the only time people come to our schools. They stand in line, vote, then go. As they leave, they say, is this how a school should be? Tcha, tcha. But will they help us?'

Raghavendra remembered paying a fat donation to get his girls admitted to their private school. Would they have been worse off if Baale had taught them? He looked at him again. Baale in his loose white shirt and white pants. The insides of his fingers coated with a permanent layer of chalk dust, like a limestone cliff, straight and strong. Baale got up and peered over Raghavendra's shoulders. Raghavendra smelt the fresh sandalwood powder and scented oil in his hair.

'Who will help us? I have sacrificed my whole life to teach these poor children. But that hasn't stopped me from continuing with my own research.' He paused, waiting for Raghavendra to turn and acknowledge him. 'My own research on Vedic mathematics. Will anybody help me to publish it as a book? Nobody. After all, I am just a schoolteacher in a poor government school.'

Raghavendra got up, worried that Baale would go on about Vedic maths. He had heard it many times before.

Baale's wife, whenever an opportunity presented itself in frilly clothes, would say, 'My husband is writing a book about ancient wisdom. Everybody seems to have forgotten our history.' She would stare at whoever was with her, peering at them as if they too had forgotten their history.

Baale took a sheet of paper from the top of the table and pulled out a pen from the inside pocket of his shirt.

'See? Solutions of quadratic equations can be found through this method also. What I want to show is that we can learn mathematics better if we use these methods.'

Raghavendra tried to focus on the squiggly forms that suddenly found life at the tips of Baale's fingers. How they squirmed, danced and pleaded. Baale was lost in his own words. He strung them in numerals, and spoke in the accent of numbers.

'I have finished my book, but where are the publishers? You don't know how many people I have gone to with my book.'

Raghavendra didn't want to know. He had been an indifferent student, finished school by the grace of Udupi Krishna. Never read a book in the last few years, maybe going on decades. He had no idea of mathematics, publishers, or even the Vedas. He remembered bits of prayers, leftovers from daily prayers said with his father. He hurriedly got up and peered out of the window as if somebody was calling him. No luck! Baale got ready to speak further, but Raghavendra had had enough. The whole day was becoming a nightmare. He said the only thing that could stop Baale. 'Now, about the tap . . . '

'What?'

'That tap. I have fixed a plumber and he wanted to come today. But I told him to come in a few days' time.'

'Few days' was a carrot dangled to shut Baale up.

'Ah! About that! Yes. I think you should wait. I think I will manage to get my own connection soon.'

Raghavendra had jumped from a fire into a volcano. In desperation, he shouted through the window, speaking to an imagined ally, 'What? You want me to come there? I am coming right now.'

He pushed Baale out with him, pulled the door shut, and hurried out of the house. Baale saw his wife's face peering out of the window of their house. He imagined her raised eyebrows and waved to them, mustering a cheer he didn't feel.

At the nearby Hanuman temple, Poornima felt dislocated from her present, even as she went around the shrine with her daughters. Her thoughts were on poor Archana. Normally, she would have sat with the girls in the temple courtyard, watching the evening life circumambulate them. But on that day, she had no patience, not even with her gods.

The three of them walked back to their house in the continuing drizzle. Suhasini had a small blue umbrella for herself, while Poornima and Sanjeevani huddled under a big black one. Some of the spokes were bent at awkward angles, and the first holes on the fabric of the umbrella, created by cockroaches, could be seen. Raindrops stood in a queue around these holes, waiting for the time when they could lazily fall through rather than flow down the sloping sides. Cars, big cars, had begun crowding the tiny lanes of their locality. They rolled majestically through the slush and rain, depositing Rorschach patterns of mud on those who braved to walk the streets. Poornima cursed the cars and what the city was becoming. Sanjeevani looked at her and said, 'Amma, you are so old-fashioned.'

The rain had also washed Archana's street and its surroundings clear of any residual rose petals of grief.

That night, as Poornima was cleaning the kitchen platform, Mrs Bhat came to the window. Her round face, a caricature of the full moon, suddenly rose into Poornima's view.

'Oy,' Mrs Bhat whispered, 'are you cooking so late?'

'No. Cleaning.'

'Did you hear about that girl?'

Archana was 'that girl' today. Tomorrow would be the turn of another. Poornima had not heard anything.

'It seems when they went to the ghat—you know now they also have the electric crematorium—there was a power cut. There were five bodies waiting in line. Imagine! A queue for dead bodies.'

It was not pleasant. Not at all. Each of the bodies had come from different parts of the city. The power had been cut in the morning and was expected back anytime. So, every time a new entourage came to the ghat, they were told to wait. Most of the bodies came in Corporation vans, except two that were carried on bamboo stretchers.

Soon there was a big crowd at the ghat and around the crematorium building.

Other than the immediate family—those who stayed near the respective bodies—the crowd dispersed into the many corners of the ghat as they waited for the turn of 'their' body to be cremated. There was one wood fire smouldering in a corner. Burning bodies with wood was fast becoming extinct, an endangered mode of bidding goodbye to the mortal body. Wood was so expensive these days, and the process of burning was not necessarily a happy one. Stories were still whispered of how the head rose up and exploded, converting the fleshy face into a caricature of a devil's skull.

Tired of waiting, many in the crowd drifted outside the ghat. A horde of handcarts, selling anything from cut cucumbers to roasted peanuts, suddenly materialised near the entrance. Some from the drifting crowd went towards these carts, while others went to the small hotels nearby, if not to snack, to *at least* have some coffee, while the family members continued arguing with the crematorium officials. Some of them sat at the feet of the bodies, amidst the sickening smell of fading flowers, ranting against the Electricity Board and the callousness of the attendants.

A crisis that could have been managed in silence blew up into a fight when one family paid an attendant some money to break the queue, a testimony to the impatience of the living with those who were dead. Everybody wanted to go back, to quickly get it over with—this conversion of flesh into ash.

Finally, when the power came on, there was a spontaneous shout and, incomprehensibly, applause. The hotels emptied rapidly. The handcart vendors stayed for a while, partly out of curiosity, but also filled with the lethargy of the living.

'And that is how her final journey was,' concluded Mrs Bhat. A death too early in life and a cremation too late in the queue. 'The family is back only now and you can imagine how they feel.'

Poornima continued scrubbing, pouring water from a large vessel onto the kitchen platform and the floor. The floor shone like a lake upon which her footprints were little inhabited islands.

Mrs Bhat's moonface suddenly dipped and was gone. Poornima lifted her head, saw her shadow drown in a muddy puddle under a streetlight that was getting ready for bed.

5

The next water day, two days after Archana's death, found Poornima collecting water at three in the morning. Raghavendra had complained of all kinds of aches the previous night, and Poornima's protective self had let him sleep in. The night was misty and cool, and the flickering road lights reminded her of the fitful sleep that invaded even tube lights. The water pressure was low. She filled one vessel, carried it to the kitchen, poured the water into a larger container, then came back to the tap to fill the vessel again. As she came closer to the tap, she saw a woman standing there with a vessel in her hand. She was irritated: the water pressure was so low, and now she had to wait for Gowda's wife to fill her vessel. As she came closer, ready to assert her rights over the tap, she saw that it was not Gowda's wife. Hearing Poornima, the other woman turned her head to look at her. With a shock, Poornima recognised Archana's mother, Hema.

Poornima was immediately ready to be magnanimous. 'You have come *here* for the water. Please take it,' she said, as she opened the tap. There was a trickle of water, but Hema continued to stand with the vessel in her hand.

'You take it,' she said.

'No, no. You please take it first.' In her anxiety to please, Poornima did not mind that the precious water was flowing into the mossy slabs under the tap.

Hema stretched her hand, took the vessel from Poornima and placed it under the tap, saying, 'We get little water as it is.' The sound of water dripping into the empty vessel was a magnified drone in the still night.

'I didn't come here for the water,' Hema said. 'I came to meet you.'

Poornima was surprised. The two women had never found an occasion to converse. If they had slipped past each other on their routine journey of life, it was only to vaguely nod at each other.

'What can I say?' she began awkwardly. 'I was so shocked, Archana was such a sweet girl.' She suddenly wondered if Hema could follow her chaste Kannada, Hema whose Kannada shared a porous border with Malayalam.

Hema looked into the black yawn of the vessel. The drone of the water had become a continuous pattern like the sound of little children's feet dancing on the water surface.

'I come to you as a mother . . . as a mother of girls yourself. I want your help.'

'What help can I give?' Poornima whispered.

'My daughter took poison.' Hema waited for Poornima's response.

'Poor child,' Poornima countered instinctively.

'Her father was very angry with her. What to do? The girl went and became pregnant.' She waited, and when the response was only the sound of water filling up the vessel, she continued, 'I told him—her father—once it is done, what is the use of shouting and beating her? We could have taken her to a doctor. But no, it was *his* pride that was hurt. He locked her in a room and she took rat poison. Where did she get this poison? I have never bothered about rats, letting them run around where they wanted.'

'Wasn't there time to save her?'

'Save her? The obstinate child had locked the door from inside. But when her pain became too much, she opened the door. God, how scared she must have been! But my husband had locked the door from outside, as if she was planning to run away from the house. Even after the sound of her crying and vomiting, he refused to open the door. He just stood there and said that he would not be taken in by her tantrums and drama. What drama? The poor girl was dying.' She looked at the vessel, watching it till it filled to the brim. Then she turned the tap off.

'And then there was silence. Even then, he said it was just an act. By the time I managed to get past him and open the door, it was too late.'

The two women stood quietly. A drizzle began, as if it too had been listening to Hema, and had waited for her to finish. It began to coat the two short, plump women with a fine layer of liquid dust, covering them with a lace blanket, bringing them together. If one had sneezed, the other would have coughed.

It was Hema who reminded them of their duty. 'So much water above, so little in these taps.'

It was a cue that Poornima grabbed. 'How can I help you now? Whatever it is, I will do it.'

'I heard about your husband's new job. I want to ask him only one thing—to find out who made my daughter . . . the way she became. Who made her pregnant? Who was it who killed my daughter, a little innocent child herself?'

Poornima stared at her, hoping the look would express her immediate response: *What is the point now? Why discover secrets that are best left hidden?* Moreover, she had already decided that Raghavendra should start the grocery shop immediately. But then, she was also a mother of two girls. She said, 'If my husband manages to discover that boy or man, which I doubt, what are you going to do?'

'I don't know. I only want to know who he is. When I know, I'll decide.'

Poornima wanted to be honest with her. 'I will be frank; my husband is planning to close his agency and start . . . '

Hema turned her face away abruptly.

Poornima continued, 'But I will tell him that he should do what you want before he closes the agency. Nothing is more important.'

She smiled, and Hema found a gap in her sorrow that widened her mouth just a tiny bit. She turned to leave, lifting her empty vessel to her hip.

'One more thing. My husband doesn't know about this. He says he has not lost any daughter. He is trying to act as if he is the one who has been injured.' Her voice broke into little shards of anger and grief. 'I don't want him to know what I have asked of your husband. All that he is interested in now is to see how quickly he can get our other daughter married. He is worried that nobody will marry her now.' She paused and suddenly, more insistently, said, 'I will pay whatever it costs. I can even give my jewellery.'

Poornima was aghast. Matters such as these should not be contaminated with talk of money. 'No, no. Don't say that. My husband will do this for free. It's a matter of justice and it's for your little girl.'

Hema turned away, her tears now a part of the offering from the skies. Poornima bent down and turned on the tap: there was no more water. She picked her vessel and heard Hema's hesitant voice say, in English, 'Thank you.'

Raghavendra was puzzled. First, she had insisted that he stop 'all this dectective nonsense' and now she was at him to do 'one little thing for that poor girl'. And what was he expected to do? Find out who made her pregnant! And how would he do that? How could he ask people about these things? Thieves and robbers were a different matter altogether.

And to bring all this up early in the morning, even before his coffee, and when his eyes were out of focus despite his spectacles?

'No, no. I have decided to start the grocery store today.' He sat on the chair, looking smaller than usual, with the Kannada newspaper, *Prajavani*, in front of him. When he reached the end of the headline, he saw Poornima's nudging waist in front of his eyes. She pulled the paper away.

'This is the first time I have asked you for anything. All these years, you did some stupid security work. Now you are wasting time and money with Nagaraj. When I ask you, *your wife asks you*, to do a simple thing, all you can do is refuse. Is this right? This can be your last case.'

Raghavendra could not see his work as being in the realm of right or wrong. He was afraid to confess what he was increasingly feeling: boredom. The utter senselessness of anything he did.

'No, it is not right. But have you forgotten Nagaraj? More importantly, I am not a detective, really. I am just a security guard.'

She knelt beside him. 'How can you say that? You know truths better than any one of us. You are a father, and you know what that mother is feeling.'

She placed her palms on his thighs, and he remembered. He looked at her fondly, giving her a shy smile. 'Okay, I will see what I can do in the next few days.'

She got up slowly, ruffled his thick mat of hair and gave him back the paper.

'Your daughters will be proud of you,' she said, as she unconsciously walked away with a swing of her hips.

He went to the office, took a piece of cloth and cleaned the table. He sat on the chair in front of the table, elbows pressing into the wood grains. Then remembered that he had to ask Nagaraj for the key to the locked drawer. He wondered once more how he should deal with him. He decided, as the first step in this, his first and last case, to begin afresh, and walked out to meet Nagaraj.

Marimuthu was waiting at the gates of the temple. He just stood there, watching and waiting. Wasting no effort on frivolous greetings. He only spoke when he thought it was necessary. Only spoke to pass condensed messages. When Raghavendra passed him, he called out to him with a swish of his hand. It was not a command, yet a summons, and Raghavendra walked towards him with much more cheer than he had felt before.

'So, Swamiji, how are you?' Both of them were surprised at Raghavendra's use of the title 'Swamiji'. But Marimuthu was pleased.

'I want to tell you something. For your own good. It is my god's way of telling you to come here more often.' His palms swept the shrine, the glaring anthill with red flowers draped over it. 'I want to tell you what you don't know. What you should have known. I am doing this only because you are a good man. Nagaraj, that rogue, is running a chit fund. He uses your house as his office. It is not an ordinary chit fund. He cheats. He has stolen money from many people who thought they were putting money in the chit fund. He has collected a lot of money and I know most of it has been spent drinking in Venkateswara Bar.'

Venkateswara Bar and Restaurant, commonly referred to as VBR. Now infected with the ambition of Bangalore. It used to be a tiny place where workers and auto drivers would surreptitiously drink cheap liquor. But Bangalore's aspiration to be the big bad city of India had also made it the liquor capital of the country. Not just Kingfisher beer, which was already famous, but various new brands of alcohol had flooded the city. Bangalore was becoming known for its sophisticated pubs, exotic drinks, as well as exotic people. These changes rippled out to Mathikere Extension, and VBR too thought it would join the revolution with a bold new board, the name written in English. With no Kannada at all! Even the cynics of Mathikere Extension grudgingly agreed that VBR had indeed become part of the new cosmopolis.

Marimuthu continued, 'People have understood his game and are beginning to get angry. Those who have lost money are not going to sit in silence. And when they come, they will come to your house. Nagaraj will say you are his partner. It is your house, your family, that will have to pay up. Remember this.'

He turned away dramatically, pulled the towel around his shoulders tighter, and went to sit under the tree. Raghavendra stared after him, unwilling to cross the gate and enter the temple. Once past the gate, he knew Mari was the king, and he would have to prostrate to him and the gods inside. Take the offering, spread it on his forehead. Perhaps Mari would hand him flowers to be given to his wife and daughters. Which meant that the next time he would have to come back with his family.

Raghavendra called out, trying not to shout, 'Do you know where Nagaraj lives?'

Marimuthu glared at him. *He is your partner, and you do not even know where he lives! What innocence, how stupid.* But he kept quiet, and in that silence, Raghavendra understood what Marimuthu meant to say. *Come back, come inside, come with your offerings of coconut and camphor, and then I will tell you.*

On his way back, Raghavendra passed the tailoring shop. Shankar was standing inside, cutting a piece of cloth, with a Malayalam song blaring away. He called out, 'Uncle, how are you?' Raghavendra took this as an invitation, and entered the shop. He remembered what Poornima had said. 'My wife told me she gave you something to be stitched. Is it finished?' He was unaccountably shy, imagining Shankar stitching his wife's blouse.

Shankar was intent on cutting the cloth along a chalk line marked on it. 'Ah, three blouses. The pieces are somewhere here. I'll finish it today or tomorrow.'

Raghavendra looked around and saw a few blouses lying in a corner. He recognised his wife's old red blouse among them. Suddenly possessive, he said, 'Give them back today.'

Shankar finished cutting with a final smooth swish. There was a sudden pause in the music, and Raghavendra, without thinking, said, 'That girl. How sad.'

Shankar looked at him, another song began, and Raghavendra was grateful that he did not ask: which girl? As one they looked at the carpentry shop diagonally across from Shankar's. Prasanna was sitting outside on the pavement, gathering the little sun there was, making marks on a piece of wood.

'They have an order to build a special cot. Imagine! A marriage bed! Best teak with lots of carving. So what if his daughter is dead? He says his work has to go on.' Then Raghavendra remembered that Shankar and Prasanna were both from Kerala.

'Are you and he from the same place?'

'Close enough. But two of his assistants are from my hometown.' A town that had migrated, broken into little groups of tailors, carpenters, plumbers, teashop owners. Not many remained. Those who had left continued to live in the memory-shadow of that hometown, and those that stayed only thought of those who had left.

Shankar pulled out Poornima's blouse along with a green blouse piece. 'I'll make this blouse right now,' he said, smoothing her old blouse with his palm. Raghavendra stood up, not wanting to see the caress of Shankar's palm on his wife's blouse. 'No, wait. You can do it later.' He snatched the blouse and the piece of cloth, and threw them into a corner of the room. Shankar was startled.

Raghavendra said, 'Sorry, I am just upset at the way that man is behaving.' The excuse sounded like one even to him.

'Don't worry, Uncle. He will also suffer. You think that girl is going to keep quiet? She will come back to haunt him.'

Prasanna looked up at that moment and saw both of them staring at him. Raghavendra stumbled off the steps and left.

The resolve with which he had set out in the morning was fast dissipating. He entered his house, saw the main door open, the inside door closed, and immediately sensed the presence of Nagaraj. He turned into the office and saw Nagaraj putting some papers into the drawer.

'Nagaraj,' he began, and then noticed one of Nagaraj's friends sitting on the sack of rice.

'You get up from there,' he shouted, but his voice sounded timid even to his ears. The friend looked at Nagaraj.

It was clear that Nagaraj had come in peace. He smiled at Raghavendra and told his friend to get off the sack. He locked the drawer, got up from the chair and offered it to Raghavendra. From the corner of his eye, Raghavendra saw the door open a bit. He could imagine Poornima getting ready to hear what he would say to these goons.

He spoke calmly. 'Nagaraj, let us not fight. I don't want to continue this agency. This is my house. You have put no money into this. So, before we waste more time, let's close it down. I am going to open a grocery shop here.' He began to sweat lightly, his thick glasses beginning to slide off his nose. 'And another thing, please give me back the keys to the drawer of *my* table.'

Nagaraj laughed. Raghavendra looked towards the closed door and saw it opening a bit more. *God, not Poornima.* He didn't want her to fight his wars. Nagaraj put his heavy arm around Raghavendra, pulling him close. Raghavendra could smell stale alcohol, and imagined all kinds of food fermenting in Nagaraj's stomach. He pulled away and Nagaraj staggered.

'Arre, you little rat, since when do you have muscles on you? Ah? What is this about you telling me what to do? Are you my boss? I am trying to be friendly, spending my time here for your sake, so you will earn something, like a man who can feed his wife and girls. And you are asking me to leave?' Raghavendra sensed the door behind him open further. 'You know, I have even got a case for you today. See my friend here? He has a problem and I told him, don't worry, my friend Raghavendra will take care of it. And now, in front of him, you are telling me to leave. Is that nice?'

'Nagaraj, I know about your chit fund and who knows what else you have been doing. I am not going to be threatened by you. And I don't want you to come here again. Give me the key to the door and the drawer.'

'Raagu, I am telling you for the last time. I am not going anywhere. You just shut up.'

Before Poornima burst forth, Raghavendra sensed it. Felt her anger roll past him like a shock wave. He turned to ask her to keep quiet, but she had begun speaking before she stepped into the room.

'Rowdies like you think you can get away with anything? Let me see how you do it. I will get the police to arrest you.'

Nagaraj laughed. Made a move as if to grab Poornima. Raghavendra stood rooted with shock, and Poornima screamed. Nagaraj looked out of the window.

'Bastards. You talk to me about the police? Who do you think my friend here is? He is *the* police.'

Both Poornima and Raghavendra looked at the friend. Puffy face, thick moustache, a big paunch. The friend stared back at them, simulating a fierce police stare.

'I am being nice, but you people are not. You forget who you are. You forget you have two daughters. You can't forget that, right?' His friend nodded, and as if for emphasis, spat on the floor near the table.

'But I am going to be a good man, unlike you. I am going to use this office for some more time. When I am ready to leave, I will.'

Raghavendra looked at Poornima and gathered his shattered courage. 'You are not leaving later. You are leaving now. Give me the keys.'

Nagaraj looked at his friend and, on cue, they both laughed. 'This little rat is threatening us. What to do to him?' He looked around the room, saw the sack of rice, and remembered the time he had enraged Raghavendra by kicking it. His eyes lit up. He went to his friend and told him, 'Keep them there. I have to show them who we are.'

The friend walked over in the best police manner he could and grabbed Raghavendra's shirt. Nagaraj stood in front of the rice sack. He unzipped his pants, and before Raghavendra or Poornima could utter a word, began to pee on the sack of rice. When Raghavendra tried to rush towards him, the friend pushed him back violently. His glasses fell to the ground and shattered. He fell on Poornima and they both hit the wall. In the silence of their fall, they saw Nagaraj spraying himself all over the rice, as if blessing each grain. After he was done, he looked at them lying on the floor. He walked past them, Raghavendra impotently glaring at him, Poornima with her eyes on the floor, desperately holding back her tears, *the shame of it if she cried in front of him*, his friend standing over them with his legs spread and arms at his sides in the best cinematic posture of threat. Nagaraj stepped on Raghavendra's spectacles, crushing the frame, and walked out of the door.

For the next few minutes, there was only silence in the room. Poornima began to cry, softly at first, then violently. Raghavendra had tears in his eyes. He moved to hold her, but she pushed him away and went inside. Raghavendra looked at the sack of rice and the senseless waste it had become. He looked outside, heard the sounds of the mundane rituals that had come to define life outside his home. He looked at his hands, recognising their weakness with shame. He got up, picked up the pieces of his spectacles and put them on the table. He then got hold of the sack of rice, shuddering to touch any part of it, and dragged it across the room.

He was panting by the time he reached the door. He found he couldn't lift it over the one-inch doorframe. Felt the impotence of his physical weakness, and gave up the attempt to maintain his purity. He knelt against the sack, feeling the wetness, smelling the strong smell of urine, and pushed it with his shoulders. It rolled over the obstruction. He continued to lean on it, rolling the sack into the small front yard. He pushed it to a corner of the yard, feeling pain in parts of his body that he never knew existed. Sweat poured down his face, mixed with tears of anger. He saw Poornima at the window of the office, watching him, crying silently. He walked slowly back, feeling a pain in his chest, smelling Nagaraj's urine on himself. He went to the backyard, threw his dhoti and shirt on the ground. He would burn them later. He walked to the well in his underwear and lowered a bucket into it. The pain in his chest grew as he lifted the full bucket and poured the cold water all over himself. He filled another bucket, emptying it on his head. Poornima came out with a new soap bar, kept it on the wall of the well. Seeing her, he slumped down. She gave him the soap, pulled water from the well, letting it flow down in cascades on his back. It was a long time before he thought he was somewhat clean.

It was a penance. He remembered his father then, telling him repeatedly of how important it was to push the body to its limits. Cold early morning baths before prayer, walking barefoot to the temples. Fasting on certain days, not even a glass of water. Cooking your own food over a wood fire after a bath and prayers. Mental solace comes from physical pain, not indulgent comfort. He remembered, too, how he had resisted those lessons. The pleasures of the body were too immediate, more easily available than the solace of the mind. Perhaps this was what his father had wanted him to experience.

Raghavendra put on a dhoti and shirt, and walked to the market without his slippers. He went to Gururaj's hardware store and insisted that he accompany him to his house at once. Gururaj broke the lock of the main door and replaced it with a new one. Poornima was in the kitchen. She too had had a bath. She had cleaned the front office, had poured a large measure of Dettol and scrubbed the floor as if she were skinning Nagaraj's face. In the midst of all this, the children had come back home and sat quietly, knowing something had happened. Gururaj did his work quickly, with no attempt at conversation. After he left, Raghavendra entered his office, took a crowbar that he normally used to dehusk coconuts and used it to break the drawer. It splintered at the first smash. He pulled out the sheets of paper inside the drawer, and sat down to read them with his broken spectacles.

Around seven, Poornima called him for dinner. She had only this to say, when the children were not around, 'Go tell the police.' When he nodded, she added, 'Get new glasses also.'

That night, the power went off for two hours. In the darkness, Raghavendra sat at the window looking out into the street where life went on in the form of dancing candlelight. He saw the silhouette of the sack and knew that, if they were lucky, the rats would soon come to take it all away. Then remembered that he had still not paid Venkatappa for the sack of rice.

He felt no regret. Strength comes from penance and he knew, much too late, what he would have told his father then.

6

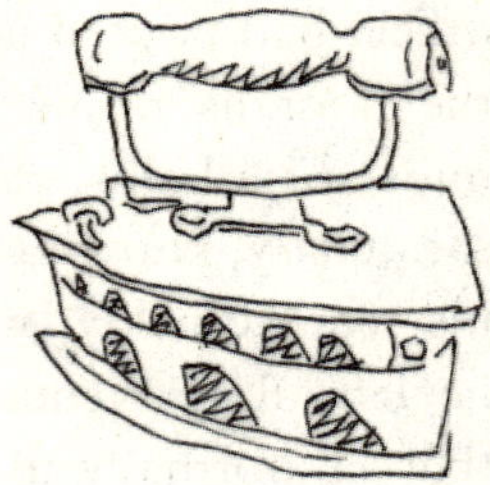

RAJESH HURRIED IN EARLY THE NEXT MORNING, communicating the urgency of his message through his speed. 'Uncle,' he began, seeing Raghavendra sitting in the office room with a cup of coffee, 'a sack of rice is outside!'

Whatever the vagaries of the South, he had never imagined that a sack of healthy rice would be discarded so offensively. The only way Raghavendra could still his shock was to tell him about Nagaraj. He had decided that it was time to take help, if not for himself, at least for the sake of his family.

'You said you had friends who would help. Is that really true?'

'Of course, Uncle. You tell me and I will call the Commander immediately.'

Raghavendra smiled. Rajesh: so dramatic and yet so spontaneous. 'No, I will tell you when I need them.'

Rajesh looked at the broken spectacles on the table. 'What happened to your specs, Uncle? Did you sleep on them?' When Raghavendra stared back at him silently, he added, 'I'll go get one for you right now. My friend runs a spectacle shop, you know, that shop—True Sight.' Raghavendra scowled. Did all of Rajesh's friends own one shop or the other? Or was it that all the shopkeepers were Rajesh's friends?

Rajesh continued, 'He will give me a discount also.'

Raghavendra had thought of sticking together the broken pieces till he gathered enough motivation to buy a new pair of spectacles. Instead, he gave in to Rajesh's enthusiasm. 'Okay, Rajesh. We'll go there when you are free.'

Rajesh was pleased. 'Uncle, I'm always free for you. If possible, I'll ask my friend to come here to take measurements for your eyes.'

Raghavendra wondered if Rajesh had mistaken an optician for a tailor. Rajesh thought about what he had just said. 'But Uncle, in case he can't . . . let me take these to him.' He picked up the spectacles and moved towards the table. He noted the broken drawer first, and then the new lock on the door. He peeped into the hall, very fleetingly (after all, two girls were inside) and shouted into the silence within, 'Don't worry, Auntie. I am here.' He looked back in anticipation of Poornima's acknowledgement, for her to come out and offer him a cup of coffee. He would refuse, saying he drank only tea. But Poornima stayed inside, silent, though with a tiny smile.

Later, around 11 a. m., the time when working people had left their homes and the streets were lazily soaking up the sun, Raghavendra stepped out into the backyard. The ladder lay on the ground near the well. He bent down and lifted it awkwardly. Poornima watched him from the kitchen window as she washed the rice, three times, before cooking it. She was still upset at what Nagaraj had been able to do in her house. Angry at their own impotence. She watched Raghavendra struggle, trying to take the ladder into the house, as the last drops of water drained away between her fingers. Then, out of compassion masked as irritation, she asked, 'Where are you taking the ladder now?'

He spoke back to the kitchen wall. 'I am removing the board.' The process of cleaning would begin with him tottering up the ladder with a hammer and without his spectacles.

'You think you can do it by yourself? You think your hand has the strength that Nagaraj's hand had when he nailed the board? You want to fall and break your head?'

She spoke too fast, and at the end of it, in the silence, heard her own regret. Raghavendra responded by throwing the ladder down. It hit the wall, producing a loud noise that caused reverberations in the big copper vessel that they used to store water in the bathroom.

Poornima came hurrying out of the kitchen, still holding on to the vessel of rice. She saw Raghavendra staring at the floor. When he heard her, he looked up.

She saw his eyes without the glasses, squinting hard, trying to see, attempting to communicate his anger to her. His loose banian and oversized dhoti magnified the hurt in his eyes. She suddenly longed to hold him and tell him she was sorry. Instead, she said, 'What is the hurry to remove that board? After all, you promised Archana's mother that you'll find out who the boy is. Till you do that, the board can remain there.'

Seeing Poornima back off, he decided on exhibiting his anger. He threw the hammer on the ground and walked past her, not looking her in the eye. 'Shouting and ordering all the time,' he muttered as he went to the door of the hall, loud enough for her to hear. In the reflection of his mind's eye, yet another slated window, he saw her walk back into the kitchen. He smiled and slipped into the office.

The board stayed, for the moment. It would be a constant reminder of Raghavendra's lost cause. Or, at least, his last case.

Raghavendra told Poornima about Marimuthu and his warnings about Nagaraj. How they had misjudged Mari, he said. What trouble they took to avoid his eyes which were often mysteriously red, as if he had applied sunna to his eyeballs.

Poornima said, 'You should meet Marimuthu and ask him about Archana.'

He refused, almost as a matter of habit. He was not going to enter into a relationship of gossip with Mari.

Especially, as he added, not with all of us refusing to even visit his temple.

Late in the afternoon, Rajesh came over with new glasses for Raghavendra. His friend had indeed worked hard, had tested the broken lenses, replaced them with equivalent ones, and had chosen a new frame. Rajesh implied that no better spectacles could be found in Bangalore—all because the optician was *his* friend. Raghavendra looked at the green frame with a concerned frown. The frame looked so heavy . . . and its colour! He tried it on. The lenses sparkled in the dim light inside the house.

Poornima saw them and began to laugh, but on noticing Rajesh's hurt-filled face, she told him that it was the best pair of spectacles that Raghavendra had ever possessed. Rajesh informed them that the cost of the glasses was two hundred rupees, and added that elsewhere, not just in Bangalore but even in Bihar, the cost would be much more. Raghavendra could only blink his thanks in reply even as Poornima gave him a piece of milk peda that she had bought over a week ago.

That evening, Raghavendra and Poornima crossed the gates of Marimuthu's temple. If Raghavendra would not go, Poornima had threatened, she would go with a plate of flowers, coconut and camphor. 'You have lost your conscience,' she told her husband. 'You who do not know the grief of a mother. Anyway, no man or snake or snake god can harm us, those of us who go with truth and justice in our hearts.'

The moment he saw them, Marimuthu got up from his place under the tree. He lifted his hands, partly as a half-hearted blessing, and partly as a command to still the sudden shattering sound of their explanations. Addressing Poornima, he said, 'I was waiting for the day you would come. Come inside.'

They bent through the doorway, the huge anthill right in front of their eyes. From the road, it had been merely a shadow of a weak bulb, but close-up it was an angry collection of stalagmites with bright red kumkum streaks all over it. Marimuthu placed his right palm over the biggest hole. *This is where the king cobra comes from, this is his house.*

As he gave back part of the flowers and some kumkum, he told Poornima, 'Next time, bring your children. These gods are powerful; they listen to each one of us.' He asked them to sit under the tree with him, wanting passers-by to note his growing clientele. Even a Madhwa Brahmin comes to worship at Marimuthu's temple!

As if to reciprocate their gesture, he said, 'So, is Nagaraj still around? Heard he made a fuss the other day in your house with his police friend. Let me tell you, I know how to control these fellows. You only have to tell me.'

Raghavendra was suddenly flustered. He had been so busy staring at the anthill in awe that he had neglected to place money on the offering plate. He looked up at the sprawling branches above him, hoping for a quick solution to his oversight.

It was Poornima who, after an irritated glance at her husband, said, 'Forget Nagaraj. We have decided to close the agency. It is not desirable to have people like him around.' She paused and looked at her husband, who was gazing at his feet. 'Days have become like this. You cannot trust anybody or anything. Look at that girl, Archana. Such a nice girl, and then she dies.'

Mari leaned towards her. 'I am sure you know the reason why.'

She pulled her sari tighter around her, suggesting rituals of the body that betrayed the state of the mind. 'They say so many things.'

'But only one reason, isn't it? And that is a temptation for all these boys and girls. Especially these days.'

Raghavendra got up. 'No, sit down.' Mari pulled him back. 'Your wife knows these problems.'

'Since I know these problems, tell me, *Swamiji,*' Poornima said, with an unnecessary emphasis, 'who is the boy who did *that* to the girl?'

Mari leaned back, stretching his back muscles so that they looked like an extension of a tree trunk. 'That would not be fair, would it? It is only the little girl who knows and who can tell. Don't you think so?'

'Maybe. But do you know who the boy is?'

'Ha! It would seem like I should. After all, I sit here the full day and watch people go up and down. I know so much about this place that you would be embarrassed to hear some of what I know.' Poornima glanced at Raghavendra, who was fidgeting now, unhappy at the turn the conversation had taken. 'But that doesn't mean I know everything.'

'Or won't tell?'

'What do I see, *Amma*?' Mari made a point of emphasising the word, suggesting to Raghavendra that his wife was safe with him, as safe as a mother could be. 'But is it important for you to know?'

'Yes.'

'Who knows the feeling of mothers?' Mari offered his words to the evening breeze. It was clear to Poornima that no answers would be forthcoming. She sprang up from the ground, watching Raghavendra struggle to follow her movements. She would be back, if needed, to find out what she wanted to know.

As they left, Mari said, 'If I want, I can know the answer in a few days. But I do not want to know.' He smiled as they crossed the gate and hurried away. Poornima's sari wound around her legs, making her walk like a keyed-up doll.

Raghavendra's new spectacles irritated the bridge of his nose. 'Poorni, why you asked that man all those questions, I don't know. He just acts as if he knows everything.'

As they neared the house, she said, 'Why don't you go to Shankar and see if my blouses are ready? But more importantly, you have still not asked him anything about that girl.' The way she said it, he understood that if he did not do it, she would immediately march into Shankar's shop and deal with the matter herself.

Shankar would bear the force of Raghavendra's irritation. First Mari and his snakes, his red towel and eyes, his sweeping gestures and familiar, conspiratorial tone with his wife. Then Shankar and the unnecessary smoothening of his wife's blouse with not a hint of a smile or even a dream.

Shankar had a new boy in his shop who was helping him with the cutting and stitching. Raghavendra leaned across the table aggressively. 'You told me you will give *it* to me earlier.'

'But you didn't come.'

Raghavendra had forgotten, what with so many things to worry about. 'You could have sent it to my house.' He looked around and saw the boy in the corner, trying to stitch a hook on another blouse. 'You could have sent it with him.'

Shankar was surprised at Raghavendra's aggression. He had thought of him as a man with no passion and no interests. He took Poornima's blouse, placed it on the table. 'This is the old one,' he said. Raghavendra was fidgeting. *Why is Shankar exhibiting my wife's blouse so everyone in the street can see them?*

Shankar spread out three new blouses that he had stitched. He placed one on top of the other, indicating to Raghavendra how perfectly they matched. He rolled them in a newspaper, tucked in the ends and gave it to him. A soft, fluffy parcel. Not noting Raghavendra's agitation, he said, 'One hundred and fifty.'

'What?'

'One hundred and fifty rupees. This is the price I am giving your madam. It is less than what I charge for others.'

Raghavendra pulled out two crumpled hundred-rupee notes and banged them on the table. Shankar sent the boy to get change, and also two cups of tea. Raghavendra refused the tea, but Shankar persisted. *Here, take this seat, sit here with me and we can watch the street go by together.* Raghavendra would have left, but he saw Prasanna from the corner of his eye, and his irritation was transferred to the carpenter. He watched Shankar pull out a pant piece and make markings on it. Always busy, Shankar seemed to say. *I have too much work to do.* From a nameless tailoring shop, he had recently uncovered a name and a nameboard: Winspot Tailors. Written in English and Kannada along with the words 'Ladies and Gentlemen tailor'. As if he was perpetually on the verge of delivering a talk.

Raghavendra looked at Prasanna, who was working on a piece of wood, sitting on the pavement. *Everybody is working except me!* He turned to Shankar. 'The fellow is still working on that cot?'

Shankar did not disguise his reaction. 'Yes, making marriage cots while his daughter . . . '

Raghavendra responded as if he had been waiting for this opportunity. 'Do you know what really happened to her?'

'She took poison.' Shankar picked up the large scissors and cut a diagonal piece.

'I heard it was because she was . . . '

'Yes. She was.'

He threw a piece carelessly into the dustbin.

'What sort of a boy makes a young child pregnant?'

'She was not a child.' Images, scissored into many bits and pieces, flashed past him. Young, giggly, childish, flirtatious. Laughing. Prodding. That was it: challenging. Her laugh was a challenge. But he kept his eyes carefully on his work.

He remembered the time she had given him her shirt as a measurement for a new one. He had been so shy while taking it. Archana had leaned across the table and looked him in the eye. Challenging! *Can you do it right, you think?* She had sneaked beneath his drooping eyelids, watched him hiding inside its folds and laughed, then turned triumphantly and walked away. Child indeed!

Raghavendra was moved to say, 'All girls are children . . . till they are married.' He looked around pensively, seeing if perchance his daughters were walking around on the street.

'What about boys? Are they children too?' Shankar asked.

'Ha! You and I know better. Look at all the boys walking on the road, their eyes always roaming, from one girl to another.' He didn't say what he thought: even at women. Married women. He had seen so many of those looks directed at Poornima. *Who says vision should not have any shame?* He might as well have added that sight must many times be hidden, covered, brought out only to peek.

'Anyway, Uncle. That is the way some are. Why blame all men for that?'

Raghavendra looked at Shankar, saw an innocence that moved him. 'You are right, Shankar. We have to see the best in people. But sometimes, when you see something happening, like to that girl . . . '

'Maybe it was all a mistake. You know what I think? I think it was an older, married man. These young girls are so foolish when it comes to these things.'

Immediately, Raghavendra felt the surging power of knowledge. An older man!

'There is nobody in this area who could have done this.' It sounded like a defence of his generation. Or of being married.

'Why not? Look at all the men. Look at fellows like Nagaraj, your friend.'

Nagaraj! Why hadn't Raghavendra thought of him?

'You really think it could be Nagaraj?' He leaned forward, the spectacles slipping on his nose. *Damn these new spectacles. Rajesh and his friends*! He was sure he had been cheated.

'What do you think, Uncle? Those fellows are drunk most of the time. Maybe the girl had a drink with them . . . '

Raghavendra jumped up. 'Don't speak like that, Shankar. Don't say such things about little girls.' Instinctively, he looked across the road. There were a few customers outside Prasanna's shop, and Prasanna was only a lumpy shadow on the ground.

Shankar looked contrite. 'It's okay. I am just saying. I am sorry. She was a sweet girl. I hope the bastard who got her pregnant . . . I hope he pays for it.' It was a speech indeed, in keeping with the ladies and gentlemen tailor.

Raghavendra got up. 'God is there,' he said. Looking out at the road for the gods to come riding in chariots. God was there to dispense justice, but wasn't around to make sure the tea would arrive. He took the packet of rolled-up blouses and told Shankar to send the change to his house. As he stepped down carefully, his loose spectacles held firmly with his right index finger, the boy came hurrying. Two half-filled glasses of tea, sloshing around, impatient to be gulped.

Shankar grabbed the change and gave Raghavendra his money. He insisted that Raghavendra drink the tea, saying, 'After all, it has already come'. As if the two glasses had come there of their own accord.

Raghavendra stood on the road and drank the warm tea. Normally he wouldn't have, but since he thought that one hundred and fifty rupees was too much for stitching three blouses, he felt he could morally afford to drink the tea bought by Shankar.

That night, lying on the floor next to Poornima, thankful that the power was on and that a grumbling fan could keep at least some mosquitoes away, he told her about Shankar's comments about Nagaraj. She was falling asleep, a slow feathered drop, but suddenly turned on her side and said, 'Nagaraj! You think that girl would ever have . . . ?' Her anger made the silence tick. *What does Raghavendra know about girls?* She opened her eyes and stared at him. Uncomfortable, he too turned on his side so that they could stare at each other. 'Nagaraj can anyway get all those other women, those prostitutes who are always out here in the nights.'

He gave up staring and slumped on his back. *How does she know about such things?* Prostitutes here? Where? He had not seen even one.

Poornima was irritated, thinking that he had gone to sleep while she was talking to him. She prodded him in the side and he twitched. 'You are wasting too much time,' she hissed. 'You are lucky Nagaraj hasn't come here yet. How much longer are you going to take to find out about Archana?' She turned her back on him. In the darkness, accentuated by his poor sight, she looked like a range of mountains at midnight.

That night, Raghavendra suddenly realised: time is not to be measured in cycles of light and darkness. Neither by water days.

Now, for him, time was accumulated in the sack of rice that had been thrown out in the open, for the rain, the sun, the rats and many other insects who had discovered a treasure trove in it. He had noticed that some amount of rice was missing each passing moment. The trail of grains led to all corners of his compound. The drizzle and the dampness had given the sack an extra heaviness that seemed to push it more forcefully into the ground.

Watching the sack surreptitiously through the open window, he decided that he would finish Archana's case before the sack got empty. Then he would buy a new sack of rice and inaugurate his grocery store. This resolution lifted his spirits, made the future accountable to him. When he excitedly told Poornima of his decision, she had only this to say: 'You are more excited about a sack of rice than that poor girl.'

7

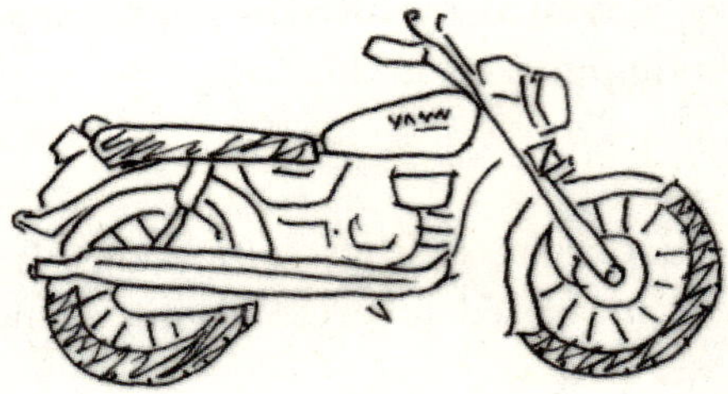

RAGHAVENDRA WOULD NOT HAVE ACCEPTED THIS FACT SO easily: he was slowly changing, transforming himself from a man who followed events to one who made them happen. He was beginning to find the true spirit of entrepreneurship as well as discovering the magic of being a detective. Before, when he worked for Paul, he was mostly a manager of men, but now he had to manage only his time, that oppressive space of freedom. So it was that when he woke to the knock of dawn on the bedroom window, already the fifth day after Archana's death, he decided that he would draw upon Rajesh, Marimuthu and Shankar to help him in his search. Somehow, this gave him the confidence that his search for the mysterious lover would not be futile.

In his newfound confidence, he left the house early, managing not to awaken Poornima. Not even waiting for his coffee, he went to meet Marimuthu, who was at the borewell, pumping water into a bucket, red coloured (*what else?*). Raghavendra stood at the gates of the temple and watched Mari pour the water over his head, so cold that he could feel the chill across that distance, a current that made him feel that he was the one who was having a cold bath. It was as if Marimuthu was saying to him, 'If having a cold-water head bath with water drawn from a well, every morning in Bangalore, is not the sign of a yogi, what is?'

The borewell itself was a minor miracle. Nobody knew how or why it came about. One day a lorry came with boring equipment. Shattered the afternoon silence into pneumatic bits and left, leaving behind gushing water. The well was dug just outside the side compound of the temple and it seemed as if it was dug for the temple. As Mari had added, by the power of the temple. Really, a truer democratic borewell could not be found in the entire city of Bangalore.

The other, not so minor, miracle associated with this event, for after all it was not enough for just one miracle to sustain the imagination of Mathikere Extension, was that no politician claimed credit for the borewell. This was indeed baffling. When even a new lamppost had to be inaugurated by the local leaders, the borewell had just come to be.

Soon after, five huts came up alongside, crowding each other on a piece of government land nearby, and a whole new civilisation sprang up along the banks of the borewell stream. The borewell now served Mari, the hutment dwellers, two bakeries nearby, and also a cycle repair shop. The little boy who worked in that shop collected water in a shallow pan in order to test for punctures. Mari once wryly told the shop owner, a sturdy man who looked like he lifted cycles for weights, that he would not be surprised if the water from that borewell would come to possess miraculous curing powers—if not for people, at least for the punctured cycle tubes.

Mari walked past Raghavendra and entered the temple, his cold skin muttering prayers of its own. He went into the anthill room and soon came out attired in red.

Marimuthu had one more ritual to perform. He sat under the tree and started praying. To legitimise himself further in the eyes of a Brahmin, he had to recite prayers, to create a religion out of an anthill.

Every few lines or so, Raghavendra recognised some Sanskrit words and his conversion was complete. *He is not even a Brahmin but he puts me to shame.* He was ready to take Mari into his fold.

Mari saw Raghavendra relax, felt his acceptance. He finished his prayers, went around the tree three times, and prostrated on the ground. He really looked like a snake then. He got up, went to the gate and whistled. The boy from the bakery a few doors away looked out. Two chai, Marimuthu said, and ruffled Raghavendra's refusal with a glance.

'Tell me. You are here to ask me something.'

Raghavendra felt a growing warmth towards this man. 'It is Nagaraj,' he replied. 'I have decided to get rid of him.'

'What? Kill him!' Mari laughed, delighting in the image of Raghavendra killing Nagaraj.

Raghavendra was shocked that Mari could even think him capable of murder. 'No, no,' he began, but Mari only laughed louder. He bent over, making cackling sounds beside the roots of the tree, talking to the roots in their own language.

'Oh, keep quiet. All I want to do is to go to the police.'

Mari made a show of jumping up, still laughing. 'It would be easier to kill him,' he spluttered.

'I found his papers on the chit fund. If he has been cheating people, then these papers will prove it.'

Mari became serious. He placed his hands on Raghavendra's shoulders and said, 'That would be really foolish. He will kill you much more easily than you can think of slapping him.'

Raghavendra sat down abruptly on the cement platform built around the tree.

Mari looked down at him. 'I suggest that you make copies of his papers. When he asks you for them, give the originals to him. Or better still, go to where he is and give him the originals.'

Raghavendra thought of telling him that Nagaraj had not come to his house even once after he had changed the lock. Then had a sinking doubt: *Did he come late in the night and discover the new lock and the sack of rice in the open?* He remembered a question he had asked Mari before, and asked it again. 'Where does Nagaraj live?'

Nagaraj lived in many places, Mari told him. He slept in his friends' houses, drunk almost every night. Otherwise, in the company of prostitutes.

Raghavendra reacted visibly. 'Prostitutes here?'

Mari asked dramatically, 'Who do you think lives in those rooms above the many hotels here?'

Most of these places had a name followed by 'Bar and Restaurant'. Venkateswara Bar and Restaurant was the most successful of the lot. The ground floor was a wine shop. A crumbling staircase, marked with paan stains, led to the restaurant upstairs. Above it were two floors of single rooms with common toilets at one end of each floor. These were the meeting places for the prostitutes in the area. Earlier, there were a few women who stood outside the Yeswanthpur Railway station, near the market. They would loiter near the pavements outside old hotels which housed travelling salesmen, medical reps, lorry drivers and traders. These women used to come from the northern part of Karnataka, which was reeling under a drought. Then, slowly, like all the other professions in Bangalore, prostitution too began to attract women from other states. Just as students came to study from Bihar and Bengal, so too did women come from these regions, brought to Bangalore by a network of men and women with associates in all the states through which these women passed. If earlier, the women were somewhat older and experienced, the sudden growth of Bangalore spurred the introduction of younger women, some of whom bypassed Mumbai to come to the dreams that Bangalore built.

Marimuthu said, 'You cannot handle this situation by yourself, saar.'

Raghavendra looked at him in surprise: *Why suddenly this saar?*

'If you want my help, tell me. But then you will have no control over what happens. It may so happen that Nagaraj may get beaten up . . . and may even die. I can help you because you are a good man, but once you enter this path, your idea of good and bad might change.'

Raghavendra was worried. Mari talked so easily of killing. He pushed his sliding spectacles back on his nose—the act reminding him again that he should complain to Rajesh about the optician—and got up. 'This is my job. My duty. I will do what I can. If I cannot, or if I feel my family is in danger, I will come to you.'

'Do that. But remember, you will have to go into the hotels and sit at tables where they serve chicken and beer. You will have to meet the girls who stay in those single rooms and share your thoughts with them. You think you can do it?'

Mari was not questioning Raghavendra's individual capabilities but was asking a historical question. Will you, a Madhwa Brahmin, step into *those* places, meet *those* people on *their* ground? Will you, a Madhwa Brahmin, sit on chairs that sweat the fried smells of meat and are coated with impatient alcoholic vapours? Will you, a respectable middle-aged man with two girls, sit in places where prostitutes have sat, leaning on the impression of their bottoms? Will you be able to raise a fist, if not to attack, at least to defend?

Raghavendra looked at him, searching for a hint of mockery, but Mari's smile showed only concern. It also meant to say: Go ahead. I will be there behind you.

He went back home, his mind imagining the melange of criminals and prostitutes in *his* locality. He would have told Poornima, look at what is happening around us. Would my father have even dreamt of these happenings in our locality? But he kept quiet, anticipating her response. As he entered the house, Rajesh came down, on his way for his morning tea. Raghavendra called him over.

'You and your friends!' He thrust his glasses at him. 'Your friend is a cheat. He has sold me this rotten frame.'

Rajesh was immediately hurt. 'My friend would never cheat me. Since you think he has done so, I will skip my tea, go to his house, wake him if needed and repair your glasses.' He took the glasses from Raghavendra and walked away, his back bristling with hurt pride.

When Poornima heard that Raghavendra had been to meet Mari, she was irritated. 'What was the hurry, going without telling me or even before having your coffee?'

Raghavendra only smiled back. How could she know how entrepreneurs think and act? That they, *us*, are not creatures of habit but creators of time?

She scowled at his condescending smile and asked him if he had talked to Mari about Archana. *Oh, how could he have forgotten!* He mumbled something; the only distinct sound she heard was 'Nagaraj'.

Rajesh came back after an hour and gave Raghavendra his spectacles. He had no words or gestures to offer him, and left, stiff and formal. Raghavendra was too scared to ask him whether he had really fixed his spectacles or had merely taken them for a walk.

Although it was not a water day, Raghavendra had this dream on the sixth day: he woke up before the alarm, remembered to turn it off, and went to collect water. The pressure of the water was more forceful that day. He looked up, and stars with dimples in their eyes greeted him. Before his vessel was full, he heard the sound of Baale's door opening. He hurriedly closed the tap and lifted the vessel. In his haste, the vessel slipped and fell back on the ground, spilling much of the water it contained. Without looking up, he angrily turned on the tap again, willing the water to gush out.

He saw Mrs Gowda come up to the broken fence, and on seeing him, hurry back to her house. He could hear her, in the stillness of the night, waking Baale. From the corner of his eye, he saw both of them standing near the door of their house, waiting for him to leave. In an uncharacteristic fit of meanness, he allowed the water to slow to a trickle. He then went inside to get another vessel. When he came back, he saw that Baale was filling his vessel and had also increased the flow of water in the tap. He felt ashamed, having his juvenile trick exposed by a school principal, no less!

Baale picked up his vessel and moved through the fence, stirring the sleepy flowers of the bougainvillaea awake. He looked at Raghavendra with reproach, a look that said, You do this to me?

Irritated, Raghavendra was moved to say: 'Remember, two weeks.' He filled his vessel and lifted it casually, as if its weight mattered little. But, along with the vessel, he found he also carried a catch in his back.

He woke up suddenly, hearing the sound of an auto blasting its horn right outside the window. It was already bright outside and he could hear the girls talking to their mother. He felt disoriented, and his body still remembered him lifting (*so effortlessly!*) the vessel filled with water.

When Poornima came into the room to take a towel from the cupboard, he told her that he had dreamt he had filled water that morning. She ignored him. He thought she had not heard him, but as she walked out of the room, she muttered, 'Collecting water fills our lives so much that we can't even distinguish dreams and real life.'

The catch in the dream had become a knot in his back by nine. He lay in bed while Poornima sent the girls off to school. The knot was alleviated by a breakfast of idlis. That was her way of atonement, even though there was no reason for her to have felt guilty.

He would have liked to go back to the warmth of the bed. But he knew that she would have none of that. She would weave her way in and out of the room, like a moth with a thorn in its wing, wanting him to get up, discovering reasons for it near the sides of the bed. If he still refused to get up, she would begin muttering. The words would make no sense, but the meaning would be clear: young men like you sleeping in the daytime! It was as if his dozing in the morning somehow made *her* an old woman.

So he went to the toilet. He passed the bedroom on his way out, leaving it behind with a wistful sigh. Only to return immediately and ask Poornima to rub a balm on his back. *In spite of the pain*, his pliant, soft back told her, *I am going to work*. She pushed him out not so gently.

He went to meet Sunil, the owner of a spray-paint shop. The shop was actually the space underneath the staircase of a crumbling two-storey house. There was a generator in one corner and a gas cylinder in the other. In between these sat a small boy whose age had withered in the spray of paint. Paint dust had gathered in the pores of his skin, and had discovered cracks and creases, those that had been hidden for his old age. His teeth had become metallic grey and when he bit into his food, it was with the sound of rusted steel. He was just one of the thousands in the streets of urban India trying to survive chemicals, fumes and stained water.

Sunil always sat under a tree opposite his shop. The tree had miraculously survived the over-crowded pavement. The boy would keep a folding chair under the tree for Sunil before he began his work. Sunil not only kept one eye on his employee, he also distributed the sight of the other eye to the many other small shops around. His biggest worry was that the boy would leave him and join the scooter repair shop nearby.

Sunil saw Raghavendra and ignored him. It was only when Raghavendra stood in front of him, his crumpled brown pants hiding the view of the boy, that he looked up. It was only after Raghavendra had said that he wanted Sunil to paint a board for him that he stood up.

'I want it to be a secret,' Raghavendra said, looking around at all the busy shops close by, knowing well that every secret in the place was a mirage.

Secrets were no problem for Sunil. They were like promises that were never kept. But to emphasise that he would do as Raghavendra wished, he took him for a walk down the road. 'Now you tell me what you want. Nobody can hear you.'

Raghavendra asked him to paint 'Sri Krishna Provision Stores' on a tin plate. He wanted red for the letters and blue for the background. 'Which blue?' Sunil asked and Raghavendra looked vainly at the sky for a patch of blue. He could only point to the clouds and mutter, 'Sky blue.' Sunil nodded wisely, as if sky blue was the colour of his mind.

'What red?' he asked, trying to tell Raghavendra that he was not a small-time shop owner but a professional who was particular about the right shades of colour.

What red? Raghavendra looked around, saw Sunil's stare stick on a girl in a red skirt walking by, and kept quiet. Sunil nodded again, wise to Raghavendra's thoughts. He wondered why Raghavendra wanted spray painting when he could have spent much less getting somebody to do a patchy brush paint job. But maybe he had underestimated this uninspiring man, who too seemed to be a professional like him.

'Since I do my job with the best paint,' he said in a lowered voice, adding a price for the secret, 'it won't be cheap.'

Raghavendra haggled a bit. They walked back to Sunil's shop. They agreed on a price and Raghavendra insisted that nobody should see the board being made. But the moment he saw the boy spraying a small steel almirah, exhibiting his art for all to see, he lost his illusions about that. Then he noticed the boy's shirt—streaks of red darting around a seabed of grey and blue. He pointed at the shirt. 'I want it in those colours,' he said, happy to have finally grasped his words with sight.

Sunil was disappointed. He did not believe that the aesthetic beauty of colours could be captured in a dirty shirt. He shrugged, his eyebrows rising and muttering their own words: *if that is what you want*. The boy sat with his head hung low, concentrating on evenly distributing the paint on the almirah, breathing the fine mist through his unprotected nose and mouth. Clouds of paint rose gracefully and settled on his head, a silvery halo for a boy who would soon become an angel.

That done, *what a surprise for Poornima*, Raghavendra went to the bus stop to wait for a bus to Yeshwanthpur. He was lucky to find a bus that was ready to leave. He pushed his way in and was crushed by the growing crowd. He felt suddenly nauseous, but before he could think of getting out, the bus had jerked forward. Two women fell off the footboard and he could hear their cries echoing in the passengers around him. The bus did not stop but sped off with a gleeful roar, leaving behind a blanket of thick, black smoke. How Raghavendra missed the safety of his bedroom then.

If ever there was a conflict in his life, it could be located in the contentment that he felt while lounging inside the house, even as the rest of the world proved their worth by constantly running around, catching buses or speeding on scooters, bikes and cycles. Raghavendra was happy to be a traffic light amidst all this motion. He would gladly have changed from red to yellow to green, and back to red again. It was that kind of comfort he desired, a cyclical order of predictable colours. He was indifferent to the chaos around him, but Poornima had tried to eradicate all such thoughts from him. She didn't want an unemployed man in the house, happy to move aimlessly from morning to evening to night. She wanted Raghavendra to occupy all the space in between. She wanted him accountable to minutes, if not seconds. But most importantly, most secretly, she didn't want him around the house the whole day because the time and space here, its homely silence, were for her alone. Raghavendra and her children only succeeded in disturbing the peaceful bond she had with her house, although she sometimes felt that it was only their noise that made the house a home.

So, it was but natural that Raghavendra enjoyed being the owner of his own agency. His desire to be a grocer, if he were ever to articulate it, stemmed from the comfort and warmth he felt sitting among the silent gunny bags filled with groceries. Customers would only be passing distractions from his soliloquies with silence. If Poornima had gained the silent comfort of a house, he would gain it in his shop.

Yeshwanthpur Police Station was at the corner of five intersecting roads. One of them led onto a highway while another went into the folded heart of Yeshwanthpur with its thousand little shops, bakeries, restaurants and markets. It was an area that defined itself with a characteristic smell of wholesale groceries (*how can anybody think that wholesale and retail groceries smell the same?*), rotting vegetables, fresh flowers, sudden whiffs of fish from the pavement, and the fresh, anonymous smell of meat from the corner butcher shops. Over this chaotic domain, there was one Eye that kept constant watch. This, as only to be expected, was the police station. For no fathomable reason, the station building had a metallic sculpture on top that resembled an eye. Nobody knew how that mangled piece of iron had come to rest on the roof of the station. The gaze of the Eye was more pronounced at those times of the day when the station was visible only through a blanket of exhaust fumes from vehicles standing patiently at the five signals.

Below, in the many rooms, were many eyes keeping watch for many things: drivers with no licence, out-of-state lorries with no proper permits, scooterists who impatiently tried to skip the signals. There was always a horde of constables hovering outside the station, waiting for one false move, and at times, for the right one. Every driver on these roads was a potential criminal and the Eye made sure that it would extract a price for even imagined traffic crimes. Only cyclists who did not stop at signals were spared monetary damage. They got one or two patronising slaps on the head instead.

The Eye also kept a watch on crimes in that area. The lockup here was famed for the violent attempts made to elicit information. It was only first-time criminals who graced the lockup, for the Eye was known to wink and in that wink pockets would be filled with money.

The bus carrying Raghavendra stopped at the signal, spewing more black smoke. A crowd pushed at him and he found himself stumbling off the bus. Before his courage could desert him, he walked up to the gates of the police station. Two constables rushed past him to catch a motor bike with Tamil Nadu numberplates. One of them pulled at the driver even as he was trying to drive away. The other caught hold of the motorbike. As an added precaution, the first constable gave a resounding slap on the back of the driver. The sound of it drowned out Raghavendra's growing unease, but before he could turn away, another constable held his hand.

'What do you want?' he asked, questioning Raghavendra's right to stand under the Eye for no reason.

'I want to meet the inspector,' Raghavendra managed to reply, trying to release his hand without being too obvious about it.

The constable pushed him through the gate and into the compound. 'Why?' he asked.

Yes, why? Could Raghavendra tell him that he wanted to complain about Nagaraj? But the constables around him looked like they were all avatars of Nagaraj.

'I have to meet the inspector,' he said again, hoping he would not have to talk about Nagaraj in public.

The constable dragged him to the door as if Raghavendra was the criminal and had been caught trying to escape on his spindly legs. Raghavendra mustered enough courage to pull his hand away.

At the first sign of assertion, the constable glared at him. 'You go to that desk and tell him what you want. You think anybody can just walk in and meet the inspector?'

Of course not. Raghavendra did not think *anybody* could do that. He had forgotten to think. Else, how could he have been so foolish as to enter the domain of the Eye? The desk was manned by two red eyes and a thick moustache. The man's paunch sloped beneath the desk as if it had grown in size while he sat rooted in his chair. If ever the man had smiled, it must have been years ago.

The constable pushed Raghavendra towards the table and said, 'He says he wants to meet the inspector!' His voice was scornful, the kind of scorn that is beyond derisive laughter. 'And he doesn't say why.'

Everybody in the room looked at Raghavendra immediately. What little humanity they had saved for their evenings with their families was lost in those stares.

Raghavendra looked at a picture of Hanuman behind the man at the desk. A picture of Gandhi was below it. He felt his fear change to aggression.

'Remove your hand,' he told the constable sternly. Looking at the man behind the desk, he added, 'You act as if I am a criminal. Is the inspector here or not?'

There was total silence in the room. The ticking of a clock intruded on the silence, basking in its moment of glory. Behind the man, Raghavendra could see a room with swinging doors. From the deference shown in the eyes that sometimes glanced towards those doors, Raghavendra knew it to be that of the Inspector's.

He nodded towards the door. 'Is he there or not?' He had begun confidently, but his voice fell to a squeak. The man behind the desk caught that momentary lapse of courage and told him to go and sit on the bench.

There were five others on the bench. An old couple sat submissively, and a fleeting glance at the woman suggested that she had been crying.

Once dismissed, also forgotten. He sat there for half an hour, the wall clock in front of his eyes now a mocking presence. It was the only object in that room which showed any sign of life. Nobody on the bench moved or was called in. They sat in silence, afraid to even talk among themselves.

Life went on around them, with people going in and out. Once, a man was dragged past them by his collar, his shirt torn in many places. As he went past, he smiled at them. Raghavendra felt a surge of energy from that smile. He got up and went to the desk. 'Are you going to tell me if I can meet him now or not?'

'Why? What are you going to do?'

'Aey, you call yourselves the police? You are servants of the people.' He spoke as rapidly as he blinked.

Suddenly, the man laughed. Unexpectedly cheerful laughter from the bottom of his paunch. The desk reverberated. All his colleagues in the room too laughed.

'Servants!' he repeated, and laughed louder. He lifted his hand, big and fleshy, as if he was going to strike Raghavendra, who took an awkward step back.

The laughter suddenly stopped. 'Go sit there,' the man shouted. Raghavendra turned away. At the door, a policeman in plainclothes stopped him.

'Why do you say such things? They won't let you see the inspector. You want to see him, pay that fellow hundred rupees.'

Raghavendra did not have that kind of money. 'No!' he said. 'I would rather complain to the higher authorities.'

The plainclothesman took him aside. 'Okay, pay me fifty and I'll take you to meet him.'

'Why should I pay you for no fault of mine? I am not the criminal here!'

'That is not the point. You can either sit here for another few hours or you can see the inspector now. Fifty rupees is only because I am taking pity on you. You remind me of my father. I have to anyway give most of it to the inspector.'

Raghavendra dug into his pocket and came up with a new fifty-rupee note. He felt ashamed giving the money to the man. He looked up furtively and saw Gandhi's photo hide behind a passing cloud of shame.

After a ten-minute wait, he was told to go in. He walked past the desk; the man had become, once again, two red eyes and a thick moustache. He pushed open the swinging doors and saw the inspector reading a newspaper.

What a disaster this whole trip had been. He had been crushed in the bus and had the sweaty smells of others rubbed onto him. Then he had been vomited out of the bus and thrown at the doorsteps of the police station like a sacrificial lamb. There, he had been harassed and humiliated and had fifty rupees taken off him. For what? Yes, for what?

It was a few minutes before the inspector put the paper down. Raghavendra stood near the edge of the desk, but when the face behind the paper refused to materialise, he sat on the chair.

Surprised, the inspector looked at him. He pulled a few sheets of paper towards him. Rang a bell on the table. A peon soon crawled in with one cup of coffee the colour of the inspector's desk. Raghavendra fidgeted as the intimidation by silence continued. After a few more minutes spent reading the nametag of the inspector, watching the peeling paint on the walls, hearing the frightened whimpers of law that had gone to hide in the walls, Raghavendra coughed. The inspector picked up a poster of Wanted men, whose photos had greyed from having been run through an old Xerox machine, and looked at them intently. Then looked at Raghavendra, as if he were one of the criminals who had materialised suddenly in front of him.

'I want to make a complaint,' Raghavendra ventured to say. 'About a man who is bothering me and my family. He is a well-known criminal, it seems.'

'Where are you from?' the inspector finally asked, his voice as curly as his hair, filled with well-oiled innuendoes and accusations.

'Mathikere Extension.'

Immediately, the inspector showed interest. He took his stick and tapped it on the table.

'Who is it?'

'He is called Nagaraj. He comes to my house and threatens us . . . '

'Nagaraj?' Once again, silence filled the space between them. 'Are you sure it is Nagaraj?'

There are many Nagarajs in this world, he seemed to suggest. *For you to come and disturb my time* . . . 'What is his initial?'

Once again, Raghavendra's ignorance about Nagaraj, his own partner, came to haunt him. He lost any pretence of maintaining his dignity. He pleaded, 'I don't know what his initials are. But I beg you, please do something about it. I have a wife and two little girls . . . '

There! He had said it again! Family, family. What kind of a man was he, to use his family to beg for favours?

The inspector mellowed. 'What do you do?' he asked. Looking at Raghavendra, he knew it was all going to be a waste of time.

'I am going to start a grocery shop,' Raghavendra replied. 'You are my only hope.'

'Ah! That is true. That is there. I have to take care of so many things. But we will see.'

Raghavendra refused to get up. He wanted the inspector to do something. Anything.

'Can you send someone to talk to Nagaraj?' he asked, summoning his last reserve of energy.

The inspector rang the bell again and picked up the Wanted photos. When the peon slithered in, afraid to break the silence with the tread of his footsteps, he said, 'Send *him* in.'

'Him' came in, hurrying through the swinging doors. His eyes were all for the inspector, suggesting to him that his sight, no, his whole life, was for the inspector's sake alone.

'Sir,' he said.

'Do you know any fellow called Nagaraj in Mathikere Extension?'

The man, already at attention, froze and looked at Raghavendra. Simultaneously, they recognised each other. If memory had eyes, Raghavendra would have seen this man, once again, standing over Poornima and himself, glaring at them, simulating a face of terror.

'You,' Raghavendra began. The look on the man's face stopped him.

The inspector, oblivious to their exchange, said, 'Go with him and talk to that Nagaraj. He is creating trouble for him, it seems.'

The man leaned closer to the inspector and whispered. When the whisper threatened to become a growl, Raghavendra got up and walked out, unable to speak. Justice had lost its voice. And all that he had to say was sacrificed to the rhythmic creak of the swinging doors that he pushed at, violently, on his way out.

Even the crowd in the bus on the way back refused to give back the voice to his anger.

8

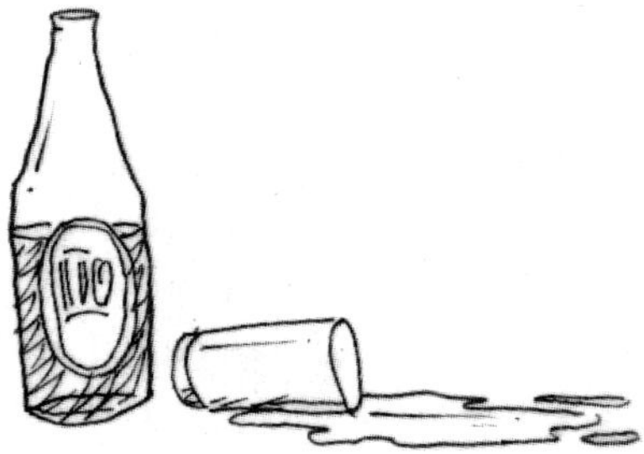

Anger was a stage on which Raghavendra strutted around, speaking his lines, all that he would have liked to tell the inspector. He wrote dialogues in his head and acted them out with ferocious intensity. Tired after his mental performance, he fell asleep, finding no words even for Poornima. But his crumpled face and angry snores had their own story to tell. She realised this and felt a sudden affection for him. She closed the windows and stood in front of them to shelter him from the sound and light that had invaded the late afternoon. When he tossed and turned, she soothed his murmurs by hiding them in the warm folds of her sari. In the afternoon, she would wake him up with good, strong coffee. Forget the cost, forget the good habit of drinking tea in the afternoons.

When he did manage to speak, quickly, before the girls came back home, before the impatient chatter of their footsteps rang the bell for the evening, he told her about his visit to the police station.

Her response was typical: 'I've told you before, there is no justice for us. Therefore, you cannot uphold justice for others. Except this one time. You take the help of Rajesh and find out what you can about Archana. And then we will forget this part of our life.'

She had not stopped speaking. But the fan, already creaking under the pressure of low voltage, suddenly stopped. Poornima said, 'I will also help. I can ask some people . . . and maybe some of Archana's friends.' She had a ray of doubt. 'I am sure she had friends, don't you think?'

Even then Raghavendra was lethargic. Couldn't find the right words to convince her of his desire or ability to discover who Archana's lover had been. As a final bait, she said, 'I'll call Rajesh now and tell him. You just go with him.' She stopped abruptly, staring intently at him, and he heard what she didn't say: *If you don't, I'll go with him.* When he didn't reply even to this provocation, she went out and called Rajesh, one step on the staircase, one eye on the road, and one ear for the echo of her own voice.

When Rajesh came down, a towel around his shoulders, they could see he had been dozing. He walked in, still holding onto a residue of his hurt, now coloured by the reddish tinge that bordered his towel. Poornima spoke to him in Hindi, gathering together a few words she had absorbed from the many Hindi TV serials and making a garland out of them. Rajesh wanted to reciprocate that gesture and found an immediate smile for her.

Raghavendra had had enough of Poornima's intrusions. He told Rajesh sternly, 'I need your help. I have promised to do something which is not to my liking.' He glanced at his wife, who looked out of the window, searching for her daughters. They would soon be coming back from school. 'This is not really our business, but Archana's mother wants to know who made Archana pregnant.'

He stumbled over his thoughts, not wanting to talk about a pregnant teenager with a young man like Rajesh. Rajesh was delighted. He pulled the towel tighter around his shoulders and said, 'Haan, you should do that, Uncle. After all, you are the detective of this place.'

When he said 'detective', it sounded like a series of clicks of his teeth.

'And not to worry. If you had asked me this before, I would have told you all the answers. Three students, all from Bihar, live in the house next to Archana's.' He ended with a flourish, 'They are all my juniors.' The way he said it, it was obvious that being a junior was as good as being a slave.

Raghavendra was not surprised to hear about more students from Bihar. From a science and technology hub, Bangalore had become an education hub. Students from all the other states flocked to the state of Karnataka, to its many private engineering and medical colleges. The nineties were fuelled by a drive of students from Bengal and Bihar, all of whom found some means of paying capitation fees and joining the growing number of colleges in Bangalore. Some sold their father's land, some their mother's jewellery. Initially, it was the boys who came in droves, but soon, the girls started coming in large numbers. To accommodate them, the owners of small houses in Mathikere Extension started renting out one room and half a toilet or better, half a room and a common toilet.

'Of course, they pay a heavy rent, but what do they care? Rich fathers in Bihar, not like mine.' The look he gave Raghavendra and the glance around the room said: *not like yours, either*.

Raghavendra was relieved. He could now do something rather than sit around waiting for the power to suddenly come back, or dozing on the chair.

'You think they will know something?'

'If they don't, nobody here will.' Rajesh slipped out of the house and as he went past the door, the two girls came in, their voices swinging rhythmically in tune with their schoolbags. Rajesh was emboldened enough to pat the younger girl's head and say something in Hindi. He had wanted the pat to be a blessing, an imitation of adulthood, but Sanjeevani only felt tickled and embarrassed.

Raghavendra felt a bit foolish as he set out with Rajesh. He was always uncomfortable going to a stranger's house. The strangeness was not only in the people he didn't know; it inhabited the house itself. The rooms were not where they were in his house; the TV intruded into his eyes, and even the chairs and sofas kept suggesting to him that he didn't belong there. As for the people in the house, the less said the better. People were always strangers to him.

Worse: as they entered Archana's street, memories came back to him as hazy little flutters in his stomach. Archana's house stood forlorn, away from the community of other houses. The door was closed, hiding the insides from prying eyes. As if there lay Archana in a corner, on a coir mat, covering her shameful eyes from others.

Oblivious to Raghavendra's mood, Rajesh walked along with a spring, and out of his receding footsteps flowed a song. Or at least a hum, a remembered melody that had Manisha Koirala doing dainty dances in a heavily brocaded green dress. He walked to his friend's house and opened the gate confidently. As they walked past the gate, Raghavendra saw Prasanna come out of his house and look at him. His expression froze when he saw the two of them, then his eyes flitted to his neighbour's house. If his look could have reached out, it would have pulled Raghavendra into Prasanna's hold and choked him.

Prasanna stood glaring at them as they rang the bell. When the bell did not work, Rajesh banged on the door. Raghavendra looked back. Prasanna was still standing there, staring, as if challenging them.

Finally, one of the boys opened the door. He had obviously been sleeping. His blurred eyes questioned Rajesh. *Arre, everybody sleeps in the afternoon.* Seeing Raghavendra, the question turned into a puzzle.

Raghavendra pushed past Rajesh and hurriedly went inside. The living room was a mess. Unwashed clothes were draped on chairs, cigarette ash spotted the floor, and grime decorated the walls. A door led into a small kitchen. Raghavendra could imagine the sink filled with unwashed vessels. The whole house was coagulated with dust. The chairs and a lumpy sofa looked tired. They were all waiting, the boys, the furniture, the floor and the kitchen, waiting for the maid to scrub and clean, and the cook to wash.

And in the meanwhile?

Rajesh's friend, Kumar, went to the toilet and washed his face with water from a big plastic drum. As he opened the toilet door, a strong smell of urine escaped past him and ran out of the door. Kumar turned his face as if he was able to see the trail of that smell.

Rajesh went into the kitchen and called out, 'Uncle, you want some tea?' His friends were all like this, he seemed to say. *I may live in a room in your house, but all my friends' houses are also mine. This is the way we Biharis are*. Raghavendra did not want tea; he just wanted to leave. Before he could get up, Kumar was back. He was extremely solicitous. Old people never came to their house, and that too a local man! He picked up an already opened packet of bhujia and poured it onto a plate that was spotted with oil and some leftover pieces of little fried bits.

'Please eat, Uncle,' he said and shouted out to Rajesh, 'Make some tea for us.'

Raghavendra refused to touch the bhujia, but Kumar, oblivious to this, went on eating. Rajesh came out with three cups of tea. The tea was milky and served in chipped and darkened ceramic cups with a design of roses on them.

How should Raghavendra begin? How could he stomach talking to this boy about Archana? Before he could gather his thoughts and come up with a question, Rajesh told Kumar about Raghavendra's quest. He spoke proudly of him and how, although he looked like a weakling (this in a rapid aside in Hindi), he had been asked to solve the *mysterious* case of Archana.

Kumar was surprised but also excited. Life as a student in Bangalore, although filled with sufficient distractions, including periodic visits to the racecourse, was quite monotonous. Nothing really exciting happened. No dacoits, no gun fights, no 'manly' events ever took place here.

Seeing Kumar's obvious glee, Raghavendra was worried. He told him that their enquiry was to be a secret between them. When he saw Kumar's eyes darting around, he knew it was a futile request. Kumar got up from the cot he was leaning on and, taking Raghavendra's hand, pulled him towards a window. From here, they could see a room in Prasanna's house. The windows of the room were closed.

'See that, that is where she would stand, combing her hair . . . '

With a song on her lips. Her hair full of oil that she would keep massaging. The scalp, occasionally visible, would shine, and even light would rush to hide in the fragrant warmth of the coconut oil. See! That is also where she would dress, with the windows wide open, waiting for the breeze to caress her back and her corner-gaze searching for the boys. For me, Kumar would have said, as he stood watching through the crack in the window, only for me.

The timing of these rituals was strictly followed. Once Prasanna left the house, the windows would open, light would bounce in, and the songs would begin. Only the stray shouts of her mother would disturb the silence. How many classes Kumar and his friends had bunked in order to share stealthy, fleeting glimpses that would pass as they had come, in a sudden bang of the windows.

'And what about her sister?' asked Raghavendra, forcing himself to listen to Kumar, willing himself not to hate him at that moment. More: he wanted to know, so that he could make sure the windows in his house were barred against any such exhibitions by his daughters. Thinking of them, he feared that they would be easy prey for these boys.

'Her sister? She is such a . . . straight thing. We only hear her voice, see only her back, and we even have to imagine her face.' He spoke poetically, he thought, and paused for applause.

'Archana was special. She was like a bird full of joy. Her sister is just the opposite.'

Raghavendra's thoughts arose as fast as Kumar's lilting words. Were two sisters always doomed to be like this? Would Sanjeevani be the silent one, forever in the acoustic shade of her gregarious sister? God, how fast Suhasini was growing! Should they move out of this locality into one where there were no college boys? What would Poorni say?

Raghavendra shook himself out of his daymare. His daughters would never become like Archana. The sense of optimism filled him with relief, and he walked back to his chair.

'Do you know why she died?' he asked.

'Haan, she was pregnant,' Kumar replied easily.

'How do you know that?'

'Arre, Uncle. You think we can't hear what we can so easily see! You think we did not hear the shouts and screams of her parents?' Watching Raghavendra sharply, he added, 'Ha! You are thinking how we could understand Malayalam. Not to worry. A Malayali friend who stays in the hostel was here that night. Poor chap, he had started joining us at the window, watching that girl as if she was his own! Just because she was a Malayali, he thought he had a better chance with her than any of us. I think he fell in love with Archana.' His gaze swept past the room, lingered on the TV and a few bottles of booze lying behind it. 'That fellow told us everything.' How Kumar laughed then! Laughing louder at the thought that such love would never be reciprocated.

'What did he hear?'

'He heard all that could be heard.' Kumar did not add that the screaming had erased the meaning of the words. Anger had warped the words, the sounds had become twisted. But the Malayali boy had also heard enough to know it was not only *his* heart that had reached out to her.

'Can you believe it? The night before the girl's death, we were all sitting around this window listening to her father shouting. And when this boy realised what had happened, he got tears in his eyes. Immediately, he left the house. He didn't even speak to us in college the next day.'

'And then what happened?'

'Well, I think the father was beating her and her mother was trying to stop him. Then we heard the door of the room close. I think they locked her in.'

They had heard more, but their eyes were fixed on that window, willing it to open, wanting Archana to call out to them (no, to *me*, each of those boys thought), to come and save her. That would have been worthy of a Hindi movie. That would have made their treks to the local cinema hall worthwhile.

Leaving Bihar was not just about getting away from their families or communities. It also meant a kind of freedom that only they could understand and experience. Hordes of these boys wanted to come to Bangalore as if it was a foreign land. It was foreign, no doubt—the language, the food, the way the locals behaved, their soft nature. But still, Hindi was a bridge on which they could meet. They laughed at the way the locals spoke Hindi but never thought for a moment that they should learn Kannada. That would have been beneath them; not just beneath their dignity but also below the dignity of their language. To accommodate them, the locals had started speaking in broken Hindi. The shopkeepers, who would always charge these outsiders more, thought speaking in cracked Hindi was worth the extra money they could make. To pander to the tastes of these students, several small joints had opened all over Mathikere Extension. They advertised themselves as UP Mess, Bihar Hotel, Bengal Cafe (the Bengalis always wanting to be different and more sophisticated), Punjabi Dhaba. It was not just a flood of students but also tonnes of wheat flour that made their way to Bangalore. Oh, that and something else which the locals had never heard of nor liked when it was offered to them: bottles of mustard oil. Soon, Mathikere Extension would be partitioned not just according to regional identities but also oils with different smells. Keralites with the smell of coconut oil, Tamilians with gingelly oil, Kannadigas with groundnut oil, North Indians with mustard oil. The nation may as well have been a large oil depot with the different states put inside huge steel drums labelled with the names of different oils characterising each of them.

But the window did not open. Even whimpers barely escaped through the cracks. They waited and waited in the dark room (one roommate had the great idea of turning out the lights when their spying began) till a TV programme and the local rum caught their attention.

'But then, how did she die?' asked Rajesh, wanting to insert himself between their thoughts.

'I think she took poison. We heard more shouts and banging on the door past midnight.' Kumar's voice trailed into silence. He didn't want to tell Raghavendra how they had all been drunk, how they had been singing along with a song playing on TV, how they had almost missed the climax of Archana's life.

As Kumar leaned drunkenly against the window, disjointedly connecting the words of a song, he had hazily heard sounds from the other house. He thought he could hear Archana shouting to be let out, and the sound of vomiting. But he had been too drunk to think clearly.

And then, mercifully, there had been silence—both from Prasanna's house and his internal voice. He had gone to sleep leaning against the window, his deep breaths reaching out a helping hand to an already dead Archana.

'You know the rest,' he added guiltily.

Raghavendra's eyes went back and forth from the window to Kumar, as if somewhere in the space in between lay the answers.

'Do you know who made her pregnant?' he finally asked, after a long pause punctuated by the sounds of stray vehicles on the road.

'That we don't know.' Kumar felt sad, and was briefly afraid that he was showing it. Asserting his macho self, he added, 'Could have been anybody. I wish it had been one of us.' The moment he said it, he knew he had been unnecessarily cruel. Rajesh got up and stood over him.

'You don't have to say such things,' he told him in a mixture of Hindi mixed with the gurgling sound of the Ganga.

Raghavendra got up immediately. He wanted to leave the filth of the room and run to the shelter of his house. There, he would first close the windows and tie them with a string. Safety lay only in the darkness of his own room.

Rajesh's silence, as they left the house, was an apology for Kumar's last words. But as they walked back to their house, he consoled Raghavendra, saying that they would soon find Archana's lover. He tried to explain to him that this was how college boys were—*they say these things, but you know*—even as he suggested that he was not like them.

They passed Prasanna's shop. Prasanna sat still in the shade of the shop, staring at Kumar's house. He transferred his gaze to them as they walked past. Raghavendra walked faster, feeling Prasanna's eyes drill holes in his back.

Poornima was not only disappointed but also furious. Not just at Prasanna, or Kumar and his friends, but also at Raghavendra's inability to have somehow found the answer. Did she think that the answer was there, hovering near her husband's eyes, and that he had somehow missed it? But she also realised that her anger stemmed from his hesitant description of Archana and the window that bared her spirit to peeping eyes. She knew he was not saying all that he had heard and was irritated at his fear. She read his mind and knew that, even as he was narrating his visit to her, he was only thinking about their daughters. Her anger rose from her irritation that Raghavendra continued to link his daughters' actions to Archana's. *My daughters are not like that—and how dare their own father think that of them.*

Raghavendra was tired after an eventful day. He had already forgotten his visit to the police station—*just this morning!* He was ready to eat his food, tickle his daughters and go to sleep. But Poornima's irritation drove him to seek out Nagaraj and take a fateful step that would have its own repercussions. In one way, it could be said that Poornima catalysed it, but it could also be said that this step was always the most obvious one for him to take.

Troubles were like a sandpile, thought Raghavendra. When he felt that one problem had been solved, multiple others cropped up in its place.

Unexpectedly, old Patil re-opened his tiny grocery shop, opposite Raghavendra's house, that night. He had just returned from Dharwad, where he had gone with his family for an extended visit. Patil's store was always dark and dingy, with not even a nameboard. His only enterprising act in all these many years had been to start selling vegetables along with his limited stock of groceries.

Raghavendra, like most people around, had pitied Patil and once, in a fit of generosity, had insisted that he would help him bring vegetables from the main market in Yeshwanthpur. So the two of them would go regularly to the market, and Raghavendra would bring back two canvas bags filled with vegetables on his cycle. In the early days, he was so keen to help Patil that he bought vegetables from him, foregoing the wholesale prices at the market.

Patil's family sat at the shop the whole day. They had bought an old black and white TV, and now all their attention was directed to it. When customers arrived, their gaze too would go to the TV screen. If they had the time, they would even make passing comments on the programme while asking for hundred grams of tomatoes and some free chillies and coriander leaves alongside.

Before Patil and his family had left for Dharwad, he had requested Raghavendra to keep an eye on the shop. At the time, Raghavendra was still working for Paul, and his desire to be a grocer was a forgotten dream.

But now, when he saw the shop open and a hesitant yellow light on, he felt a passing wave of regret. How could he tell Patil that he was going to be a competitor to him? He could see Patil moving, slowly peering into one sack after another. It was just a matter of time before he would have to go over to meet him.

The rain began soon after eight. It poured heavily for an hour. Raghavendra sat with his family in front of the TV, trying to discover hidden springs of humour within himself, so he could laugh at the stale jokes. After a while, he tuned out, smiling only in response to the sudden laughter from his daughters.

When he looked outside again, around nine, Patil's shop was closed. Now that the rain had been subdued by the night and wet spray illuminated the streetlights, he was ready to leave too. He gathered up Nagaraj's chit fund papers, put them in a plastic cover and placed it in his cloth bag. Poornima saw him to the door, patted his bag instead of him and told him that she would stay up for him. He left with the thought of her sitting at the window, watching the streets, waiting for him to appear out of the rain. It would have given him a romantic twinge when he was younger, but now . . .

Marimuthu was getting ready for bed when Raghavendra reached the temple. Mari walked to the gate, exposing himself to the drizzle. Raghavendra felt humbled; his umbrella seemed like a luxury and suddenly felt heavy.

'I have come to take your help,' he said, twiddling his umbrella uneasily. Mari was gracious. He asked no questions but came out immediately. Looking at the way Raghavendra was dressed—in pants and a baggy shirt hanging over his soon-to-be-bulging waist, a bag on his right shoulder, he knew that he was out on a mission.

'I want to meet Nagaraj and return his papers to him,' Raghavendra said. 'Will you take me to his place?'

Mari peered at him. 'I will not meet him, but I will take you to the places where he might be.'

Raghavendra nodded his thanks and tried to offer the shelter of his umbrella to Marimuthu. But Mari had no need for such contraptions; he had already walked ahead, his footsteps singing in the rain.

They first went to Venkateswara Bar and Restaurant, which was on the main road. The wine shop was on the ground floor. A dirty curtain partitioned the room into two. Those who had no time to sip their drink, to imbibe spirits in darkened rooms, could go past the curtain and gulp it down. There was no place to sit in this inner sanctorum, just a wooden shelf on which they could rest their glasses. If needed, they could also buy a plate of masala groundnuts garnished with onions and chopped green chillies.

A stairway near the curtain led up to the restaurant. The lightbulb had steadily worn its brightness down.

What had been a 40-watt bulb now produced light like a 10-watt one. The regulars noticed the bulb had not yet fused—three years and still going strong. They were all justifiably proud that their very own Mysore Lamps made such durable bulbs.

Outside every one of these restaurants and bars would be a stall selling cigarettes and paan. The men manning these stalls—their mouth red from consuming the product they sold—were the sentinels of these places. Unlike doorkeepers, who greeted people coming in, these men greeted those who left. And when regulars came to them, there would be no exchange of words, just a transfer of cigarettes of a particular brand or the usual paan. Entrepreneurship had impacted this profession too. The growing popularity of gutka, tobacco-laced spiced betel nut packaged in shiny little sachets, had made millions of people around the country switch from chewing betel leaves containing tobacco. They only had to empty the packet into their mouth, without having to chew the betel leaves. They still had to soften the mixture in the mouth and spit it out, but somehow it had become a national craze. So too had the ritual of spitting the red juice from the mouth. They had given different names to these concoctions; Paan 420 was the most popular of them all. Four hundred and twenty was a special number in the Hindi imagination, playing on the fact that 420 was also the number of the Indian Penal Code that referred to cheats. When there was a national obsession, film stars could not be far away. Already, a growing number of them were advertising these tobacco products.

Raghavendra, needless to say, had never visited any of these stalls. He would not be caught standing near one of them. The pool of red spit near the stalls was particularly distasteful. As Marimuthu walked briskly towards the paanwallah, Raghavendra tried to hide himself by bringing the umbrella to rest on his shoulders, making him look like a black, overgrown head walking on two thin legs.

The paanwallah was dry, except for the red spit that kept drooling from the sides of his mouth, thanks to a big plastic umbrella stand supplied by one of the cigarette manufacturers. When he saw Marimuthu approaching him, he spat behind him, with a careless turn of his head. When he recognised Raghavendra, who was standing behind Marimuthu, he took a red cloth (once white, before the paan mixture made it bleed) and wiped his mouth.

Mari went under the plastic umbrella and stood next to the man. It was clear that what he wanted to say was only for those fleshy ears.

'We are looking for Nagaraj. Is he inside?' His left eyebrow traced an arch that went right into the innards of the restaurant.

'No,' the man replied. 'He left with two of his friends sometime back. He has gone to Chikanna's house, I think.'

Marimuthu nodded curtly and walked away with Raghavendra shuffling behind him, grateful that they had only stopped for such a short time. As he hurried away, the paanwallah called out to him, 'Saar, I hear you are in trouble with Nagaraj. Be careful.'

Such unsolicited advice: Raghavendra hung his head in shame and the umbrella nodded for him. To be recognised and, worse, advised by this paan fellow. What had his reputation come to!

Marimuthu led Raghavendra to Chikanna's house. It was the last house on a road that had been built on a tiny bit of land. It looked like it had been squeezed out of a bottle. Through the open window of the front room, they could see Nagaraj sitting with two men who looked more like shadows. Marimuthu left Raghavendra at the gate, patted him on his back and swiftly vanished into a side street.

Raghavendra's timid knock was answered by a thin, frightened looking woman. Her eyes vanished into her lashes when she saw Raghavendra. The folded umbrella dripped water and he felt as if he was wet from the inside. The woman stared at him till he managed to say, 'I have to meet Nagaraj.'

She turned immediately, as though afraid that he would say anything more. Soon, one of the men came out.

'Who are you?' he began, then peered at Raghavendra and went back inside, looking astonished. The beginning of Raghavendra's answer trailed behind him.

He was back almost immediately. 'Come,' he said brusquely, having hidden his astonishment in his wildly growing moustache.

Raghavendra followed Chikanna into the room, his bag staking its presence by gently lapping against his thighs: *Let me in first, me first.*

Nagaraj sat sternly, a king with a glass of liquor in his hand. Raghavendra squinted to see better through the coughing haze of cigarette smoke that filled the room. For Raghavendra, Nagaraj would always be a tub of sweat and stale alcohol. His two friends were two huge mounds filled with water. He could almost imagine poking them and watching the liquid flow out.

Chikanna spoke on behalf of the others. 'What gave you the courage to come here?'

Raghavendra went up to Nagaraj and offered him the plastic bag containing the original papers of the chit fund. He could see the thin woman trying to hide behind the door. Unaccountably, that gave him courage.

'All your papers are here. I thought you would want them.'

Nagaraj took the bag and tossed it aside, then leaned back on the dirty single sofa and stared at Raghavendra.

Finally, he spoke. 'Come and have a drink!' The others began laughing loudly. Raghavendra once again saw the woman shrink beyond the door.

'No, I am leaving.'

The third man in the room jumped up and grabbed Raghavendra's arm, then pulled him down onto a rickety chair beside him.

When he looked up, Raghavendra saw that it was the policeman. He struggled to get up, holding on to the tottering armrest. The policeman pushed him down again and spoke to Nagaraj.

'See this fellow. He has the audacity to complain to our inspector about you. And now he dares to come here—'

Nagaraj threw the remains of his drink at Raghavendra's face. The stench of strong liquor went into his eyes and dripped from his glasses. On a reflex, he put his tongue out and a few drops of whisky stole onto it. Even then, *even then,* he could not spit on the floor of the room. He swallowed his saliva, removed his glasses and dried them on the strap of his bag.

'Don't think you can do whatever you want and get away with it.' He looked around the room and thought desperately. 'It's only a matter of days for you.'

The policeman came close to him and poured his drink all over his head. 'Now you are threatening us, are you, you miserable Brahmin bastard!'

Raghavendra turned his head away. He looked through the open window and thought he recognised Marimuthu outside it. He regained his words, sounds floating on passing clouds of courage. First that woman and now the shadow of a man.

'I am going to the DSP. Neither you nor your inspector can do anything then!' That had been an inspiration, one that had no basis to it. The DSP was just another caricature lost in the bowels of policedom.

But it shut them up for a few seconds. Raghavendra pushed himself up again and stood in front of the policeman. He could smell himself: stale whiskey souring on his body as if the whiskey drops found *him* distasteful.

Nagaraj looked at the policeman and said, 'He is talking too much.'

The policeman lifted his hand and got ready to swing it at Raghavendra.

Raghavendra knew that the slap was coming. He knew it was going to be a thunderbolt. He turned his head towards the window, not wanting to see what would hit him but in doing so, inadvertently offering his cheek. He thought he saw Marimuthu jump up and throw something.

A stone flew in and hit the policeman's head. Raghavendra closed his eyes as he heard, no, felt, the resounding knock of the stone. The man's hand dropped before rushing to his head. Blood and booze knocked him out cold. Nagaraj and Chikanna stared at Raghavendra, wondering what magic of his had felled the man. Before their brains could respond, he left. The woman waited near the door, keeping it open for him.

He thought he saw her smile. He picked up his umbrella and walked out into the drizzle, hoping it would rain and cleanse him of the alcohol. He looked for Marimuthu, but there was no one on the streets. He heard Nagaraj shouting for the woman to bring a towel. He saw him come to the window. The rain suddenly increased, and the sudden barking of dogs gave voice to his joy.

His body was drenched and cleansed by the time he reached home. He saw Poornima dozing at the window of their office room, and waved to her dreams. As he entered the house, Raghavendra realised that he had not once worried about catching a cold despite being drenched in the rain. He went to the bathroom, poured cold water over himself, scrubbed his body with a new bar of soap to remove the last stale, alcoholic smell of his fear. He came out of the bathroom to find Poornima waiting for him with a puzzled look.

'Nothing to worry,' he declared jauntily. 'Just a little bit of slush.'

Poornima came close to him and took a deep breath. Worried, he asked, 'What is it?' Could she smell the alcohol that had been thrown on him? Would she dare to think he had been drinking?

She frowned, knowing something was off, but before her quivering nostrils could detect any imagined smells, he said, 'I think the girls are calling out to you.'

9

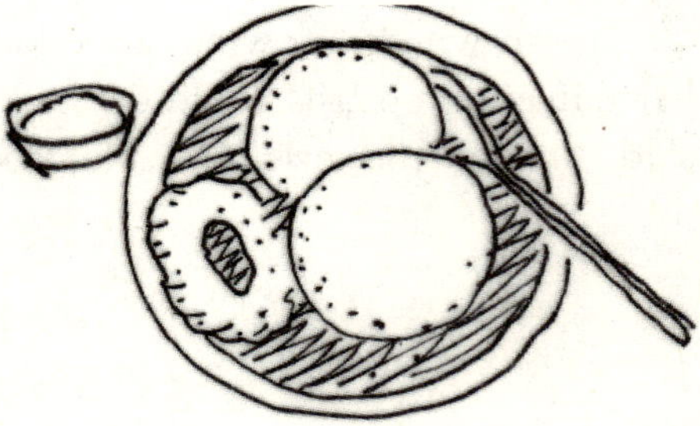

THE SEVENTH DAY AFTER ARCHANA'S DEATH DID NOT begin well. Poornima had woken in the morning to collect water. The tap was completely dry. She shook the pipe, placed her ear near the mouth of the tap. Even the distant gurgling sound of the Cauvery had frozen into an eerie silence. The sky was clear and it was as if the clouds had been sucked into the emptiness of the taps.

She stood near the tap for a few minutes. When she saw a light come on in Gowda's house, she picked up the empty vessels and went back to her home. From her window she saw Baale's wife trying in vain to elicit water out of the tap.

She went into the kitchen, aimlessly washed a few vessels with a few mugs of water. She then paced up and down, looked out at the streets, wishing that the magic of the morning could remain a permanent feature of their locality. *How silent and peaceful it was!* After some time, she went back to the tap. Not even the hint of a flow. She knew that no water would come that day. She went back to sleep.

Baale Gowda knocked on Raghavendra's door after seven that morning. As a matter of principle he refused to use the calling bell, believing that a knock on the door was the proper way to announce one's arrival. He had resisted installing a bell in his house (despite his wife's protests), somehow contriving to suggest that it was not part of 'our' ancient tradition to use electric bells.

Raghavendra was reading the newspaper. He had woken with a lightness he had not felt in a long time. He had jumped out of bed at the sound of the first whistle of the pressure cooker from Bhat's house. He drank his coffee with a song on his lips—all because of a well-aimed stone! How he had underestimated Marimuthu, how liberating to know that he didn't have to carry the burden of his struggle alone.

Gowda wasted no time talking about the headlines in the morning's newspaper. He spoke rapidly, his words in a hurry to get to school and occupy the principal's chair.

'Did you cut the water supply today?'

Raghavendra was puzzled. 'What happened, no water today?' he asked needlessly.

'No. And my wife thinks your wife collected water and did something to the tap. I cannot believe the things you people do.'

Raghavendra couldn't believe it either. He called out to Poornima, who appeared drying her hands on her sari. When she saw Gowda, her face discovered a hidden frown.

'Did you collect water today?' Raghavendra asked.

Poornima guessed the reason for Gowda's visit. 'I tried to, but there was no water in the tap.'

'He thinks you stopped the supply after you collected the water.' Raghavendra felt magisterial. In matters of justice, even his wife was answerable to his stern voice.

'Why or how would I do that?' she countered. 'All these years they have been taking *our* water. Maybe he should tell his wife to get up earlier. I mean, you can either sleep or collect water.' She turned her voice towards Gowda and continued, 'Don't you men think so?' She tossed her hair and went back in. As she walked away, they heard her murmur clearly, 'Disturbing me for useless things! Ha!'

Raghavendra was embarrassed, as was Gowda. The two men had intruded in a long simmering battle between their wives. To make up for Poornima's outburst, Raghavendra offered Gowda coffee. Gowda immediately refused. He didn't relish the thought of communicating Poornima's message to his wife. To delay the inevitable, he asked Raghavendra about the agency.

'Going on,' Raghavendra replied. 'These jobs are tough, you know.'

'Life itself is tough. Look at me. Have to run the school, deal with money problems . . .' He looked around the office and added, ‘And my own research work, I have told you about it?’

Raghavendra’s spirit of atonement allowed Baale to continue, even though he had heard him before on *his* mathematics.

‘I have almost finished showing how modern mathematics can be derived from the Vedas.’

‘Yes, yes, you have told me that before.’

‘Now I have sent it to a famous mathematician . . . in that institute, you know, Tata Institute.’

No, Raghavendra did not know. And frankly did not care for mathematics, science or the Vedas. Their Extension stood at one end of a famous science institute, but no locals were allowed entry into it. Raghavendra had first heard of it from Rajesh, who told him that it was a blessing that Raghavendra’s house was so close to the place. Imagine, he had said, great scientists are just around the corner from your house, his tone suggesting that these scientists were like the plumbers or electricians who were always around the corner in Mathikere Extension. He wanted to give the impression that he could go in and out of that institute as he pleased. Raghavendra himself had managed to do so only once, when his auto took the road through the campus because the main road was closed due to a sewage leak. The roads were dug up and sewage had overflowed into built and unbuilt houses. Raghavendra remembered thinking then how useful it would have been to have an institute that worked to improve the roads and sewage in their locality. All he remembered of the sprawling green campus was buildings with the names of subjects he remembered from his school days. Like his school learning, these buildings merged one into another in a meaningless row of names.

'I am sure that the person from the institute will recognise your greatness,' he said hurriedly, making his comment sound like a blessing. To stop Baale from talking further, he shouted, 'Suhasini, get a cup of coffee for Uncle.'

Gowda got up as if to leave, then sat back. He was sure Poornima would not offer him coffee. *How little Raghavendra understood women!* When the coffee did not materialise, his honour would be saved.

Surprisingly, Suhasini came out with a cup of coffee in the only ceramic cup they had at home. Two had been bought for the kids, but the younger one had broken hers.

The cup of coffee offered to Gowda was partly a peace offering on Poornima's part; partly to tell him that she was above her neighbour's fallibilities.

Just as Gowda left, Patil came in, stooping as always. He went into the house, patted the girls, and told Poornima that he had received some 'wonderful' rice from Nellore. As he shuffled out, he reminded Raghavendra about going to the market. Raghavendra stayed silent, unable to find a response in his guilt. Patil's eyes, too weak to discover new sights, did not see the slowly disappearing grains of rice outside Raghavendra's house.

Raghavendra, in continued good spirits, walked the girls to school, on his way to check on the nameboard for his grocery store. Sunil took him for a walk again, promising that he would get the board in two days. On the way back, Raghavendra waved to Soumitro and said quite unnecessarily, 'No tea.' He had decided that he would first meet Marimuthu, thank him, and buy him chow-chow bhath as his offering of thanks. Although he had puzzled about this dish, a mix of savoury and sweet, he knew that it had become a quintessential marker of the city, particularly in the stand-up restaurants. As if the dish was a declaration of the nature of the city, or perhaps of the nature of these restaurants that would soon pervade every part of the city.

Marimuthu was reading the newspaper when Raghavendra walked into the temple compound with a growing smile on his face.

'What can I say, Swamiji,' he began. 'If you had not come to my help, who knows what would have happened?'

Marimuthu was embarrassed. He did not want Raghavendra to tell others about his deed. He said, 'I don't know how I helped you. All I did was leave you at the gates and come back here.'

Raghavendra understood. He nodded and said, 'I am going to have tiffin. Why don't you join me?'

Marimuthu joined him. There was a rush at the darshini, although it was early in the morning. Marimuthu said, 'How much of eating goes on. Incessantly. Even the pause between munches sounds impatient!'

Before they parted, he said, 'If you still want to know the name of that boy who destroyed that girl's life, go to Shahi theatre and ask somebody there. That is where all these girls go with their boys.'

Raghavendra nodded. He was surprised that he had forgotten to think of this most obvious possibility. Bangalore might be a pensioner's paradise for some and a garden city for others, but for the young it was the theatres that defined their city. Long before Bangalore became famous for its pubs (they were mostly called bars then), it was famous for its theatres. It was the city where the latest films in Kannada, Hindi, Tamil and Telugu ran in hundreds of big and small theatres dotting the city. Befitting its status as a gentlemanly city, it also attracted the latest English films. Many Kannada students learnt to speak English by watching these films, while also learning to walk and dress the way Indiana Jones did, and to sing like ABBA. For those who came to Bangalore from other states, films were an immediate, nostalgic connection to what they had left behind. And for young couples, theatres were increasingly the only places, like parks earlier, that gave them some privacy.

Raghavendra wanted to show his gratitude to Mari. So he told him about his plans for the grocery store but told him not to tell anybody else.

On his return home, he went straight to Rajesh's room. Rajesh had made his bed, lit an incense stick, and was looking forward to vadas for breakfast in the college canteen. It was the only South Indian dish that he respected, not the idli and not even the dosa. Vadas were deep fried, as any respectable dish had to be. When Raghavendra knocked, Rajesh insisted that he come in and sit on the one broken chair. He could have added something about Raghavendra not providing a proper chair in the room. Instead, he told him that if only there were a kitchen, he would have made him parathas and tea.

Raghavendra asked him, 'Do you know a theatre called Shahi?'

'That theatre? It's beyond the main market.' He looked at Raghavendra in mock surprise. 'You've lived here for so long and have even built a house. And you don't know where the theatre is?'

Raghavendra stared at him, scowling. Several new theatres had sprung up to accommodate the growing number of young migrants in the area. Some survived only for a short time before a new building replaced it. He told Rajesh, 'Take me there. I need to visit the place.'

'Why? You want to go watch a movie?' Rajesh laughed happily at the thought.

'Yes. And you are coming with me.'

'Uncle!' Rajesh stared at him, surprised. Wasn't Raghavendra too old for the movies? And then it struck him. 'Oh, is it to do with your Case?' Every time Rajesh mentioned the case, a spirit of joyousness seemed to enter him. Raghavendra could imagine all his friends sharing his mirth in the college canteen. *Oh-ho, that old man and his case! These locals!*

'What is funny about that? I am already close to the finish.' When he was irritated, Raghavendra spoke only in Kannada. But Rajesh understood all that he was supposed to understand.

'The shows are at 10.30, then 2.30 and 7 p.m.' There was also a 'night show', where the timing and the film they actually showed depended on the theatre manager. Rajesh could not bring himself to imagine Raghavendra watching the night show. 'Which one do you want to go to?'

Raghavendra was afraid his enthusiasm would drain out over the day. '10.30 show,' he replied.

'Oh! Then I have to miss my class.' Rajesh paused, but Raghavendra remained silent.

'For you, Uncle, I will even miss my class. Come, let's go and I'll also show you the best place for parathas near the theatre.'

As they left the house, Raghavendra could hear Poornima opening the door. He didn't want to explain that he was going for a movie—what excuses you find, she would have said—and hurried on. With a knowing glance over his shoulder, Rajesh followed.

After Rajesh had his paratha and walked around the kitchen of the hotel, just to show Raghavendra that he knew everybody in the locality, especially those from the North, they went to the theatre. It was a long hall with a tin roof. A line of stragglers stood around the ticket stall, waiting for someone to move. Rajesh did not want to stand in the queue.

'I'll go to the manager's office and get some good seats for us.' He waited for Raghavendra to respond appropriately.

'You know the manager!' Raghavendra expressed the right amount of surprise, although the feeling of guilt about watching early morning movies overrode any other emotion in him.

Rajesh walked in confidently. He told the doorman that he wanted to see the manager, and was promptly sent back to the queue outside.

He came out, still grinning, and told Raghavendra that the manager was not there. 'But,' he added, 'I know the ticket man. Don't worry.'

Worry! Raghavendra's unease had only increased, seeing a horde of thin, scrawny, listless men. They stood silently, as if even their sense of anticipation had gone to sleep. Partly torn posters of a Hindi movie were stuck in various places. Posters that were printed in red, the angry face of a man with a gun, and a woman in a dancing costume. Raghavendra was convinced that the men in the queue were all unemployed, so when he saw a few women hurrying towards the ticket stall, he turned his face away in surprise—and found Rajesh's in front of his nose.

'You are surprised, Uncle, that women are coming?' Rajesh paused dramatically, then continued, 'They are coming for customers.' His voice was lubricated with unadulterated glee. *What is Rajesh so happy about?* Raghavendra would have left, not wanting to share an event with *these* women, but the ticket man had come and there was a sudden movement in the queue. Raghavendra took some money and gave it to Rajesh, who, at the counter, tried a smile and a greeting in Hindi, but got a stony glare in reply.

As they went in, Raghavendra told Rajesh he wanted to talk to somebody about Archana. They looked around the decaying lobby and saw the man at the entrance to the viewing hall, waiting to collect their tickets. Thankfully, he was a Kannadiga. Raghavendra did not want to get caught in more language games.

A bell rang and the attendant asked them to find their seats. He closed one door and drew a curtain across the other half. Not knowing what he should ask, Raghavendra blurted, 'Where do you live?' Rajesh pushed aside the curtain and tried to peer inside.

'Just two streets away.'

Raghavendra explained where his own house was, even as the attendant plainly showed his disinterest.

Raghavendra said, 'I run an agency and am looking to hire a young man like you.'

That got his attention. The attendant sent a group of boys in hurriedly, closed the other door as the film began with a deafening blare.

'I'll do any job you like, sir.'

Raghavendra was pleased. 'Ours is not an ordinary company. We are a detective agency.' He paused, wondering how to explain what being a detective meant. But he needn't have worried.

Stars came to light the young man's eyes. 'Please, sir, that is a job I will be very good at. I have always wanted to be like the police. But what to do, so much competition, and exams to write. And then, so much money needed to bribe to get the smallest job in the police station.' His grimace seemed to put a figure to the bribe needed to become a constable.

Rajesh had opened the door a little and stuck his head in. The attendant smiled—any other time, Rajesh would have received a hard slap on the back. Raghavendra told Rajesh to go in and watch the film. Rajesh happily vanished inside.

'What is your name?'

'Yediyurappa.' He waited expectantly, as if ready to change his name if Raghavendra so desired.

'Good. Very good. You see, I am looking for a man who has sharp eyes and watches everything around him.'

'I do! I do!'

'I am sure.' Raghavendra looked him closely in the eye. 'Did you notice the people who went in just now?'

Yediyurappa had not. He was indifferent to the constant flow of people. He was as bored as the people who came to watch movies in Shahi at 10.30 in the morning.

'Yes,' he replied. 'You saw a group of four men who came together? They belong to a gang. They are responsible for most of the thefts here.' Caught up in his imagination, he refused to pause. 'Another set who came, they are auto drivers. Or so they say. Then there are the women—ha! They are not good. You know what I mean.' The way he (and Rajesh) smirked when they talked of the unaccompanied women in theatres (and not to forget, restaurants), it was clear what they thought of them.

'But tell me, do you remember people who have come here before?'

'Yes, I do. Completely. I always keep watching for people like this.'

Was he implying that only crooks, gangsters and prostitutes visited the theatre? Raghavendra stared at him, already feeling tired of the game he was caught in. He wanted to go back home and lie down with all the windows closed. He had never imagined, in all his years of living in Mathikere Extension, that such places and people existed. And now, when he saw them, he had no energy for their stories.

'Let me be frank, Yediyurappa. I am here to find out something, and if you can help me with this, I will definitely give you the job.' He paused, struck with a worry that this man might visit his house and pester him for the job. Then he cast the worry aside; let the fish nibble on it for all he cared. 'You see, there was a girl near my house. She died a few days ago.'

Yediyurappa perked up. This is what his dreams were made of, in flesh and blood, and not on cinema screens getting stained with water leaks and the overflowing blood of actors.

'Of course, I heard that some girl had died. She took poison, right?' He stopped and looked at Raghavendra, confused. Had she died some other way? Did Raghavendra expect him to say: 'Or was she murdered?'

The ticket man came up to them before Raghavendra could reply. He looked surprised to find the attendant talking to a customer, that too, a respectable middle-aged man. Yediyurappa said, 'Sir, he is a friend of my father's.' The ticket seller walked away without a response, unhappy that a customer was more interested in chatting than in watching the movie.

'So, what do you think, sir?' Yediyurappa said. 'Was she murdered?'

'Don't worry about that now. All I want you to remember is whether she came to the theatre with any boys?'

There! He had said it. He had wanted to say men, but had been too ashamed to say the word aloud. Boys were a mistake he could accept more easily.

Yediyurappa thought furiously. There were so many boys and girls who came, slinking in together, hiding in the shy glances of each other.

Raghavendra added, 'She was a Malayali. Young girl, maybe sixteen, very bright, always laughing, short and slightly plump.' The stutter in his voice at the end seemed to express his surprise that he remembered so much about that girl.

'Malayali? Why didn't you say so first? Of course, there was this girl who came here more than once.'

'There were no other Malayali girls?' Raghavendra could not help sounding sceptical.

Yediyurappa sensed it. 'Yes sir, I see what you mean. There are so many Malayalis here. Little more time, they will take over the entire place. There were other Malayali girls and boys. But this girl was special, exactly as you described her. The other girls were thin, with no happy smiles. But this girl, sir, she would smile even at me!'

Looking at Raghavendra's frown, he added, 'As a friend, sir, only in a friendly way. She was always with this man.'

'Man? Do you know who it was?'

Yediyurappa wished that he had been more inquisitive and not so enamoured of that smile.

'Sir, I don't know his name. But if I see him again, I will know. He was always neatly dressed, very shy fellow.'

Raghavendra was disappointed. 'Think more. Was he also a Malayali?'

Yediyurappa had never heard the man speak. After seeing Archana's smiles, his sight was all for her receding back. How it had beckoned him!

'I am sure he was also a Malayali. I have never seen these Malayalis talk to anybody else.' He paused and stared into the distance. 'He had a thin moustache, short hair.' Even as he said this, he was disappointed. Maybe he should have lied. Conjured up a real villain, big and strong and mean looking. His confusion told Raghavendra that no more insights would be forthcoming.

Raghavendra patted him on his shoulder. 'If you think of anything more, tell me. And tell the boy who came with me that I have left.' He scribbled his address on the back of his ticket and gave it to Yediyurappa.

As he turned away, Yediyurappa found his voice again. 'I remember him because they were both so well dressed.' He didn't add 'compared with the others who come here', but his accompanying glance towards the closed door of the theatre said it all.

The ticket seller stood near the entrance. He was reluctant to open the door, unhappy that a customer was leaving. As Raghavendra walked out, he could hear screams from the movie hall. The action was well and truly on its gory way.

Meanwhile, two important events had occurred, the repercussions of which would drastically alter Raghavendra's search. Prasanna had been extremely disturbed when he saw Raghavendra at Kumar's house. For some reason, he had a profound dislike for Raghavendra. Was it to do with him being a 'local', walking around as if the locality belonged to him in a way it would never for Prasanna? When he heard about Raghavendra's agency, he had sniggered, but when he heard that Nagaraj was a partner, he felt uneasy. With Nagaraj as a partner, Raghavendra's status had definitely changed.

He remembered, too, the feeling of guilt when Raghavendra looked at him as he entered Kumar's house. Prasanna was sure that Raghavendra's (first and only) visit to Kumar's house had something to do with Archana. So, the night after Raghavendra's visit, the seventh night as measured by the clock of the departed Archana, he decided to visit the boys next door. He looked around first (he was always looking around these days, waiting to hear suspicious whispers behind every plant), then up at the open window of Kumar's house, through which he could hear the stray remnants of a loud song. He walked to Kumar's window and tried to peer into the darkness inside. His tightly leashed anger uncoiled itself. How well he knew why these windows were always open. Lechers, especially these North Indian boys, waiting to have a glimpse of the women in his house. He took a small pebble and threw it at the window.

Kumar was lying on the cot watching Hindi movie songs on TV. He noticed the shadow of Prasanna and sank back into the cot. When the pebble hit the window bar and rolled inside, he went to the window.

Prasanna was aggressive. 'Hey! Why do you fellows throw rubbish on my grounds?' He spoke in broken Hindi, not happy that he could not shout at him in angry Malayalam.

'No, Uncle, we have not thrown anything there.' Except our hungry looks, he might have added.

'Arre, come closer and look!' As Kumar tried to squint through the window bars, Prasanna caught his hand. Surprised, Kumar tried to pull his hand away, but Prasanna tightened his grip.

'You . . . beggars! You think I don't know what you have been doing, sitting at this window and staring at my house?' Prasanna's anger garbled his words. He was spitting as he spoke, and Kumar, for all his bravado, was scared.

'I am first going to complain to the police, and then tell your house owner to throw you all out. You think this is Bihar?'

Kumar was, by now, petrified. He knew how the police harassed North Indian students. Whenever there was trouble, they would round them up, take them into the lockup, and practise their body blows on them.

'No, Uncle, I don't know what you are saying.' His wrist hurt as Prasanna pressed it relentlessly. Prasanna could not bring himself to say what he knew, that these boys had been watching his daughters and, he was sure, his wife too.

'You know what I mean. And look at what you did yesterday! You think I don't know? You were talking to your friend and that man . . . '

His fingernails made scratchy marks on Kumar's wrist. 'Uncle, please leave my hand. I had nothing to do with that man coming here. They came suddenly.'

'That is what you say. I know what you people did. Sat and gossiped about my family. But you too have mothers and sisters, you bastards.'

'No. I promise you. That man only wanted to know about your daughter's death. I told him I know nothing. I promise.'

'You are lying. I know that man asked you for something else.'

'No. Yes! He wanted to know why she died'—the pressure on his wrist increased—'and who made her pregnant!' Kumar stopped, his eyes full of tears from the pain on his wrist.

Prasanna pushed him back, shouting, 'If I ever see this window open again, I will kill you all with my bare hands!'

Prasanna was so furious that he went up to his terrace and started pacing up and down. His footsteps tattooed an angry pattern for Hema and Megha in the house below.

If they had looked up at the ceiling, they would have seen ferocious images forming on the hard concrete.

Prasanna's fury would soon hide inside a trove of ideas. He thought of Raghavendra, that owl-like, ugly man with the smug expression, trying to teach morality to those around him. The image only inspired more anger. What right did that man have to ask about the death of his daughter? Didn't that stupid fool realise that he had another daughter who had to be married off? And who was he anyway, to ask these questions?

New ideas arose from his tumultuous thoughts. The problem, as far as Prasanna was concerned, was clear. Why should he be worried about Megha's marriage? He looked out from the terrace, saw the world around him, the shops that were still open and beckoning with their weak yellow lights, houses with white tube lights hiding behind closed doors, the intermittent sound of vehicles and, suddenly, Shankar stepping out of his shop. His mind was surprisingly clear. Prasanna stopped pacing. He knew what he would do next.

Soon after nine that night (around the same time that Raghavendra left to meet Marimuthu), Prasanna left his house, resolved to put an end to Raghavendra's mischief. Shankar was still in his shop, cutting and stitching his dreams into new clothes. Prasanna was pleased that Shankar had so much work to do.

He asked him to close the shop and join him for dinner. Shankar was more than surprised: An invitation to dinner from a man whose behaviour always bordered on unfriendly? When he hesitated, Prasanna told him that they could go to Venkateswara B&R. He paused, and in that silence, Shankar knew that the dinner would also include drinks. He quickly pulled down the shutter, the clatter it made scattering the few dogs that were roaming around looking for after-dinner gossip.

That night, it was not the people of Mathikere Extension who conspired among themselves. It was time itself, that kind of time which placed poor, innocent people in locations of its choice and then waited for them to play their roles. So it was that Prasanna and Shankar were seated in the bar when Mari asked the paanwallah about Nagaraj. If Prasanna had looked out of the window, he might have recognised Raghavendra hiding under his black umbrella. But that night, Prasanna was focussed only on Shankar.

The restaurant was almost full. As Prasanna entered, he put his arm around Shankar, gently leading him to a place next to the window. They sat opposite each other. Prasanna ordered a full bottle of rum—the only drink worthy of us, he told Shankar, who wondered what the 'us' meant. Did Prasanna mean to place them together as Malayalis or only as neighbouring shop owners? He promptly forgot his own query as soon as he heard Prasanna ordering butter chicken masala and rice.

The first drink vanished fast. Shankar remained silent, a silence that somehow seemed accusatory. Sensing this, Prasanna said, 'You are thinking how I can eat and drink when my daughter is just dead and gone? No, no, don't deny it. But we have to go on living, right?'

Shankar nodded vaguely, afraid that Prasanna would get emotional in public about his daughter. But Prasanna began talking about Shankar's shop and how it could be expanded. 'We Malayalis,' he said, 'have to stick together and help each other. You may not know this but I have sent you many customers, those who came to my shop.'

By the time they had finished a second glass, the noise in the restaurant had increased. Before the food appeared, the two of them had consumed more liquor and were already in the first haze of drunkenness.

Prasanna beckoned Shankar closer. Shankar leaned across the table, his sight beginning to blur. *How could I have thought so meanly of this man!*

'I want to tell you something very important, Shankar.' Prasanna was struggling not to slur. What he had to say had to be clearly spelt out. 'You know I have two daughters. Now I have only one, but what to do? The younger one went bad somewhere.'

Shankar tried to focus his eyes on him. Prasanna's anger was apparent to him, although he seemed quite drunk.

'But we have forgotten that, haven't we? Now I have only my oldest daughter. She is not like the other one. Do you agree?'

Shankar nodded immediately.

'Why is she not like that one? Because she is dignified, matured, cooks well, and is lovely to look at . . . Lovelee,' he added in accented English. 'Any man who marries her is lucky. You agree?' Prasanna caught Shankar's chin with his strong fingers and shook his head from side to side. 'Don't you think so?' Tears filled his eyes.

Shankar had seen her—of course he had seen her. She was so unlike Archana, but she was nice to look at, tall and straight, with a rare smile. He gently removed Prasanna's fingers and said, 'Yes.'

Prasanna paused and looked around, as if getting ready to say something to the group of drunks at the next table. He had come here to ask Shankar a question, but he realised he could not bear to hear a negative reply. He was here as a father and being a father was even more than being a man. He said, 'Shankar, I am asking you for the first and last time: will you marry her?'

Marry her! Shankar was shocked. This was the last thing he had expected. He clasped Prasanna's hands and said, 'Are you asking me this seriously, sir?'

'Of course. I want you to become my son-in-law. I promise you, she is not like her sister at all. She is obedient and would not even have spoken to any boy. Please believe me.'

Shankar stopped him. 'Don't say anything more. I will be the happiest man if I marry her.'

Prasanna pushed himself up from his seat, went around the table and hugged Shankar. The tears that had threatened to flow for a long time finally found their release on Shankar's shoulder. Shankar emptied the bottle into their glasses and lifted his hand in a drunken toast. He had never imagined that the death of Archana would lead him along this path.

Thus it was that the father proposed his daughter's hand in marriage with the help of Indian-made rum. Thus it was that the father resolved one problem and as a bonus secured a son-in-law. In that moment, Prasanna did not think of his daughter whose life he had offered across a messy table laden with glasses and plates with discarded bones; nor of his wife, who in the midst of grieving for the loss of one daughter would have to accept the potential loss of the other. His only thought in that momentous instant, a still portrait of cunning time, was of Raghavendra. And how he had stymied his potential for creating trouble.

This act would have passed as just one more event in a confused locality, but the night was not yet done. Venkateswara B&R had to live up to its reputation of being the meeting ground for conspiracies and partnerships in Mathikere Extension.

Shankar and Prasanna were about to leave when Nagaraj and Chikanna entered. Prasanna saw Nagaraj and their eyes met. Nagaraj turned away derisively. Prasanna was a man of no consequence, and moreover, was an outsider. Seeing Nagaraj, Prasanna was reminded of Raghavendra and his inquisition of Kumar. He pushed Shankar back into his chair and remained standing as Nagaraj passed by. Nagaraj's arrival was indeed timely. Now that Prasanna had taken care of one problem (yes, Megha was first a problem and then a daughter), he, in a moment of drunken clarity, had found a way to take care of the other problem too.

He greeted Nagaraj in Kannada and said, 'You and your friends should join me for a drink. At least one!' He called out to the waiter and asked for a bottle of rum.

Nagaraj was puzzled. Chikanna, finding any excuse for a free drink worthy of attention, sat down heavily next to Shankar.

'Yes, sit down. We need as much drink as possible.' They had just left Chikanna's house. The stone had caused some bleeding but no major damage. The thin woman had bandaged the policeman's head carelessly, hoping against hope that the wound would fester and grow. Nagaraj and Chikanna had helped her put the man into bed and left immediately. Their solace would be their B&R.

Prasanna was polite to Nagaraj. He believed that Raghavendra's snooping was known to him. And he would much rather deal with him than Raghavendra. So, by the time Nagaraj sat down, he knew what he was going to say.

'Sir,' he began, and Nagaraj was pleasantly surprised. 'You know that I am a simple man who has had the terrible fate of seeing my daughter—the younger one—dead. You are a big man, but why do you want to cause pain to me?'

Nagaraj was puzzled. What trouble? Then he understood: was this fellow in the chit fund scheme? Not that he remembered, but before he could speak,

Prasanna continued, 'I am sure your agency has more important things to worry about. What is gone is gone. Why continue with it?'

Nagaraj was irritated. 'Hey, talk straight. I don't know what you are saying.'

'This evening, your friend Raghavendra came to my neighbour's house. He asked the boy there how my daughter had died, and . . . '

'And what?'

'You know sir, my daughter took poison because . . . '

'We all know. She was pregnant.'

'Unfortunately, my fate. What I am asking you, sir, is: why should your friend continue to bother me by going around asking who made that girl pregnant? It's over. Why should a man of your stature do this?'

Nagaraj kept quiet. He had no intention of letting Prasanna know how things stood between him and Raghavendra, but was also curious as to why *that idiot* wanted to know about Archana's lover.

'Don't worry,' he replied politely. 'I will tell my partner not to bother about this matter.' He turned to Chikanna and said, 'Why does that fool not do what I tell him to?' He gulped his drink down.

Prasanna thought that this was a signal for him to leave. Shankar had fallen into a semi-doze.

After a short pause, Nagaraj asked, 'So do *you* know?'

Prasanna stared back at him. This was the question he had been hoping for. He leaned close to Nagaraj's ear and whispered dramatically, 'You know that boy who lives above Raghavendra's house? That Bihari bastard. He is the one.'

Oh! How easily, how cunningly, Prasanna had managed to introduce a name, that smug smiling face of Rajesh, into a vortex of trouble! How effortlessly he had thought of offering Rajesh as a sacrifice for Raghavendra's nosiness. This was worthy of the other magic trick he had performed that night, trapping Shankar into marriage with his daughter.

Nagaraj remembered Rajesh, and how he had been tripped by him that night, not so long ago.

'That beggar,' he began. Feeling a sudden lightness, he too got up and placed his hand on Prasanna's shoulder. 'Don't worry, my friend. I will make him pay for it.'

Even as Prasanna and Shankar stumbled drunkenly through the streets, their hearts were singing. Each for different reasons. Prasanna did not manage to enter his house. He collapsed outside his door and it was only past midnight that his wife found him. Even in his stupor, he had a smile on his face. As for Shankar, he managed to open the door of his single room and crumpled on the bed. In his dreams, instead of Megha, it was Archana who giggled and talked to him.

10

After Raghavendra had left for the movie hall, Poornima made her way to the grocery shop. She found only Ahmed there. The others had gone for their prayers, he told her, happy to suggest that his duty towards the shop was greater than that towards his god. Poornima wanted turmeric powder, but before he handed her the packet, Ahmed asked if her husband had solved the case. He felt guilty even while asking the question. Archana had almost been forgotten, and his straying mind had entered the bodies of other girls who had come to the shop since then. Poornima nodded enigmatically and informed him, 'Soon, very soon.' Later, after the story had come out and been distributed around the locality, he would tell anybody who cared to listen that it was he who had first asked Raghavendra to solve the case.

On his return, Raghavendra gave an account of his morning to Poornima. He told her of his trip to the theatre and how Yediyurappa might know who the man was if he saw him.

'All that the man said,' Poornima responded sarcastically, 'was that Archana's friend was well dressed. As if all of us are not?'

'Haan, you would think that. But how many young men are there who are thin and with a thin moustache?'

She remained silent.

'So now you want me to walk around the city looking for every young man with a moustache! Ho, ho. You really think I have nothing . . . '

'Enough, enough. I will think of something else.'

'Sure, you do that.' Unexpectedly, Raghavendra remembered the final words of Yediyurappa. 'You know, if that fellow was well dressed, then maybe Shankar would have noticed them.'

'You think Shankar looks at how people are dressed?' She had always seen him with his head bent, scissors in hand, staring at the piece of cloth in front of him as if it was a complex puzzle. She understood his intensity at work. The competition was fierce, as there had been a deluge of tailors recently; every third shop was that of a tailor.

Raghavendra was provoked to say what he hadn't intended to. 'Why do you give your blouse for stitching to Shankar? Aren't there any women tailors?' He wrinkled his nose, the very thought smelling bad.

'There are no women tailors here. All the women's stitching is done by men. You are becoming so narrow-minded as you grow old.' Saying this, Poornima walked away, having wounded Raghavendra in his weakest spot: *Growing old indeed!*

After lunch, Raghavendra lay on his bed with all the windows closed. He had, that morning, insisted on moving the dressing table (nothing fancy, just a small table with powder cans, combs, elastic bands and some forgotten ribbons on it) away from its place beneath the window. The window only looked out onto Baale's house, but he wasn't taking any chances. Didn't Baale have a son? However small he was now, wouldn't he grow older?

The groaning fan churned up dust in his mind. He fell asleep, tossing restlessly. In his sleep he could hear nomadic packets of sound, the vendors from outside the house and the sounds of cleaning within.

Around five, he went with Patil to the market. On the way back, he told him about his desire to set up a grocery store. He tried to imply that his shop would not be competition but a complement to Patil's. There was no response from him. After Raghavendra helped him unload all the vegetables in his dark store, Patil said, 'It would not be correct for me to ask you to come to the market again.' His words filled with hurt, he added, 'I am sure you will be busy buying things for *your* shop.'

As Raghavendra tried to protest, he stopped him and put his hands on his shoulders. 'You have been so good to me.' And added in English, 'Very much thanks.'

Raghavendra wanted to tell him that starting a grocery shop was not a parting, it was not the death of either of them. But Patil shuffled into the shop, sat down next to his wife and began telling her about the new competition. Raghavendra hurried home before she could turn her eyes towards him. He wouldn't have been surprised if she had discovered tears in her eyes for his benefit.

He went home, irritatedly washed his feet, and told Poornima, 'This stupid grocery store is not worth it. Now everybody thinks I am their enemy.'

It was much later, when he suddenly got up that night after the fan had stopped, that he asked himself: *Why do so many people want to sell groceries?*

The day was not yet done with its deeds. Raghavendra set out just as darkness was beginning to fall. He had spent the evening with his daughters, trying to reassure himself that all was well with them. He had also decided that they would not watch TV any more, especially not those popular film song sequences that had men and women gyrating suggestively. The girls didn't protest; they merely giggled some more, and he had no response for that. Poornima told him not to worry so much, adding in an aside that not all girls would become like Archana.

Later, he went to Shankar to ask him about his clients, those who had thin moustaches. Shankar was standing outside the shop, a shining silhouette under a cloudy sky. He was feeling great, a song on his lips mouthing the Yesudas song playing loudly in the shop. When Raghavendra walked up to him briskly, Shankar looked guiltily at Prasanna, who was sitting outside his shop as usual.

Prasanna had been waiting for this moment. Before Raghavendra could say anything to Shankar, he had crossed the road and stood next to him. Prasanna had not shaved from the time of Archana's death, a perverse ritual for a man who claimed that he had not lost a daughter, and the grey prickly hair on his face poked questions at Raghavendra.

'Ah, Mr Raghavendra,' he began, surprising Raghavendra with the use of his name and the suffix. Mister was so *English*.

'I have been waiting to meet you,' Prasanna continued, gently pulling him out of the range of Shankar's inquisitive eyes. 'Come and have tea with me.'

Raghavendra followed him, a surprised look on his face. Prasanna took him to a bakery (*run by a Malayali, who else?*) and pointed to the stale, oily puffs and wrinkled buns on display. There were three trays of buns. One of them contained sweet buns, the middle tray was filled with masala buns, while the last one had the famous Bangalore potato buns.

'Why don't you have something?'

Raghavendra refused the offer. Prasanna asked for two puffs and two teas.

'How can we just have tea?' Prasanna asked.

The puffs were cut into two pieces each and Raghavendra stuffed one of them into his mouth. Flakes fell on his shirt; he rubbed them away and found an oil stain instead. *Great, Poornima will love this*!

There were two stools in a corner of the bakery. Prasanna nudged him towards them. What they would talk here would be sheltered from prying ears, thanks to a tape recorder playing Hindi film songs.

'I know you are surprised,' Prasanna began. Raghavendra shook his head as if he was trying to clear the pasty dough that had stuck to his teeth in many places.

'I also know that you, god knows why, are going around asking about my daughter's death.'

The tea came in two glasses, three quarters full. The steam from it rose slowly and fogged Raghavendra's spectacles.

'I have also talked to Nagaraj and he says he doesn't want you to bother me further. After all, what is it to you how that girl died? And why are you going around talking to people about it?'

Prasanna's voice had turned aggressive. His reserves of sweetness had been exhausted in the first few minutes. Raghavendra's silence, the sight of him crouched on the stool, his eyes hidden behind thick spectacles, infuriated him.

Raghavendra had no answer to give. Although surprised at the sudden shift in his mood, he did not want to tell Prasanna that it was his wife who was the source of his actions. Who knew if she would be beaten and locked up too? Unable to answer, he just stared at Prasanna dumbly.

'You can't even talk? You sit silently like a buffalo while I am wondering why you are causing trouble for me. But never mind. I am not wasting any more time warning you. Nagaraj can take care of that. What I want to tell you is that I know the answer to your question.'

'Which one?' Raghavendra forced himself to look nonchalant and sip the over-sweet tea.

'First, I have some good news. I am telling you this not because you will share in it. After all, you only want to create trouble for my family. But I have taken care of one problem. I am sure you will be happy to know that I have fixed the marriage of my elder daughter. Does that disappoint you?' Prasanna wanted to convey to him that he was a good father, a father who at the first opportunity had found an honourable husband for his daughter. As if underlining the fact that Raghavendra was yet to accomplish this task.

Raghavendra placed his glass, with a thin layer of tea still left, on top of the small refrigerator nearby. He nodded, cast aside Prasanna's sarcasm and said, 'Yes. That is good news.'

'Do you want to know who the boy is? Or, since you are a detective, you already know?' Prasanna was being only partly sarcastic. He wondered if Raghavendra had, *somehow*, heard.

'No, but whoever it is, I am sure your daughter will be happy.'

'You don't worry about that. The boy is none other than our tailor, Shankar.'

Raghavendra was surprised, very surprised. 'Oh, that is very good. He is such a nice boy.'

Prasanna mellowed. Raghavendra seemed so sincere. But he persisted, 'I know you have been asking who made that girl pregnant.'

Why was he going on referring to Archana as 'that girl'? Raghavendra remained silent.

'You see, I very well know who that beggar is. And don't think that he will escape me. But since I don't want you going around asking your stupid question again, I will tell you. Actually, if you think about it, you are yourself a cause of that pregnancy.'

Raghavendra looked up at him, his anger slowly rising.

'Don't act so surprised. You rent your rooms to boys you don't know. And that sidekick of yours, that Bihari fellow, you think he is a nice chap, ah?'

Rajesh? Raghavendra felt slightly uneasy. The puff was doing things to his stomach.

'Haan, Rajesh. Your sidekick. Do you know what he has done?' He stopped and looked up, as if the answer would resound from the heavens. 'He was the one who made *that* girl pregnant.'

Triumphant Prasanna, giving his tea glass regally to the boy who was hovering around, crossing his legs and leaning back on an imaginary backrest. How easily, how casually, he had referred to his daughter as that girl, with not a break in his cunning voice!

Shocked Raghavendra, his eyes rapidly blinking in tune with the shock he felt. Rajesh? *Ridiculous*.

When finally he could speak, he said, 'You are wrong. It cannot be Rajesh.'

Even as he said it, doubt had knocked, entered and filled his being. Rajesh, who lived on top in his house, and his own two daughters down below!

'Arre, how do you know? I am telling you, he met this girl in his friend's house—the house you went to the other day. The boys there told me. But it is not your business any more, it never was. You can throw him out of your house yourself, or . . . '

Prasanna waited before delivering a final thrust, what he had dreamed of telling this nosy man, over and over again.

'Or do you want your two daughters to also become pregnant by him?' When Raghavendra showed no reaction, he leaned close to him and gleefully added, 'Maybe he is already doing something with them!' He laughed happily and got up from the stool, leaving it rocking on its uneven legs. On the way out, he slapped the back of the man at the counter heartily, his victory lighting his way.

Raghavendra swallowed his hurt and fear. He got up slowly and walked out without being aware of what he was doing. The man at the counter called out to him, 'Hey, you haven't paid.' Raghavendra turned back and apologetically handed over some faded, sticky notes. The man was not pleased, a feeling that clearly showed on his face. What is wrong with me, thought Raghavendra, that they all look at me like this? He looked back at the man, but found that he had no energy for a forgiving smile. All he saw was the man's curly, oiled hair and black, thick moustache.

Moustache!

Instantly, his heart felt light. He was released from the curse of doubt. He smiled back at the man with such openness that the man felt oddly guilty. Raghavendra walked back home with more than a bounce in his steps. For he knew, with absolute clarity of vision, that Rajesh had never worn a moustache.

11

RAGHAVENDRA WOKE UP TO YET ANOTHER DAY, HIS EYES tired after the excitement of the previous night. When he had come back home, Poornima and the girls had been watching a movie. They had refused to budge from their seats in front of the television, their eyes glued to the film, which had been released earlier in the year and was called *Shanti, Shanti, Shanti*. Feeling left out of their little circle, he had eaten his dinner alone and gone to sleep.

He had woken around three, his ears immediately searching for the sound of water. Then he remembered that it was not a water day; the Corporation had announced this in the paper the previous day. Having woken, he perversely woke Poornima too, telling her it was a water day.

She snapped at him, 'You read the paper for hours, read every word in it, yet you did not see the news that water would not be supplied to our area today.' Irritated, she turned away from him, but Raghavendra was not done.

'You know, last night I met Prasanna. And do you know what he said?'

Poornima ignored him.

'He has arranged for the marriage of his elder daughter to *your* tailor, Shankar. He is so scared that nobody will marry her after what Archana did, he decided to get her married to Shankar.'

Poornima turned towards him, peering into the hazy darkness, searching for a lost joke.

'Oh, now you are awake. Shankar immediately agreed, he said. Why not? Now they can combine their two shops.' She could see the shadow of his gleeful nod.

Raghavendra continued, 'He also told me something else. He knows who made that girl pregnant.'

Now she was truly awake. As she sat up, he put his right arm beneath his head and looked up at her happily.

'You want to know, don't you?'

'Don't play stupid games at this time of the night,' Poornima countered.

'Games, is it? Not when you hear what he said. The boy is—'

He waited for Poornima to say something. But she lay down and turned away from him.

'Rajesh.'

She jumped up again. Her sari pallu followed the movement and came to rest on her lap. Raghavendra looked at her chest. She covered herself, saying, 'Don't be stupid. It cannot be Rajesh.' She thought for a moment. 'He cannot speak one word of Malayalam. Do you think that girl would even have looked at him?'

Ah, is that another proof? How clever Poornima is.

'Moreover, Prasanna is a rotten man. He is trying to cause trouble for you. I hope you shouted at him or maybe even slapped him.' Looking at Raghavendra, she realised: *no, that you cannot do*. 'I hope you were not foolish enough to believe him.'

'Of course not. Don't I know Rajesh?'

'I don't know what you know or don't know.'

She lay back again, and they were silent for a while. Then she said, 'You see, it cannot be Rajesh. He doesn't have a moustache.'

She turned towards him triumphantly.

Raghavendra would not give in easily. 'You think I didn't think of that?'

She was about to say 'no', but kept quiet. After a pause, she added, 'Of course, if that man in the theatre and Rajesh are friends, and they made up this story to cheat you . . . '

It was Raghavendra's turn to sit bolt upright. 'Wait. Do you think Yediyurappa was lying?'

Poornima took his hand. 'Oh, you are so worried all the time. How could they have made up this story? You are the one who asked Rajesh to go with you to the theatre. And I am telling you, it is not Rajesh.'

Raghavendra looked up at the ceiling, knowing Rajesh's room was just above.

'Anyway,' she continued, 'at least Shankar has made a good catch. Now they can join the carpentry and tailoring shops. I tell you, these Malayalis always stick together.'

She pulled Raghavendra down. She hugged him tentatively as if to erase his last doubts, and soon he forgot about Rajesh and, after a few more moments, about Prasanna too.

Even if it had been an enjoyable early morning, the rest of the day proved to be disastrous. When Raghavendra stepped out to see his daughters off to school, he noticed that the rain and the rats had finally emptied the rice, and only the gunnysack remained, wet and torn in many places. He took a stick, lifted the tattered sack and threw it on the road. After he removed it, he could see a white patch of rice on the ground and imagined a world of worms wrapped around them. Throwing the sack out was like the final expulsion of Nagaraj from his house.

As he was standing in the compound, he noticed a well-built man walking towards him, peering at every house he passed. Raghavendra noticed the man's sudden glance at the nameboard above his house, and saw him walk briskly towards him. He opened the gate and came to stand in front of Raghavendra.

'Are you the owner of this . . . agency?'

Raghavendra nodded weakly. The man caught hold of his shirt.

'You cheat. Don't you have any shame cheating us out of our hard-earned money?'

Raghavendra looked desperately around him. He saw Patil walk slowly from his shop, peering at the short-sighted insults at Raghavendra.

Poornima heard the noise and hurried out. The man saw her and his anger spluttered. 'Oh, you have a family too! How do you people live off my savings without any guilt?'

Raghavendra was confused. 'I don't know . . . '

'What don't you know?' Before the man could say anything further, Poornima said, 'Come inside first.' Raghavendra hurried behind her words and the man was forced to follow. She closed the door behind them.

'Sit down,' she said, pointing to a chair in the office.

'Yes, talk. You people cheat us by talking.'

'I promise you, I really don't know what you are talking about.'

The man had a momentary doubt. 'Aren't you running the chit fund?'

'No, no,' began Poornima, but Raghavendra intervened.

'You mean the chit fund of Nagaraj?'

'Yes, Nagaraj. The chit fund is in the name of your agency. He said he was working for somebody—yes, somebody called Raagu.'

Poornima glared at Raghavendra and went inside.

'I am sorry, my friend. Nagaraj has not only cheated you but also me. I have nothing to do with that chit fund. He has misused my name.'

'I don't believe that he used your name without you knowing.'

'No, believe me, he did. I have complained about him to the police. I am even closing down this agency in a day or two.'

The man was unconvinced and looked around the room in confusion, as if searching for a place to keep his anger.

Raghavendra was suddenly inspired to say, 'See, I have a wife and two little girls. I swear on those girls that I have nothing to do with this.'

The man was immediately apologetic. 'You don't need to swear on your girls,' he admonished him. 'My name is Muthanna,' he added, offering his name somewhat like an apology. A calm, quiet man, he had lost his temper unnecessarily towards another like him. But it wasn't his fault, was it? The little money he had saved every month and given to the chit fund now seemed irrevocably lost. How could he have been so foolish? Watching him, Raghavendra could feel his doubt and confusion. He wished he could do something to help him.

Poornima came back then with a cup of coffee. The hot, strong smell further calmed the man. 'We are people like you,' Poornima added. The man nodded his approval and finished his coffee in silence.

Then he asked, 'Now what can I do? Not only me, but many of my friends have been cheated. They want to go to the police, but I know what the police are worth.'

Raghavendra nodded his head vigorously and asked, 'But how did he cheat all of you?'

'We are the fools. We gave money once a month for the fund. There is a lucky draw and whosoever is selected can take all the money in the fund. For the last many months, the winner was always a stranger. By chance, we found out one day that the names of the winners were all fictitious and Nagaraj was pocketing the money.' He paused as he remembered: 'Oh, a couple of months back, a man called Raghavendra won. That must be you!'

Seeing Raghavendra's shocked face, he managed a smile.

Poornima was quick as usual. 'But my husband started the agency with Nagaraj only a month or so ago.'

'Earlier, it had nothing to do with the agency. We got suspicious and discovered this only last week. When one of my friends met Nagaraj, he said it was your agency that was in charge.'

Poornima murmured distinctly, 'Thief.' The way she said it, the word became an unutterable curse. Raghavendra looked at her in shock and the man smiled again. *This man is too dumb to do this.* He looked approvingly at Poornima in her faded sari.

Raghavendra said, 'This is not correct and I am sorry that my name has been used in this manner. I will set it right.' He was suddenly struck by an idea. He hurried outside and called out to Bhaskar. It was Rajesh who peeped out, and Raghavendra asked him to send Bhaskar down. When Bhaskar came down, it was with a look of surprise. He had had no interaction so far with Raghavendra, other than paying the rent.

'Bhaskar, I need some help from you.' Raghavendra spoke in a mixture of Kannada and English.

'Anything, Uncle.'

'I have some papers. They are full of numbers and calculations. You are good at that, I think?'

Bhaskar smiled shyly, but confidently.

'I want you to read them and tell me what you think.'

'Give them to me anytime, Uncle.'

'Can you do it now?'

Bhaskar looked at his watch and agreed, as if the watch had to first give him permission. After all, what were a few numbers for an algebraic brain? He was sure he would need only a few minutes to do whatever Raghavendra wanted him to do.

The few minutes became two hours. Bhaskar left his room only once, to call his office and inform them that he would be late. He was fascinated by the simplicity of the scam.

Muthanna left after more promises from Raghavendra that he would somehow try to help him. He left with little confidence, resigning himself to the unpleasant fact of having lost all his hard-earned savings. When Raghavendra said that it was a 'computer brain' that would help them, the two men shared a hesitant smile that said, yes, we are ignorant of these things, we are the older generation.

Muthanna had added, 'My son—he is in fourth class—he already knows compooters.' Already, Bangalore was fast transforming from a 'garden city' to a 'compooter city'.

Raghavendra was glad when the man left. He was getting tired of speaking so much. Each day, he had to find new words in different languages to communicate. It was no longer possible to live in Bangalore knowing only Kannada. It was necessary to know English, Hindi, Malayalam, Tamil,

Telugu, and who knew what else! The vegetable sellers spoke Tamil, the rice merchants Telugu, the garment shop owners Hindi, the employees at teashops and bakeries Malayalam, leaving only the workers at roadside cycle shops and darshinis—tiny, standing-only restaurants selling the world's best idlis, vadas and dosas—to speak in Kannada.

He told Poornima, 'Poorni, speaking in all these languages just to pass time! If we had remained in Udupi, no such problems.'

She had harrumphed. *You and your Udupi.* But she was secretly glad that her girls were speaking English so well, or so she thought.

But Raghavendra was not done. 'Do you know what Mari told me? That within the next ten years, Kannada speakers will become a minority. We will be taken over by the North Indians.'

Seeing Poornima dismiss this with a smirk, he continued, 'You think you can get your food then? Your idlis and dosas? It will all be North Indian food. And you have to speak Hindi. Or who knows what language? How would you like that?'

Poornima liked that very much, thank you. She wanted to eat something different, talk to people in other languages. Her daughters spoke in English with each other, and in Hindi with some students at school. How proud she was of them, and here was her husband blabbering about idlis and Hindi.

She wanted to give him a suitable riposte, but found that her Hindi did not rise to the occasion. Instead, she said in English, 'No problem.'

Bhaskar came down before lunch and explained to Raghavendra (and a hovering Poornima) the mechanics of the chit fund.

'There is no doubt that one person has taken all the money every month.'

Raghavendra nodded sagely, provoking Bhaskar to ask, 'Do you know who it is?'

He began to nod assent, but Poornima pinched him sharply in the back. So he converted it into an oscillating no.

Bhaskar added, 'If you show this to the police, this man will surely be arrested.'

Poornima laughed. 'You are young,' she said. As if to atone, she asked, 'Will you have coffee or tea?'

He drank neither, but settled for a plate of excellent kodbales instead.

Before he left, he informed them, 'I had wanted to tell you this earlier. My parents have almost fixed my marriage. Maybe in two or three months. Then I will vacate your room.'

Bhaskar had finally made it, not just in the eyes of his parents, but also in the calculations of his in-laws. In their eyes, he was the perfect catch. He had moved away from sultry Madurai to Bangalore, a foreign place which was cool all the year around, where the vegetables had rosy cheeks. He was a computer engineer, and the dreams that were building a new Bangalore had wafted all the way to Madurai. It was not his parents who had found a girl for him—it was the girl's family that had tracked him down. They approached his father with a proposal laden with sweets, hopes and promises. Their daughter had just finished her BSc and was waiting, like a thousand other girls, for her parents to find a boy for them. Secretly, she hoped that she too could work in that magical city that had entered the world of Tamil films, which she watched on a tired, dusty TV in the hot confines of her home. The refrain for her and her friends was simply this: if the boy was not in the US, then at least in Bangalore.

Poornima and Raghavendra stood at the door watching him leave.

'So unlike Rajesh, no?' they both said at the same time.

Maybe it was all a matter of timing. Poornima went to Josephine's house to get an extra litre of milk in the afternoon. She used to get milk twice a day, but had discontinued that practice. Earlier, they had bought fresh cow's milk from the milkman who came twice a day. But then, the milk had increasingly become more watery, which added a new worry since the water, given the scarcity of it, was quite assuredly of dubious origin.

For the past few days, the girls had been clamouring for a sweet. So, Poornima had decided to make some coconut burfi. She knocked on the door of Josephine, who opened it after a few sleepy moments. 'One litre,' Poornima said apologetically. Josephine walked back to a barely functioning refrigerator for two half-litre packets.

As Poornima thanked her and turned to leave, Josephine spoke. 'I have been hearing things. You be careful of that boy in your house.' *Oh no! Not her too!* Poornima tried to act as if she hadn't heard. But Josephine spoke louder, daring her to run away and let the whole street hear her.

'I am talking about the North Indian boy,' she said loudly.

Poornima turned back. 'What about him?'

'He made that girl . . . the girl who died? . . . pregnant.'

'That is false. I know he didn't do it.'

Josephine stared back at her. 'How can you be so sure?'

Poornima had nothing to say. The look that Josephine gave her seemed to suggest she was being too protective of Rajesh. *Why? I say, why?*

'I will tell my husband,' she said, running away from uncontrollable rumours.

That evening, four men came to Raghavendra's house. Poornima had finished making the sweet but was not happy with the way it had turned out. *Right from the time I got the milk, the sweet has been cursed.* The children were now licking the top layer of the pieces of burfi in their hands, even as their eyes lazily skimmed their books.

One of the men called out to Raghavendra. When he came out, they asked, 'Where is that upstairs boy?'

He had no idea.

'We have come to take him to the police station. He has destroyed our girl. Either you throw him out or else . . . '

From the way the man spoke and looked, Raghavendra knew he was a Tamilian. In an act of bravado, he said,

'You try doing anything and you will be the one in the police station. This boy is innocent. Don't spoil his life. Tell Prasanna that he should stay out of our lives.'

Poornima, listening from behind the door, felt like clapping.

'Oh, that is the way, is it?' The man turned around and loudly told a few passers-by on the road, 'This man supports that rascal who has killed our girl. Should we keep quiet?'

Patil, in the opposite shop, quickly turned off the TV and shut his shop. A crowd gathered.

'Do we keep quiet? Ah? Ah?' For each question, there were ten nodding answers.

'This is what happens if we let North Indians into our locality. Ah?'

A few from the crowd left. They looked, all too obviously, like they were from the North.

'They think this is Bihar. We should castrate the bastard and send him back to that state.' The man's cronies clapped.

Raghavendra walked out to the gate and said, 'Who is this fellow to talk? Ask him where he is from. He cannot even speak Kannada properly.' Another part of the crowd hooted. Inspired, he continued, 'If you throw out people from other places, how many of you will be left?'

The Tamilian and his friends were getting fidgety. The language issue was one they would not debate. Their leader, attempting to reassert himself, raised his voice. 'That is not the point. This boy has spoiled *our* girl.'

Baale Gowda came hurrying into the circle. He said, in a manner befitting a headmaster, measured and calm, 'Relax, friends. We are all civilised people.' He looked at Raghavendra with a frown. 'We can deal with it without getting angry.'

Suddenly, a young man at the edge of the crowd took a stone and threw it at Raghavendra's house. It hit the board, loudly declaring its presence. Raghavendra had seen the man bend down, throw the stone and try to move away. He pushed past the group, caught him by his shirt and pushed him to the ground. He stood above him, his silhouette a poster hero. No one in the locality had ever heard Raghavendra raise his voice. But at that moment they heard this mild, middle-aged man in a dhoti and a loose shirt shout, 'You touch a stone, I will break your bones!'

Poornima came running behind him. Everyone expected her to pull Raghavendra away; instead, she spat on the man who lay on the ground, looking more abashed than angry. This was a shame neither he nor the crowd could react to. The mob dispersed. Raghavendra took Poornima's hand and walked briskly into his compound. The man who had thrown the stone vanished.

The crowd had vanished but it left behind a stain of its presence, which, in little knots here and there, would stay on for days to come. What had remained unvoiced in Mathikere Extension was finally out: a linguistic conflict between the Kannadigas and the others. And Raghavendra would be seen as a man who spoke for his people.

Whatever Prasanna had hoped to achieve by sending his friends to attack Raghavendra, it hadn't worked. His insane anger towards Raghavendra could only rebound on him. His attempt to publicly accuse Rajesh was not done on behalf of Archana, but only as a means to insult Raghavendra. However surprising it may seem, he had no interest in getting justice for his daughter. She had truly been expelled from his angry mind and was only an excuse for his injured pride. But why he hated Raghavendra so much would continue to remain one of the unsolved mysteries of Mathikere Extension.

Rajesh was walking back home that night with just a teeny bit of worry. His test in thermodynamics had not gone too well. He had (ever so casually) tried to look at the answer sheet of his neighbour, but surprisingly, the teacher seemed to be extra vigilant that day. Not that his performance had got his spirits down. After dinner at Guptaji's mess—more potatoes—he had gone to his friend's house, and they watched two Hindi serials. Life was fine as it was, and as always he looked forward to the next dawn. No unnecessary angst of cyclic water days for him.

As he turned from the main road into his street, he saw Nagaraj with two men. A smile blossomed readily, even for them. Before he could pass by, one of the men, who had a bandage around his head, stopped him.

'Come,' he said in English. Nagaraj took his arm and led him towards Chikanna's house. Rajesh went along happily, assuming they needed his help with something or the other. *At the rate at which I am helping others, how can I concentrate on my studies?*

Chikanna's wife let them into the house. Rajesh was taken into the room where Raghavendra had met Nagaraj and his friends.

'Drink?' asked Nagaraj, but Rajesh shook his head. Even though all his friends drank and most of them smoked, he had always refused to indulge himself. This was another lesson his father had taught him well.

The man with the bandage, yes, the policeman, picked up a stone that sat on a table and showed it to Rajesh.

'You recognise this?' he asked in heavily accented Hindi.

It was a fist-sized stone. Rajesh shook his head with the puzzled dawn of a smile.

'You don't? Not even when you threw it at me?'

Rajesh laughed. 'Uncle, I don't throw stones at people.'

'Didn't you come with that fool Raghavendra the other night? And threw this stone at me through that open window?'

Raghavendra had been here! Rajesh was impressed. The room looked like a mini version of Venkateswara Bar and Restaurant.

'No, I don't know when Uncle came here.'

'Do you know who I am? Do you think you and that old man can play games with us?'

The stone still tightly clenched in his fist, he gestured to Nagaraj and Chikanna, who sat comfortably, with filled glasses in their hands.

'You don't think we know all about you?'

Rajesh was beginning to get worried. Unexpectedly, Nagaraj spoke. 'You are from Bihar?'

Rajesh nodded vigorously.

'And you come here and put sight on our girls?'

Our girls? Put sight?

'Don't act as if you don't understand, you fucking Bihari. We know you made that girl pregnant.'

'What?' Rajesh looked around him, looking for reasons for this attack on him. 'Uncle, who are you talking about?'

'That girl who died. Remember, the one who committed suicide?'

'No, Uncle. I have not even talked to her.' In truth, he had not once managed to produce one of his ubiquitous smiles for her. And even if he had smiled, mostly for himself, that would not have made her pregnant—*would it?*

'Don't lie on top of what you've already done. We don't like you fellows coming to our city and behaving as if you are in Bihar.'

'And worse,' continued the cop, 'we don't like you throwing stones at me. If you have the guts, do it to my face.'

Rajesh, poor chap, short and squat, whose face came up to the neck of the cop, had no idea what to do. He was suddenly afraid to even get up.

'Come on, I am waiting. Do it to my face.'

'I promise you, Uncle, I have not done anything to you. Let me go.'

'Go? Where? Come on, hit me.'

Rajesh felt the menace in the room. Looking around, he noticed that the door had been closed. He saw Chikanna get up to close the windows.

He folded his hands. 'Please, Uncle, I beg you, don't do anything to me.'

The cop bent forward, showing him his bandaged head. 'Look at what you have done.' He showed him the stone. 'I'll tell you for the last time, we don't want outsiders like you here.'

'I'll leave immediately, Uncle. Don't worry.' He turned towards the door, hoping that it would have miraculously opened. Just a passing trouble, they might have said, as they invited him to leave.

The cop's hand swung in an arc. 'You too can see what this stone does to you.' His words, uttered loudly in Kannada, added to the force of the stone as it cracked Rajesh's skull. Blood shot out, and Rajesh fell on the edge of the sofa before crumbling to the ground. The cop kicked him on his stomach as he lay on the ground.

Chikanna shouted out to his wife. The door opened, and she came in and looked at Rajesh. The blood was flowing freely now, mixing with the dust on the floor to form a reddish-brown paste.

'Hurry up, you deaf woman,' he shouted. 'Get a bandage.'

And more softly to Nagaraj, 'Is he dead?'

The cop put the stone on the table, sank heavily into a chair, and poured himself a drink.

Rajesh did not look like he was dead. The woman bandaged his wound with trembling hands, hiding her tears well inside her. So much water had accumulated inside those tired little eyes.

After some minutes had passed in silence, Nagaraj asked Chikanna to take a look at Rajesh, who was now lying on his back. Chikanna tried to nudge him with his foot. 'Arre, you have killed him,' he said, suddenly scared.

'Killed him? Ha!' The cop bent and checked Rajesh's pulse. It seemed to be beating, and to his drunken thoughts seemed to say, I am fine, how about you?

Nagaraj got up and told Chikanna and the cop to take Rajesh away. 'Go and dump him in front of Raghavendra's house. This will be a lesson to all of them.'

Chikanna was still worried. 'He won't die, will he?'

'Coward! You are such a girl.' The way Nagaraj spoke, he seemed to be saying, *I won't be surprised if you get pregnant*.

It was past midnight when Chikanna and the cop picked up the still unconscious Rajesh. Chikanna was sure he was dead, or soon would be. The sky was surprisingly clear, the dogs had gone to sleep, and the tube lights along the road kept a lonely vigil. They carried him to Raghavendra's house, which lay in darkness now. Noiselessly, they opened the gate and placed Rajesh on the ground, right outside the door. Chikanna was trembling. The cop looked around, ready to poke out any prying eyes. They turned and left quickly, and under the first lamppost they passed, Chikanna stopped and pissed, letting all his guilt flow out with an audible sigh.

12

The alarm went off at half past three. Poornima awoke, turned it off. She nudged Raghavendra, but he would not be bothered that morning. Irritated, she got up clumsily (but still he wouldn't awaken), collected the empty vessel, turned on the outside light, and opened the door. As she stepped out, she saw Rajesh lying close to the door. She dropped the vessel in shock, breaking the silence of the early morning. Her first thought was: *God, is he drunk?* Then she saw the blood matted over his head, soaking past the crudely tied bandage. She cried—tough Poornima! Ran into the house, woke Raghavendra and pulled him out. Without his glasses, he could only see a form, a lump of human shaped flesh on the ground. He bent down, peered at Rajesh's face, and thought he lay with the peace of the dead.

Tears flowed into his eyes, driven by a strange emotion he had never felt before. Poornima found her voice and shouted, 'Don't keep staring. See his pulse.'

When Raghavendra placed his palm on his chest, he could feel the calm breath flowing in and out. I am here, here, inside here, it said, and Raghavendra found purpose in his pain. He ran up the stairs and woke Bhaskar. His gasping breaths told a story of their own and fearing the worst, Bhaskar hurried down the stairs. He looked at Rajesh, thought he was dead and gone. He looked at Poornima, who found the strength to say, 'We have to take him to the hospital.'

Bhaskar, befitting a computer brain, moved as fast as he thought. He ran up the stairs, picked up the key to his motorbike and ran down before Raghavendra could form a sentence. He pushed the motorbike forward, stopping near Rajesh.

Seeing Poornima twisting her emotions into a braid, he added, 'Don't worry. He will be fine.' Even to him, his voice and its message seemed like an illusion.

Bhaskar and Raghavendra lifted Rajesh onto the seat of the bike. Bhaskar manoeuvred himself in front of Rajesh and Raghavendra sat (after pulling his dhoti up to his knees and still in his banian) behind Rajesh, crushing him between the two of them. Rajesh's head gently lolled on Bhaskar's neck. The bike started at the first kick (befitting the slogan *'Hamara Bajaj'*), and raced up the empty road. Poornima stood at the gate, watching them leave, seeing Raghavendra's dhoti flying in the breeze.

They stopped at the nursing home at the end of their street. Nobody was around to answer their knocks. Without wasting any more time, they went to another one, close to the market. Luckily, there was a doctor there, on night duty. When he saw them, he called out to the nurse, and they vanished into a room with Rajesh. A long time later, the doctor came out and asked the two of them to come back after a few hours. When they asked how Rajesh was, he said, predictably, 'You go home and pray.'

Poornima did collect water that morning. The tap was dripping, so she knew Baale's wife had woken up earlier. She used the water to first clean the bloodstains on the ground. However, even after a thorough scrubbing, Rajesh's cheerful spirit continued to gleefully stain the ground.

Lights came on in the houses around them. Poornima, after having collected another vessel of water, sat outside, looking at the clear sky. Two cyclists rode slowly by, and soon a procession of empty carts went past the house on their way to the Yeswanthpur market. It was just past four; the dawn was still an imagination. It would come, would come soon enough, and then she would go back to the cycles that constituted her life. But until then, she just wanted to sit in the hazy darkness, staring at their dreams being slowly shattered.

Raghavendra went back to the hospital at eight. On the way to his office, Bhaskar had informed Rajesh's friends about what had happened. Rajesh had been shifted to a special room in the hospital, and Raghavendra was allowed a peek inside. Rajesh seemed to be sleeping, still apparently at peace. He was hooked up to a drip, and there were empty injection syringes in the waste basket beneath his bed.

A nurse asked Raghavendra to fill out a form. 'You have to pay two thousand rupees now,' she told him. 'We'll give you the final bill later.' She seemed to be suggesting that it would be a long haul for Rajesh.

Raghavendra's new worry was where to get the money. He reached home and found three of Rajesh's friends waiting to meet him. He asked them to sit in the office and went inside to ask Poornima if she had some money in the house. She had very little, and when he told her about the advance to be paid, she thought: *Who will pay us back if something happens to him?* She felt a passing wave of guilt, but that was carried into the same question on Raghavendra's frowning face.

'Don't worry,' she said, 'we'll pay the money and leave the rest in the hands of god.'

Meanwhile, Rajesh's friends waited in the office, too impatient to stand or sit. Their bodies were partly in motion, partly in stillness. They were hankering to do something, anything. The most animated among them was Bindra, who looked like their leader.

When he was introduced as such by one of the boys, Raghavendra said, remembering Rajesh's stray comments a few days back, 'Oh, you are the Commander.' He received a curt nod in reply. He continued, 'Rajesh is doing better. I've just come from the hospital. I'll go back there after a visit to the bank. I have to pay the hospital an advance.'

Bindra put his hand up. 'No, sir. He is our friend, our brother. We will take care of the money.'

Raghavendra was moved to protest. 'No, no. It is nothing.' He felt a little ashamed at the sudden sense of relief.

Another of the boys spoke up. 'Uncle, Commander will take care of everything. Please don't insult us.' All that was lacking in Bindra was a camouflage outfit.

The boy continued, 'All that we want to know is, who did this to our brother.'

Raghavendra looked at the three of them. They were so intense, as if they were an army in themselves.

'Forget it, already there has been enough trouble.'

'Sir, you don't understand. It is a matter of our self-respect . . . and that of our state. We are not like you people.'

No, we are not like you, you soft people. We believe in revenge, believe in giving and taking respect. If we sit quietly now, it will only get worse. And what will happen to the prestige of our Commander? People will spit at him for not protecting his friend!

They would have said all this, if only Raghavendra had been proficient in Hindi.

Instead, the same boy said, 'You don't know our Commander. Even the police are afraid of him.'

Raghavendra looked at Bindra: lean, neatly dressed, with hair that lay shyly cuddled around one another.

He remembered Nagaraj's friend, the cop. *How these boys exaggerate!* An indulgent smile crept over his face. Bindra recognised the smile and read its insulting message. Affronted, he got up to leave.

Poornima came in with three cups of coffee. Bindra, still upset, refused to drink the coffee. But when Poornima insisted, he gave in. *Respect to women comes before revenge.* He blew on his coffee to cool it, thinking about his next action.

In between sips, he said calmly, 'It is better if you tell me who did this to Rajesh. I can anyway find out, but I am asking you—politely.' Raghavendra was impressed by the sudden shift in his voice.

So he told them, in a voice broken into words of Hindi, Kannada and English. He told them about his search, and about his problems with Nagaraj.

'I don't know if this was the work of Nagaraj. You see, even Prasanna is spreading the rumour that Rajesh got his daughter pregnant.'

The friends exchanged more than glances. 'Not Rajesh, sir,' one of them immediately replied. 'If they said that about one of us, it would have been fine. But not him.' *Fine? What do they mean?* Raghavendra was puzzled, but he knew better than to ask them about it.

Instead, he said, 'I know that. But what is done is done. Don't worry, I'll take care of Nagaraj.' Even as he said this, he was aware that he had no idea what to do. He had thought that he would give the copy of the chit fund papers to Muthanna, who could do what he wanted with them.

Bindra and his friends left. Before leaving, Bindra told Poornima, pointedly ignoring her husband, 'If you have any problems, *any* problems, just call me.' His assurance left a mark on the house, telling all who saw it that the house was under the Commander's protection.

Under my protection: this would be Bindra's epitaph. He came from a farming family, from one of the poorer regions of northern Bihar. He was an excellent student in school, but by the time he finished his twelfth grade, he knew he wanted to be more than a good student. He was already something of a local leader, and the local politicians had taken note of him. But he was not interested in being yet another sidekick to a politician. He wanted to be an engineer, wanted to be in Bangalore, a place that had drawn many youngsters from that region. Once he came to Bangalore, he realised that it was a city that had not lived up to its potential. It was effeminate, a weak and passive excuse of a city. It had the potential to become a Delhi, to gain the prosperity of Bombay with the valour and machoness of Bihar, but everything here was too slow, too polite, too laidback. He even made fun of Kannada, describing it as a language that was spoken too slowly, without any urgency. It was not surprising then, that when the first troubles began between the Bihari students and the locals, with the police supporting the latter, the students turned to Bindra. They called him 'Commander', a name befitting his status, for he had for some time now been selling country-made guns that he brought from Bihar. He stopped attending classes, although he continued to be registered as a student at the engineering college. By the time he came into Raghavendra's life, he had established himself as a person to be feared in that locality.

Bindra and his friends went straight to the hospital, three of them sitting on a brand-new bike (Yamaha, no less). They jauntily parked the bike outside the gates, walking in as if they owned the place. The receptionist told them where Rajesh's room was, but added that they should come back later, during visiting hours.

Bindra's friend, the one who spoke on his behalf (the other's job was mostly to nod), said, 'You don't know who he is? He is Commander Bindra.' The receptionist had not heard of him, and frankly thought that the puny looking fellow did not merit another thought.

She replied bravely, 'He could be the prime minister for all I care.' For all she cared, indeed. If she had met Vajpayee on the road, she would not have recognised him.

Bindra leaned over the desk and pulled out a thick wad of notes. His friend spoke for him. 'He will now pay the advance and then go to see our friend. You understand?' When he spoke in Hindi, it became clear who they were. Bindra handed the money to his friend and walked towards the rooms.

The nurse who was leaving Rajesh's room got a frown from Bindra. He lifted his eyebrows questioningly and she replied, in a lilting voice filled with the swaying coconut trees of Mangalore, 'He is much better. He is sleeping. The doctor says he will survive.'

Bindra pulled out a hundred-rupee note and gave it to her. She refused, and surprised herself by blushing when he insisted that she take the money. 'You have given me good news and I am only giving you a small gift.' She gave him a shy smile, but Bindra's eyes were already roving around the corridors of the hospital.

One of Bindra's friends went to inform Poornima that Rajesh would survive, although he had not yet regained consciousness. Poornima was so delighted that she went to the kitchen to bring him a piece of the burfi she had made. The boy tossed it into his mouth, his munching face asking for more. She got a plateful and after eating all the pieces, he said, 'As soon as Rajesh wakes up, you should send him some khichdi. Nicely mashed.' As if he were passing judgement on the quality of her burfi.

Bindra was restless in the hospital. He had walked up and down the corridors, glaring at the nurses, nodding to the doctors. He decided that he would not waste more time than was necessary—as if time was his to waste. He could have waited for Rajesh to tell him the name of the man who had so grievously broken his skull. But when he saw Rajesh sleeping so peacefully, he had a feeling that it would be a long time before he opened his mouth. There was another reason for his impatience. For Bindra, it was only action that defined a man. There was no point in waiting for Rajesh to tell him who had beaten him; he would discover that by himself.

So it was that he left the hospital with his friends, heading for Venkateswara B&R. The restaurant was just opening for business. The owner was seated at the cashier's table, dressed in a loud lungi and a loose T-shirt that had 'Chicago Bulls' stamped on it, with a red angry bull snorting at the customers. Seeing Bindra, the man got up from his stool. Bindra asked him to come inside, into a corner of the kitchen, with (yet another) movement of his eyebrows.

The owner knew Bindra well. Just a few months ago, Bindra had supplied him with a country gun brought from Bihar. It had cost a lot, but it seemed as if the power of a gun had given him more courage that led to his growing paunch.

Bindra told him about Rajesh. Each word was a container of restrained anger. The owner acted as if he knew Rajesh well, making it a point to remember to treat Rajesh well the next time he came. *If he comes!* Bindra then asked him about Nagaraj.

What could the owner say? Nagaraj was protection for him. Especially because of his policeman friend. Since Nagaraj and his friends were locals, it helped to keep him happy. Although the owner was a Kannadiga from Shimoga, wasn't he still some sort of an outsider—at least to Nagaraj? He told Bindra that Nagaraj was a nuisance, but what could he do? Nagaraj and his two friends never paid the bills for their chicken and booze. But the owner had long realised that they were worth every rupee lost to him, if they could save him potential trouble. And thanks to the cop, no other policeman came by to collect money from him.

Midway through these stumbled explanations, Bindra stopped him. 'I want to know where these fellows stay.'

The owner looked around the kitchen. Dirt and grime had steadily accumulated over the years, and the smell of meat and booze had become condensed matter that settled inside every available hole in the walls. He did not want his words to find places to hide in that grime. More importantly, he was worried about the two cooks, whose ears were live radars that communicated (later, much later) what they heard and what they guessed.

But Bindra is also dangerous!

So, he whispered to him, 'These days, Nagaraj is with Chikanna. They eat here at night, then go to his house.'

After some hesitation, he asked, 'Are you also involved with that Raghavendra, his agency?' Bindra dismissed the question, sending it sprawling into the big aluminium vessels, now totally black.

'Don't worry about all that,' his friend spoke for him.

The owner asked them to stay for lunch. His strained smile suggested that the meal would be free. Bindra refused, forcing the others to nod in acquiescence.

Grateful, the owner added, 'I will tell you something, but you should promise never to say that I said it. Chikanna has a wife, a thin, ugly woman. She told the paanwallah's wife that Raghavendra went to Chikanna's house a couple of days back. It seems that Nagaraj and his friends threw their drinks on him—imagine, on that Brahmin fellow! And as the policeman was about to hit him, a stone came flying from outside the window, breaking that beggar's head. You see what I'm telling you?'

Bindra saw it all clearly. He also noticed that the two cooks had left the kitchen.

'I want to tell you more, but I want more than a promise of silence from you.'

Bindra nodded. He knew what was coming.

'One of my friends wants a gun like the one you sold me. Of course, he thinks it's too expensive, but I told him you would give me a discount. What do you think?'

Bindra thought the man was going to take his cut while selling the gun. But he didn't care. He nodded again.

'Okay. The story on the *roads*,' the owner continued, turning his head to look at the streets past the decaying walls, 'is that Rajesh was taken to Chikanna's house last night.'

'The wife?' asked Bindra's voluble friend.

'I am not saying anything. You want her to be beaten up?' He continued, 'So Rajesh was in that room with those drunken bastards.' He paused, waiting to let the insult sink in. He knew that Bindra was noting every inflection.

'And they had some argument.' He stopped and looked around; the cooks had come back. *Had they gone to the toilet together again?* The owner herded his words around him like they were cows entering Bindra's, yes, only Bindra's ears.

'The policeman hit Rajesh with the stone.' There! He had finally said it, knowing that it was a gamble that he had taken. If this story got out on the *roads* . . .

Bindra shook the man's hand. 'You have done the right thing. Now you should keep quiet about all this.'

The owner nodded vigorously. His lips would become mute, and all that he had to say would be swallowed into his tongue. But Bindra knew that if he did not confront

Nagaraj soon, it would be Nagaraj who would be in the kitchen listening to the tired whispers that would gradually settle into dirty rumours.

Poornima went to Marimuthu's temple while Raghavendra took a nap after lunch. Marimuthu was sitting under the pipal tree, surrounded by a few men. Seeing Poornima, they all stood up. She went up to Marimuthu and said that she wanted to do a pooja. She hesitated. The men left, reading the hesitation as their dismissal. Poornima added, 'For Rajesh, the boy who lives above.'

Marimuthu nodded sagely.

'I told your husband to be careful. But now Nagaraj has taken it out on that boy.' Seeing her surprised look, he added, 'I know everything.'

He went to the anthill. She placed a fifty-rupee note as an offering. From a shaky cupboard, Marimuthu pulled out a coconut and broke it on the ground. He began murmuring prayers, offering pinches of kumkum to a picture of Krishna. Poornima was surprised, for she had thought the anthill was the deity here. Little did she realise that this was Marimuthu's way of acknowledging her roots.

As Poornima left, reassured by Marimuthu's calmness and dignity, he called out to her: 'Tell your husband that I will come and meet him.'

That was indeed a grand gesture, for Marimuthu never left his shrine to socialise with people. Now he was sounding like a priest who made house calls, like the last few doctors who still did that in Mathikere.

Prasanna heard about Rajesh before lunchtime. One of his assistants had gone to the hardware shop in the market. The shopkeeper there had asked about Rajesh, indicating that he should have known all about Rajesh since they shared a locality, if not a friendship. The assistant had promptly come back to report the news to Prasanna.

Prasanna stopped work, suddenly worried that he would be seen as a suspect. He had started his morning with a needless worry. His friend, the hot-blooded Tamilian with whom he had unwisely shared the claim about Rajesh, had come to his house early in the morning to tell him about how he had taken a few friends to deal with Rajesh. Instead, it was Raghavendra (and his wife!) whom they had had to confront. His entire description was influenced by an unsaid thought: What was happening to Kannadigas these days that they were able to find these hidden reserves of aggression? Hearing him, Prasanna was perturbed. He had mentioned Rajesh as the culprit only to shut Raghavendra up. He had not expected his friend to act in such ill-advised haste. Archana was becoming public property, for people to use according to their needs.

When he heard about Rajesh being in the hospital, Prasanna became even more worried. Under what drunken influence had he told Nagaraj? His worry began to gather an appetite: what if the locals came to beat him? What if Shankar refused to marry Meghalatha? What if . . .

He hurried home, scurrying ahead of his doubts, to his stoic wife. Along with a spicy lunch, he only got angry looks from her. Hema was still in the throes of grief, not only from Archana's death, but also from hearing about Megha's marriage that had been fixed without any discussion with her. Shankar was a nice boy, no doubt, but what was the hurry? When Megha heard of it, she had retreated further into silence. Even the sound of her footsteps was lost in the lament of her mind.

As Prasanna walked back to his shop after lunch, he came to the conclusion that he had to do something to undo his mistake. He saw Shankar standing outside his shop, looking very pleased with himself. He called him over and told him to meet Raghavendra, to communicate the message that he was very sorry to hear about Rajesh.

'Make it clear to him that I had nothing to do with this. You understand?' Shankar nodded, the memory of having met Nagaraj and his friend that night in the bar still hazy in his mind. He looked at Prasanna with a newfound fear. He had clearly underestimated the man all along.

Prasanna said, 'Better go see Rajesh in the hospital. Buy some fruits when you go. If Raghavendra is not there when you go, wait till you can meet him and give my message.' It was not easy for him, this gesture towards Raghavendra, but Prasanna knew that sometimes in life one had to bend to avoid a bow.

Shankar walked away, irritated. *Didn't Prasanna know the cost of fruits these days?*

Prasanna shouted behind Shankar's back: 'And don't take bananas. Buy apples.' Prasanna's assistants, hearing that shout, snickered. Already ordering his to-be-son-in-law like he ordered them around! Not good, not good at all!

Inconsequential events turn stories on their head. Poornima had wanted to accompany Raghavendra to the hospital in the evening, along with the two girls. But the girls refused to go, nor would they let her leave. The younger one, in an attempt to make her stay, even managed to look ill. She went to her father and asked him to feel her forehead, claiming she had a fever. Perturbed, he asked Poornima to stay back.

Poornima knew why the girls wanted to be at home. The cartoons on TV had lately become an addiction. But Raghavendra tightened his resolve (with a faded leather belt, no less), leaving Poornima muttering, 'You call yourself a father and yet you don't know the first thing about your daughters.'

He bought two packets of biscuits from Patil, whose peering eyes still looked at him with suspicion. Shankar, standing outside his shop, watched him leave, deciding that he would follow him soon.

Ten minutes after Raghavendra left, Yediyurappa came in search of him. He had thought up a convoluted story about his search for Archana's lover. He was planning to tell Raghavendra that with the help of unnamed sources, he had discovered that the girl's lover was involved in brewing illicit liquor. Then he would say, 'Forget him, sir, he is too dangerous for us. But if you want me to do any other work, I will gladly do so.'

Yediyurappa was so convinced he would get a job with Raghavendra that he didn't turn up at Shahi for his ticket collecting duties.

When Poornima opened the door, she saw a young man nervously practising his thoughts, tossing them around for the final story. He asked for Raghavendra, and she curtly told him that he was not available.

Yediyurappa realised that this was Raghavendra's wife. He wanted to impress her too. So he said, 'Madam, your husband had asked me to find out about some matter.' When she remained unresponsive, he added, 'About the girl who died.' He did not know where Archana had lived, otherwise he would have offered a glance towards her street.

'Sir asked me about some boy and I want to tell Sir something.' He was not sure if detectives' wives were privy to their secrets.

Poornima looked at him sceptically. 'Why, do you know who that boy is?'

Once more, the hand of fate showed its lines of wisdom. Yediyurappa somehow knew that she would throw out his story, along with him. Look at her! She stared at him as if his presence itself was in doubt. Intimidated, he merely said, 'No, Madam, I just want to ask him . . . ' Ask him what? He thought furiously and could only come up with ' . . . some details, you know.' Suddenly inspired, just as he imagined the door slamming on his face, he added, 'I met a friend who might know the man.'

Poornima was too tired to think through his stutters. If Raghavendra wanted to deal with him, that was his problem. So she told him to go to the hospital to meet her husband. As he left, she said, 'Close the gate when you leave.' She banged the door shut, the resultant breeze (*angry, wasn't it?*) driving him on his way.

Shankar had bought half a kilo of apples of the cheapest variety he could find. The fruit seller was irritated by his bargaining, which reflected his obvious reluctance to buy the apples. He told Shankar, 'Who else buys apples these days, except for sick patients?' Hinting clearly that sick patients deserved better than visits from *cheapos*. Shankar was surprised at the man's observation. *Who knows what else he knows about tailors!* When he put the apples in a paper bag, Shankar insisted on a plastic one, thinking that he had to maintain some shreds of dignity.

Raghavendra was surprised to see Shankar in the hospital, then amazed when Shankar dumped the fruits in his hand.

'This is for Rajesh,' Shankar said, trying to mask his discomfort at being in a hospital. He had come to give a message to Raghavendra, which did not include having to hold Rajesh's hands.

'This is very nice of you, Shankar,' Raghavendra replied. He took an apple from the bag and gave it to Shankar. 'I heard you have become engaged. Here, take this.' Shankar took the apple and pushed it into the pocket of his pants. He fidgeted, hating the suffocating smell of Dettol all around him.

Shankar was clear that he did not want to see Rajesh. What if his duty included having to touch him, for who knew what germs he had on his body? Raghavendra noticed that Shankar was intent on leaving. He walked with him to the lobby of the hospital, assuring him that he would tell Rajesh about his visit.

It was only then that Shankar said, 'I should tell you, Uncle, that our carpenter, Prasanna, is very disturbed by what happened. When he saw I was coming here, he told me to tell you that he had nothing to do with this.'

Raghavendra was ready to forgive anybody—at least for the present. And, after all, Shankar was going to be Prasanna's son-in-law.

He replied, 'No, no. I never thought that he had anything to do with this.'

Precisely at that moment, Yediyurappa came in hesitantly. He had never entered a hospital before, and was struck by the smell and the blue-white colour all around. He caught sight of Raghavendra in the lobby, talking to a young man. As he came closer, the young man left, in a hurry that was all too obvious. Yediyurappa stared at Shankar, wondering if he too had come for the job. They passed each other, Shankar smiling as if pleased that he had managed to escape from the hospital so soon.

Raghavendra was watching Shankar leave when he spotted Yediyurappa. He walked towards him, but Yediyurappa had eyes only for Shankar. When Raghavendra touched him on the shoulder, he turned and said, 'Sir, that is the man who was with that girl.' His eyes opened wider at this discovery, and the hairs on his arms stood up to salute them. There was no need to make up a story, after all.

Yediyurappa's face was one kind of proof of what he said, however shocking it was to Raghavendra. They both stared at Shankar's fast fading form, soon to be lost among the teeming many who walked up and down the streets.

Before Raghavendra could doubt him, Yediyurappa grabbed his arm and said earnestly, 'Believe me, sir. I promise on my mother. That man who was talking to you now, he is the one.'

Raghavendra did not even think of asking Yediyurappa what he was doing in the hospital. He saw it all as a pattern, one that mixed beliefs and fate into well-ordered paths. He suddenly remembered Poornima's comment that Archana would not look at Rajesh because he did not speak any Malayalam.

'Do you know who he is?' he asked. 'He is the tailor on our street.'

Yediyurappa took this inconsequential information as proof of Raghavendra's belief in him.

'This is the work of god,' he said, guessing correctly that god played an important role in Raghavendra's life. 'Otherwise, why would I see this man now, after two days of searching for him everywhere?' It was another matter that the only place he had searched was his daydreams. 'I went to your house to ask about the job. And your wife was kind enough to send me here. Look at the timing.' He stopped, looking deeply into Raghavendra's eyes, as though searching for a sign: Applicant Successful. Through the lenses, he could only see Raghavendra blink.

He continued, 'Imagine if I had been five minutes late!' Raghavendra nodded. He had finally understood it all. Truth was like this. It may get delayed sometimes, but it could never escape the hold of time.

He was confused by both this sudden insight and Yediyurappa's claim about Shankar. He took him outside and they went to a bakery next door. Thankfully, it was an Iyengar bakery, run by a 'pure' Kannadiga, who put an excess of coconut in everything. After they had eaten the potato buns and drunk coffee (*yes, coffee, leave the tea to the Malayalis*), he was consumed by guilt. He had cheated this boy, but at the same time, he couldn't stop thinking of how Shankar had misled him.

Afterwards, he took Yediyurappa to the bus stop where people sat on a half-cemented wall, squeezing themselves into a tired line. In the anonymity of continued chatter, of people and vehicles, Raghavendra told him the truth about his agency. It was going to close down, *any time now*—as if the agency was a bus they were waiting for. And a grocery shop would take its place.

Yediyurappa refused to look at Raghavendra. He was indeed feeling let down: from a detective to a grocer! He looked at the watch of the man sitting next to him, saw that it was too late for him to go back to Shahi theatre, and realised that this was yet another job lost.

But Raghavendra's fountain of ideas had not yet dried up. He thought of Paul (*Why? Because of a bald man he had seen munching a bun politely while they were at the bakery?*) and decided that he would ask him to hire this boy.

He patted him on the head and said, 'Don't worry. I will tell my friend, who has a security agency, to hire you. You will be a security man.' When Yediyurappa looked away, he added, 'You will have a khaki uniform, a cap, and maybe, if you are good at the job, a gun.'

Yediyurappa jumped off the uncomfortable seat. 'A gun!' he exclaimed. Thankfully, the word became yet another chaotic sound that enveloped them before anyone else could hear it.

'Not immediately. Paul will decide at the correct time.' Poor, gentle Paul, who would rather allow himself to be beaten up than use a gun.

Raghavendra sealed his promise by saying, 'You come to buy your groceries from me and I will give you a much cheaper price than anybody else.'

This was his offering of thanks to Yediyurappa for having created more trouble at a time when he had thought that all his problems had finally been put to rest.

That night, with no prior indication, Rajesh discovered his consciousness. The first thing he saw when he woke was the tube leading to his hand. He tried to move his head, but it felt like it had been tied to the bed. His eyes shot from one side to another, seeing a nurse bent over a table, hiding what she was doing with her graceful back. His eyes fixed on her bottom, and he slowly realised that he was in a hospital. That shocked him, for he had never thought of himself as someone who needed doctors.

The nurse turned, as if she felt his eyes boring into her. Rajesh, from who knows what depths, conjured up a smile for her. She brightened at this display and immediately hurried out. Soon, one of Bindra's minions came in and grabbed Rajesh's hands, massaging them as if they were his own.

Rajesh had much to ask, but even as he tried to form the words (how difficult it seemed now) the nurse put her fingers over his lips, closing them. What a pleasure! Rajesh exchanged a delighted glance with his friend. He would sacrifice speech for the feel of a nurse's fingers on him.

The nurse sent Rajesh's friend away. She drew the curtain around the bed and picked up a syringe. Rajesh happily tried to turn over, ready to offer his bum to her. She gently turned him back and gave the injection in his arm. Rajesh survived this with another happy smile. So what, he asked himself, suddenly finding the hidden words that seemed to flow with the liquid injected into him. As if the nurse had read his thoughts, she lightly patted his hip before leaving.

13

Poornima was aghast when Raghavendra told her about Shankar. When he added that these were the ways of fate, and after a respectful pause, of god, she was confused.

'What fate? What god?' she murmured angrily.

Raghavendra mistook her words for questions that needed to be answered. He said, 'That is the way the universe works. We cannot understand its patterns.'

Poornima was not at all pleased. She was the one who had read picture books on astronomy, ever since Suhasini suddenly showed a deep interest in that subject. She had shown her mother the colourful pictures of galaxies in a book that she had borrowed from the school library. Poornima had guiltily snuck up to the terrace one night to see the traces of those pictures in the night sky, but all she saw were the patterns she made by connecting various points of light. All the galaxies were well and truly hidden, if not out in the void, at least inside the picture books. She didn't want to say this to Suhasini. Instead, she told her that she should go to the terrace every night and look at the stars.

And here is Raghavendra telling me about patterns in the sky when he cannot see the patterns in front of his nose.

Raghavendra saw that Poornima was about to say something. He quickly jumped in. 'I meant that justice is like the patterns of the universe. Everything is a pattern—here and there.' 'There' had become the entire universe cupped in his palm. 'Things happen in ways that are as mysterious as the stars.'

Poornima petulantly walked into Suhasini's room, took the picture book of the universe and thrust it at him. 'Maybe you should first read something.'

But all said and done, she was pleased. Pleased that her husband had done what was expected of him. He had even justified his luck by invoking cosmic patterns—she had seriously not expected that from him. Only after the surprise had passed into the vortices of impatient time did she remember Shankar's engagement with Megha.

'Why did it have to be Shankar?' she asked morosely.

Yes, why did it have to be him? She might as well have said what she had fleetingly thought: Why him, when there were so many other boys and men whose roving eyes hoped on behalf of their groping hands?

Raghavendra told her that they should forget the whole incident. That is also the way of fate, he wanted to say, but couldn't find the courage to give voice to the words.

Poornima felt a mother's pain and would not keep quiet. 'If this had happened to your daughter, would you say the same?' she asked. Raghavendra, predictably, was irritated. *Why does she connect every disaster associated with any girl to our daughters?*

He tried to turn Poornima's worry on its side and put it to sleep. But she kept nudging him. Justice had once again crept into her thoughts and refused to let her sleep. For her, there was no justice without retribution. The only retribution that she could think of was not allowing Shankar to marry Megha.

Raghavendra refused to respond to her arguments. He was immensely satisfied that he had solved a case (*his first and last one!*) and a peaceful sleep was his due.

The rain returned that night and fittingly, the power died. The fan came groaning to a stop. Mosquitoes hurried back in, signalling that Raghavendra's sleep was surely lost. Poornima was pleased. She said with a hiss, 'You deserve this. When you try to act as if that girl's life is not at stake, this is what happens. This too is god's way of telling you to do something.'

Raghavendra was confused. Did she mean that god spoke in mysterious ways, through lightning and thunder, no doubt, but now also through gadgets like the fan?

The next morning, Poornima continued to try and get Raghavendra to commit himself to some action. The questions of the night had transformed, in daylight, into nagging. He refused to budge, even when she gave him his morning coffee with less sugar.

When the newspaper came, he took it to the office and hid himself behind it. He deserved every bit of relaxation, didn't he? But Poornima followed him and tried to read the paper along with him, intruding between the lines, trying to find gory stories of girls who had died and women who had been killed. Although not part of the headlines, such stories could always be found hiding in between bandhs, accidents and stale political speeches. When she read out one such story loudly, Raghavendra folded the paper, thrust it at her, and locked himself in the bathroom.

Bindra's friend came by at 7.30 a.m.. He had sped over on his motorbike, and now hurried into their house with a breathlessness that seemed to suggest that the effort was all his and not that of the bike. Rajesh had regained consciousness the previous night, and told his friend to tell Auntie that he wanted to eat her vadas. As if regaining consciousness was nothing more than regaining memories of food. Nothing like Auntie's home-made vadas, Rajesh had managed to say gleefully, insisting that Poornima make them for him.

Poornima was in no mood to indulge this fantasy. 'Anyway,' she told the friend sternly, 'it takes time to soak the dal and then make the vadas. Ask him to eat idlis and not any oily stuff.' She sent the friend away, asking him to buy two idlis from the nearest darshini. 'No more than two and remember, no chutney,' she cautioned him. In her heart of hearts, she felt like she had indeed behaved like a mother to Rajesh in his moment of trouble.

By the time Raghavendra came out of the bathroom, Poornima knew what she should do. Since her husband would not take any action, she would herself tell Hema and see to it that the marriage was stopped. She realised that some things were better left to mothers, and all things, in general, best left to women.

As she was serving Raghavendra his breakfast, she could not resist saying, 'Nobody is asking you to do anything about that poor Megha. But I would have thought that, at least to clear Rajesh's name, you would want to do something. Anyway, better leave it. You concentrate on your shop. Go to Venkatappa and tell him to send the provisions soon.'

Raghavendra was relieved that Poornima had finally realised justice was only about forgiving and forgetting.

When Raghavendra met Bindra in the hospital, he was reminded once more of justice. He told Bindra about Shankar, and the first thing Bindra said was that Shankar should confess. 'Rajesh's name, *our* names, should be cleared of this charge,' he added ferociously. Seeing Raghavendra's doubtful look, he said, 'If you don't want to do it, I will.' So it was with a confused mind that Raghavendra went to meet Venkatappa, but even in that confusion, he knew he would not interfere any more in the matter.

Like a good omen, the signboard for the grocery store was delivered that afternoon. Sunil carried the long tin sheet, painted in red and blue, proudly exhibiting his artwork to anybody who cared to see it. And there were many who saw it, as they stood on the side of the road or peeped from inside their home. They knew about Raghavendra's shop even before he decided to tell anybody. The message would be transmitted rapidly, would even reach those who had missed seeing Sunil's march down the road.

Raghavendra was unhappy when he realised how brazenly Sunil had carried the sign through the streets. But looking at the finished work, he also felt a sense of pride and contentment. His dream was finally coming true.

That evening, he first went to Muthanna's house, discovering it hidden at the back of a compound, where many rooms served as individual houses. It was perpetually dark, and what Muthanna saved in rent, he paid for electricity. He was one of those who would have said, 'Thank god for the power cuts.'

Muthanna had just come back from work, and was sitting in the hall, drinking coffee. His little son was massaging his thighs.

Muthanna insisted that Raghavendra have coffee with him. Raghavendra gave him the papers on which the details of the chit fund were written. Bhaskar's analysis of it was clearly written. Raghavendra felt proud, as if he had been the one who decoded the scam. He told Muthanna that if he gave these papers to the police, they would have to act. Even to him, his words sounded like a prayer. Muthanna was so grateful that he would have asked his son to massage Raghavendra's legs too, but Raghavendra was sitting on the edge of his chair, visibly uncomfortable in a stranger's house.

Muthanna told Raghavendra that his detective agency was the best thing to happen to Mathikere Extension, implying that the Extension would now be safe with Raghavendra to take care of it. That was when Raghavendra told him about the grocery store. Muthanna was disappointed and showed it by asking his son to stop massaging him. He wanted to ask, what makes a man open a grocery store when he could be the master of criminals? But he kept quiet, and fleetingly thought of opening his own detective agency. One look at his wife, now pregnant with their second child, dissuaded him from fathering that thought.

Soon after this, Raghavendra went to meet Marimuthu, swinging his umbrella, daring the rain to flood him. The clouds floated by, ignoring him. Marimuthu was pleased to see him, and glad to hear about Rajesh. 'Our prayers never fail,' he said, without telling him that Poornima had visited his shrine.

Raghavendra once again told Marimuthu about his grocery store. He asked him to suggest a good time for the opening of the store. He also insisted that Marimuthu conduct the pooja for the inauguration. 'With your blessings,' he said, 'I am sure we will do well.'

Marimuthu was moved. His legitimisation was now complete. Instead of using an almanac to find the best time for the opening, he sat in meditation, his ears pried open for the secret sounds that the parrots had left behind. He opened his eyes and saw Raghavendra gazing at him solemnly. He gave him the right time for the pooja and a list of pooja items that Raghavendra should have ready. Neither of them realised that Mari had chosen the thirteenth day of Archana's death for the beginning of Raghavendra's new career.

Later that night, Bindra came by on his bike. People looked at him with a grudging respect, even as some felt that he had 'fallen' by dealing with a gangster. They derived a vague satisfaction from knowing that Raghavendra's success was also his failure.

Bindra told them that Rajesh was intent on leaving the hospital, and had insisted on having his meal from Guptaji's mess. Seeing Poornima's shocked look, he told her, 'Don't worry. We were in his kitchen to make sure he made clean food with good provisions.'

He saw the red-and-blue board on the table in Raghavendra's office. He squinted his eyes to read the English lettering, wondering why Raghavendra had not got it done in Kannada. In Bihar, such a thing would not have been allowed. Raghavendra, mistaking the query in Bindra's eyes, told him about the inauguration of his store and insisted that Bindra grace the occasion. Deep down, he still wanted some protection from Nagaraj.

Bindra once more asked him to meet Shankar and make him confess to Prasanna. Raghavendra stuttered and stumbled in response. Bindra could see Poornima's irritation at this indecision. He decided that he would have to do the job himself. He removed a pistol that was tucked in his hip and looked at it closely, making it clear to Raghavendra what his next step would be. Raghavendra was alarmed and immediately decided to accompany Bindra. He had no desire to find Shankar in the hospital along with Rajesh.

Shankar was busy with two women in his shop. The player was blaring Hindi film songs. The movement of the scissors seemed to be synchronised with the beats of the song. He ended with a quick flourish and looked up at Raghavendra. When the two women left (*why do so many women come to him?*), Raghavendra introduced Bindra to him.

'He is a friend of Rajesh's,' he said. Bindra, to emphasise that messages were not only spoken but also acted upon, pushed aside the cloth on the table and sat on the table's edge. So unnecessary, thought Raghavendra, but he plodded on.

'You see, he is very unhappy about the rumour.' He waited for a response, but Shankar remained silent. 'About Rajesh and that poor girl who died.'

Bindra stared at Shankar, trying to intimidate him. Shankar's thoughts were lost in the intricate stitches of his mind.

'You should remember, Shankar, all that Bindra wants is that everybody should know that Rajesh is innocent. Right?'

Bindra caught hold of Shankar's hand, pulling him closer towards him.

'Correct?' he asked in strongly accented English.

Shankar found his lost voice, discovered it in the folds of the new cloth that was strewn all around, ironed it till it could speak clearly. 'Yes. But it was Prasanna who said it was Rajesh. He knows best, doesn't he?' Along with his voice, he had also found some spirit.

'We will come to that,' Raghavendra continued, afraid to let Bindra speak, or worse, act. 'See, now it is clear that Rajesh was not involved.'

He made Shankar sit on the plastic chair. How long ago it seemed, that rainy night when he had himself slumped in it. He leaned against the table, confident and mature, or so he thought. 'Very Unclely,' Rajesh might have said.

'You know about my detective agency,' he began, but Bindra was impatient. He put his boots on the table. The muddy remains on the soles left behind a map of Mathikere Extension on Shankar's table.

'You also know that I was asked to find out who made Archana pregnant.' Raghavendra remembered that he had asked for Shankar's help. How could he not have guessed? In that silence, from which his next thought would arise, he realised that justice was indeed blind, could not see the truth even when placed in front of her eyes.

'You know that, don't you?' He felt uncomfortable talking to two mute men and wanted some response. Shankar finally nodded.

Bindra said, 'Sir, enough of the story. Tell him.'

Raghavendra raised his palm, a wall of calmness, before Bindra's eyes. 'I had no luck with my search. Till I went to the theatre. I think you know the place—Shahi, isn't it?' Shankar did not even look up. Raghavendra had hoped for a flicker of the eye, if not a murmured response.

Bindra patted his pistol, still hidden in the back of his pants, and demanded, 'Arre, say yes or no.' Shankar nodded slightly.

'Good. The doorman there had seen Archana with a young man, well dressed, thin moustache. But how does that help? All young men today are like that. See, even you are like that, no?"

He was amazed at the casual manner in which he spoke. This was far better than shouting and beating somebody. He could see Shankar slump further down in his chair.

'Anyway, that information was of no use. I gave up the search and then, as you know, some mad fellow broke Rajesh's head. So sad, don't you think? But it was also good in one sense. You came to the hospital to meet him and were also kind enough to bring some apples.' He turned to Bindra. 'Wasn't that good of him?'

Raghavendra was himself surprised at his cunning talk. All this time, he had thought of himself as a tired old (*no, middle-aged*) man and now here he was, in the company of the local bandit, speaking as if he were a lawyer on TV! *Poornima should see me now.*

'But as you were leaving, the doorman from Shahi also came to see me. Poor boy, he wanted a job in my agency. In fact, you passed him on your way out. You probably did not recognise him, but he recognised you only too well.'

He turned to Bindra for the final denunciation. 'You see, that boy clearly remembered that it was you who visited Shahi with Archana.'

Shankar lifted his head to see Raghavendra addressing Bindra and felt a surging sense of hope. Bindra was shocked: *Me? With Archana? What is wrong with the old man?*

Raghavendra shook his head impatiently. How had his final summation failed so miserably? 'No, not you, I was talking to Shankar.' But looking at me, Bindra thought, staring at him.

That exchange was enough for Shankar to gather his courage and pocket it into nice little words. 'This is a stupid story. I did not know that girl. You think I would agree to marry her sister if I had done what you say I have?'

Bindra jumped off the table. 'Enough talk!'

He pulled out his pistol and aimed it at Shankar.

'Chutiya, I don't care what you think. No point in wasting time talking to you. We don't want your confirmation. I want you to clear Rajesh's name.' His Hindi was straight out of a screenplay, but Shankar had eyes only for the pistol. *Mad Bihari, he might even shoot me!* Shankar desperately looked to Raghavendra for help, but Raghavendra was looking outside, hoping that nobody on the street could see Bindra's gun.

Shankar drew his last ounce of bravery from Raghavendra's worry. Surely even Bindra would not shoot him in public?

'Don't try all this goondagiri on me. Go ahead and shoot if you dare.' Even as his words stumbled out in confusion, he saw Bindra's fiery stare and felt a growing sense of fear. But he had not finished. 'For a stupid girl's mistake, you will kill me? And then both of you will go to jail. For what?' He hurriedly got up, pushed past

Raghavendra, and went out into the street. In the open space, he rediscovered his courage. 'Now shoot me!' he said dramatically. Seeing their hesitation, he continued, 'So what if I went around with that girl? It was her mistake also, don't you see?'

Raghavendra stared at Shankar, unable to reconcile his knowledge with the proof at hand. All this had seemed like a game for him, a way to pass time, but now he was confronted with proof that demanded action from him. If he could have spoken then, he would have said that there was no way to pass time without being overtaken by it, without being consumed by its mischief. He looked at Bindra, thought he saw him ready to fire his pistol. He caught the pistol and tried to force it into Bindra's pocket. Bindra was ashamed of Raghavendra's fear. *This is what comes of dealing with these old localites.* He walked out of the shop and came face to face with Shankar.

'You think we can never catch you? You have to walk these streets, right? And one night, me and my friends will be there. If you want to live, better tell that carpenter the truth. If I hear anybody mentioning Rajesh's name again, I will take care of you.' He jumped on his bike, started it with an angry roar and shot past them. If the gleeful exhaust of the bike could speak its mind, it would have said, Thank god for Yamaha.

Raghavendra followed those foggy words home, with not a glance at Shankar. Now it was no longer a matter of right and wrong. He realised that it was only the issue of delayed justice that really made matter out of morals: from right or wrong to life or death.

14

Poornima was clear that it was not enough to think of justice or merely speak about it. Justice should be acted upon; this belief, for Poornima, arose out of her emotional responses. She believed that speaking the truth would necessarily lead to justice, without realising that truth and justice were no longer equivalent. For her, the only just act left to be performed was to somehow stop Megha's marriage with Shankar. But for this to happen, she had to speak. Her comments had not dented Raghavendra's resolve to not get any more involved in the case, but his indifference only fuelled more angry words in her. When she did speak, it would be with a halo of truth that would make her words ring true.

It seemed as if the events of the last few days were also following the calendar of water days. As Marimuthu would have said, nothing in this cosmic pattern should surprise anybody.

Poornima was up the next morning even before the alarm could think of waking her. She carefully turned it off, then silently picked up the waiting vessel and tiptoed out. Once again, there was an early morning mist. Poornima did not go towards her tap. The task of collecting water was secondary that day. She had more important things to do—this blasphemous thought occurred to her for the first and last time in her life. When she walked out through the gate, she could see the milk van standing near George's house. He himself was standing behind a wall of mist, smoking a beedi.

Poornima walked along the main street towards Archana's house. She knew there was a tap at the end of Archana's street (slowly becoming, once more, 6th Cross), hoping to find Hema there. As she reached the tap, she saw that the crowd of women she had expected to see around it was absent. Nobody stood there stretching sleepily, yawning at the stars and the street dogs, occasionally peering into the vessel to check if it was full. The tap itself was making gurgling sounds, impatiently waiting to be rid of its burden, after which it too could go back to rest for the remainder of the day.

Poornima did not know what to do. She had no desire to wait near the tap, for who knew which groggy eyes peered from which houses. She walked to the end of the road and came to a large main road, whose divider was lined with halogen lamps. Stray headlights flitted past here and there, glow-worms that reminded her of the magic of dark mornings. As she stood mesmerised, the milk van roared past her and turned onto the main road. Two sets of hidden eyes stared at her from inside as the van went past.

After a few minutes of walking aimlessly, she went back to the tap. The lights had come on in some houses, and she could imagine women walking to and fro in the darkened caves that most of these houses were. There was still nobody at the tap, so she stealthily walked further, to Archana's street. She saw the light outside Prasanna's house burning feebly. As she turned to go back to her vigil beside the tap, she heard the door open. She hurried to the tap and placed her vessel beneath it. With loud relief, the tap expelled the water within.

From a silhouette, Hema became a woman. She was carrying two vessels, one in each hand, which trailed limply behind her troubled thoughts. She had not slept properly—no, not slept at all—the previous night. The ghost of Archana, and Megha's impending marriage, haunted her.

She was surprised, and a trifle guilty, when she recognised Poornima at the tap.

Before she could greet her, Poornima said, 'Oh, no water in my tap today. Can you believe it? It comes here but not there!'

Hema could believe anything. Even if somebody told her that the water had turned to mud or even milk, she would only have nodded. She knew, like many in her locality, that the power of BWSSB was never to be underestimated. Seeing Poornima, she remembered, with some shame, how she had gone to her for help. It seemed like ages ago, but the thirteenth day had not yet arrived to finally liberate Archana's soul. Already, she was getting habituated to the rituals of daily life, and this realisation caused a tinge of guilt.

Poornima told Hema that she should fill her vessel first. With a soft smile, she said, 'After all, this is your tap.'

Hema insisted that Poornima had come first and she would wait. But she couldn't help looking around to see if more women would suddenly materialise. Poornima noticed that the water pressure was good and her vessel would soon be filled. She bent forward and decreased the flow when Hema was not looking.

She said, 'Low pressure.' The two women nodded together—*don't we know how it is?*

After a few moments of silence, which, to Poornima, lazily stretched and became inordinately long, she ventured to say, 'I hope you are doing better.' Or at least, as well as a mother could be after what had happened.

'I am okay,' Hema replied.

'How long ago it suddenly seems,' Poornima said. Afraid she had said the wrong thing, she followed this up with, 'But then it just seems like yesterday that you came to me.'

Her clever words did the trick.

Hema was apologetic. 'I don't know what happened to me. I shouldn't have bothered you.'

'No, no.' Poornima stopped, hesitant to say what she had to. 'My husband did find out what you wanted to know.'

Hema stared at her in silence, as if unable to speak. Poornima felt that she didn't want to hear what she had found out. But she was not to be denied her tryst with justice. 'I don't want to hurt you any more, but he knows who the boy is.'

Hema found a passing breeze of courage. She grasped it, turned off the tap, and stared blankly at Poornima. She had no words to stop her nor the courage to hear what she had to say.

Poornima would not keep silent. 'I don't like to say this to you. In other circumstances, I would have kept quiet. You have already suffered enough. I am only telling you this as a mother. One injustice has been done and I don't want to see another committed.'

Hema didn't understand. Instead of a name, she had got a speech!

'Who is it?' she whispered, her stomach cramping as if she was holding onto something inside her for support.

Poornima put out her hand for support and softly said, 'Shankar.'

Hema slumped to the ground and Poornima followed her. She put her arm around Hema's shoulder. 'I promise to god that I didn't want to tell you this. My husband refused to give your husband this information. He didn't want to cause more trouble for your family. But, you understand, don't you? Can you let that man marry your daughter now?'

Hema had nothing to say. She began to cry. She cried so much that her face seemed to shrink. They suddenly heard light steps, and looked up to see a curious mongrel that had come close to them, sniffing for secret scents. Seeing the two women sitting on the ground, it too came and sat next to them. The stillness of the morning was already being erased. Other women would be up by now, the parade was ready to begin.

Hema refused to look at Poornima's face. She said, 'Thank you for telling me.' She dragged Poornima's vessel aside and placed hers under the tap. When she opened it, the water surged through.

'Better pressure now,' she murmured, wishing Poornima would go away.

Little did she realise that Poornima was speaking not just as a woman or even a mother, but on behalf of Lady Justice. That morning, Poornima had lent her voice to the lady who seemed to have lost hers along with her sight.

'I am sure you will agree,' she continued in a whisper, 'that your other daughter should not be placed in this man's hands. How he can even think of marrying Megha when . . . '

Hema shook her head vehemently. She did not agree at all. She realised that Poornima would only leave when she received an answer. 'I don't think the marriage can be stopped,' she said, sounding defeated. 'Who is going to tell my husband to stop the marriage? He fixed it, he will go through with it. Does he care for my girl?'

'Forget him. You can refuse. Your daughter can refuse. How can he force you then?'

'For what? Tell me, why should we get into more trouble? Maybe my husband is right. Who would have married Megha after they heard about Archana? This boy at least seems nice. He has his own shop.' She had a sudden doubt. 'How sure is your husband that it is Shankar? Does he have proof?'

'Of course, he is certain. I would not have come to you if I had the slightest doubt. And why would you worry about who will marry Megha? Think of Shankar, what he has done, and what reward he is getting! Instead of punishment for his crime, he is being gifted an innocent girl in marriage.' Poornima stopped her outburst, struck by a sudden doubt: could Hema follow her Kannada when spoken so fast?

Hema didn't need to understand all the words. 'What crime and punishment? These are not matters in our hands.' She paused, looked at the vessel under the tap, moved it aside and replaced it with the other vessel, while dismissively adding, 'Why make such a fuss about marriage? What is so big about it? Megha will adjust. As if all of us women are so different!'

That was the ultimate barb for Poornima. Placing her and her husband (*whatever his problems!*) on par with Shankar. She realised that there was nothing more that Hema would say. She picked up her vessel and left, murmuring, 'I only want the best for your daughter.'

Hema looked at her retreating form, a vessel on one hip and an irritated hand on the other. What an insult, such agony, that Shankar had to be the man! What new torture for Megha! Hema was suddenly furious at her impotence. She looked at the two vessels, happy bubbles hiding inside their darkened mouths, and kicked them angrily. The vessels rolled over heavily and emptied themselves of the last drops of water. Hema had done what in her own eyes was unpardonable. It would be her atonement for her shameful silence in the face of Poornima's accusations.

Her thoughts, now free in Malayalam, unconstrained by the twisting tongue of alien Kannada, flowed uninhibitedly with the water. *What does she know? If this had happened to her daughters, what would she have said? Fool—believing that life only follows the clear paths of right and wrong. What is wrong in giving a life to Megha? Anyway, Archana is gone and nothing we can do to Shankar will bring her back to life. What does she know of my shame and failure? It is so easy to talk.*

Poornima heard the rolling clang of the vessels behind her. Little did Hema know that water has a language of its own. When Poornima went back home, tired and angry, she drank a tumbler of water from her vessel, and when those drops of water flowed into her throat, they spoke Hema's thoughts.

She was suddenly tired. It was really not her business to worry about right and wrong in other people's lives. She went back to bed, trying to catch two more hours of sleep.

The early morning coffee brought back the words that she had wanted hidden inside her. Or maybe it was the smug satisfaction on Raghavendra's face that catalysed it. She told him about her meeting with Hema and Hema's response. He was not surprised. In his opinion, Hema had behaved like a mother. But he kept quiet, knowing that Poornima would have asked him what he knew about being a mother.

She tried to pester him with inconsequential mutterings as he read the morning paper. What was so interesting in that stupid newspaper that he had to devour it faithfully every morning? She got no answer to her question, but found what she wanted to say.

'Fine. That woman is scared. Why blame her? But it is also not right, don't you see?' He kept silent. 'I am talking to you and you think that paper has something more important to say! Why don't you tell Prasanna? I am sure he will be furious with Shankar. Don't you think so? After all, he is a father like you.'

Raghavendra was surprised. This was, in his memory, the first time she had acknowledged his existence as a *father*. He hid his smile behind the paper, twisting it into a story that detailed yet another scam.

Defeated and unable to penetrate the stoic gaze of the newspaper, Poornima broke down and cried. Raghavendra was shocked and embarrassed. He threw the paper down and held her shoulders. How he had misjudged her! She spoke not out of anger, not even for some idea of justice, but from the pain in her own heart.

He said the only thing that could stop her.

Hiding her face in her sniffles, ashamed that she had lost her spirit (*that which took so much energy from her, how can he know that?*), she heard him say, 'I will tell Prasanna. Now stop your tears.'

Poornima went to the bathroom, threw mugfuls of water on her face and came back with puffy eyes, looking like a drowned fish.

Raghavendra had changed in these last few days. He would not have thought it possible that a few stray events could straighten his back, tidy his hair and perhaps even improve his eyesight. His mind too had been transformed: he now (routinely!) thought of right and wrong, the complexities of justice, and the complicated ways of his fellow humans. Having 'solved' the problem, and having felt Bindra's gun with his hands, his confidence had soared and was now perched on the bridge of his nose. His eyes peered over them, with a look that made it clear to all that Raghavendra was a man to be reckoned with in Mathikere Extension.

Later that morning, when the sun was up, bright and chirpy, washing away the sorrow of the last few nights, he went to meet Prasanna. He was surprised to see that Shankar's shop was closed. Prasanna was sitting in a chair inside his shop, frowning at a piece of wood. Seeing him, Raghavendra was reminded of their last meeting.

Prasanna was not happy to see Raghavendra standing outside his shop, squinting like a myopic owl. He would have ignored him, except that he suddenly remembered Rajesh. He came out unhurriedly, looking at the pieces of wood that were scattered around, making it clear to Raghavendra that he was much less important than these objects. But Raghavendra was in no hurry. His revenge would be long and sweet.

'I have something to tell you, Prasanna. Do you want me to speak here or shall we go elsewhere?' How easily he had addressed Prasanna by name, without any respectful appendage. Prasanna looked at his two assistants and hesitated. Raghavendra caught the hesitation and blew it back at him.

'You may not want the whole street to listen to this.' He spoke loudly, without the habitual nervous flickering of his eyelids. Prasanna shook his head and asked Raghavendra to follow him to the bakery. As if the bakery was primarily a meeting place and only then an eatery. He might as well have said: Why else are hundreds of bakeries strewn around the locality, no, the whole city?

But Raghavendra sat down on the marriage cot, now nearly ready. The assistants were surprised—even they did not dare to sit on that intricately carved cot. Prasanna was furious, but before he could say anything, Raghavendra said softly, 'You are the cause behind the beating of Rajesh. The police think so too.'

Prasanna looked around, trying to hide the accusation somewhere. It was not just his reputation that he cared for. He was more worried about the politics of the local.

'Sit here,' Raghavendra commanded, and Prasanna silently sat down next to him. 'I know what you did. Now the poor boy is in the hospital with a broken head. The inspector told me that I could file a report against you for attempted murder.' Was that right? He was confused for a moment. Did one file reports? Was he being credible?

Prasanna told the assistants to go and have some tea. They left hesitantly, leaving their ears hidden inside their chisels. When they came back and hammered on these chisels, the secrets would tumble out one by one: katack, katack . . .

Prasanna was trying to control his anger. He said, 'What is this? You are behaving like a rowdy.'

Raghavendra was pleasantly surprised. It was the first time anyone had ever mistaken him for a rowdy.

Prasanna continued, 'That bastard Rajesh deserved what he got for making my daughter pregnant, leading to her death. Whoever beat him should have killed him. Now you go and tell your inspector that Rajesh should be arrested for murder.'

Confronting Prasanna in his shop, in the midst of all his furniture, was perhaps a mistake. But Raghavendra only smiled. 'Yes, I knew you would say that. You see, I know now who made your daughter pregnant and it's not Rajesh. I have proof of it too.'

Prasanna was shocked. Raghavendra looked across to Shankar's shop. 'Where is your friend, oh no, your soon-to-be son-in-law?'

Prasanna had been surprised too, to find that Shankar had not opened his shop that morning. Even on Sunday mornings, Shankar was usually stitching something or the other. Maybe he had a hangover, Prasanna had thought, and resolved to tell him to go easy on the drink.

'I don't know,' he replied.

'Let me tell you why he is not here,' Raghavendra said. 'Last night, I met him with one of Rajesh's friends. This friend is no mere friend. He is a gangster, yet he is a gentle boy. Even the police are afraid of him. He carries a gun, like you carry . . . ' He looked at Prasanna carefully. 'Ha, like you carry your pencil tucked behind your ear.' Raghavendra was revelling in his new-found personality. How lovely to talk, to string words in circles. How lovely to tell stories, in so leisurely a manner.

'And why did we go to meet him? You see, because we had the proof and I wanted to tell Shankar about it. To see what he thinks.'

He paused, wanting to provoke Prasanna. But Prasanna merely stared at him

'Shankar, of course, denied it at first and then began blabbering.'

He paused again. Prasanna remained quiet.

'Okay, so you don't understand.' He crossed his legs and leaned back with the support of both his hands. 'Nice cot, this. For a marriage, Shankar told me. How does a father who has just lost his daughter work on a marriage cot with so much care? I didn't ask that, Shankar did.'

Prasanna clenched his fingers. He was afraid that he would pick something up and break Raghavendra's face with it.

'Ah yes, what did Shankar blabber? When I told him that I knew it was he who had made Archana, that poor girl, pregnant, you know what he said?'

Revenge had its moment of glory. Ferocious Prasanna, cornered in his own domain, lost his composure. His hand broke off a piece of the cot, one that he had so lovingly carved and then nailed to the side of the cot. The wood broke in two and a puff of dust came in between them. Shocked at his own action, Prasanna lifted the piece of wood. The cot tilted, and Raghavendra had to stop himself from sprawling on the ground. Prasanna raised his hand to strike him with the piece of wood, but Raghavendra scrambled up and away.

'I am sorry, Prasanna. You should keep all your anger for that tailor. He is the one who spoiled Archana. And now you have fixed his marriage with your other daughter. I only came to warn you about this. I don't care about him, or you. I am doing this only for the sake of your elder daughter. I don't want her to suffer because of your foolishness.'

Prasanna could not bring himself to hit Raghavendra in broad daylight. He threw the piece of wood inside the shop. It hit the wall and bounced on the ground. He stood up and said calmly, 'It's none of your business. My daughter will marry Shankar.'

He pushed him away, and Raghavendra tottered past a few unfinished pieces of furniture that lay near his feet. As he steadied himself, he realised that he was sweating and his heart was beating wildly. But as he walked home, he was proud of himself, proud of having behaved like a man and a father.

Perhaps Raghavendra should have dealt with it differently. But his newly discovered confidence had caused him to become like the others. He had taunted a man when he should have been careful. But why blame him? For so many decades he had been a lost soul, aimlessly shuffling here and there. He had helped people who had later treated him like dirt. So, having found his place in the blazing sun, he took full advantage of it.

But now, look at the consequences. Prasanna had been humiliated—that too by Raghavendra. His ego overrode any concerns he might have had for Meghalatha. There was no way he could have cancelled her engagement (although one that had only been sanctified over glasses of rum), knowing well that every moment of his life thereafter, he would have to deal with sidelong whispers. To add to this insult, Raghavendra, that most miserable rat in the world, would strut every time he walked past his shop. Anything was better than that.

So Meghalatha, that sombre girl in the final stages of her teenage years, she who hid her grief in her dark, brooding eyes, was well and truly sacrificed, sandwiched between the egos of two, no, three men.

For, right then and right there, Prasanna decided that an engagement was not enough. Who knew what further trouble Raghavendra would create? He looked at the cot and patted the broken joint almost affectionately. Meghalatha's marriage would be held immediately, he decided. Then he remembered that Archana had died only a few days ago, eleven days to be precise. His wife had wanted a pooja to be held in their house for the thirteenth-day ceremony. Even though she had forgone all the rituals of death for Archana, she wanted something to be done on the day of the liberation of Archana's soul.

His assistants slithered back, with questions as hairlocks on their foreheads. A sudden cloud cover gobbled the impatient sun, and Prasanna, in that moment of darkness, finally knew what he would do. Instead of a thirteenth-day ceremony for one daughter, he would arrange a marriage for the other.

15

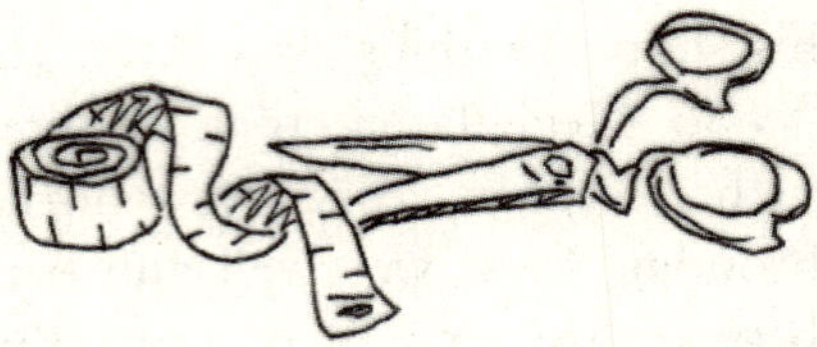

RAJESH REFUSED TO STAY IN THE HOSPITAL ANY LONGER. Early the next morning, two of Bindra's friends came to the hospital and paid the bills. Rajesh had earlier asked them to bring a box of sweets which he wanted to give to the nurses. One of the nurses removed his bandage and wanted to stick a smaller plaster on the wound. But he told her to tie a fresh bandage around his head. He wanted to go back home in triumph; the bandage trumpeting his bravery. He gave the nurse the box of sweets along with a coy smile. She patted his head affectionately, knowing that she would never see him again.

'Don't forget to distribute the sweets to the other nurses,' he added patronisingly, wanting to spread his goodwill amongst all of them. She made a face, and he wondered what the actor Suniel Shetty would have done in his place. Having no answer, he turned back at the door and waved to the nurse, who had already forgotten him and was busy removing the bedcover. Rajesh and his two friends squeezed onto the bike. He looked around, gathering all the curious stares with pride. Now all of Mathikere Extension would speak about him, and how.

The three boys reached Raghavendra's house on the Yamaha. Rajesh stood for a few moments at the gate, offering his smile to anybody who passed by. He then rang the bell. Poornima opened the door and found Rajesh in front of her, short and squat, with a grin that could split his wound. She gave a delighted shout that brought Raghavendra with his two girls in tow. They all made a fuss of Rajesh, insisting that he sit on the chair. His two friends stood on either side, like bodyguards.

Rajesh patted Sanjeevani's head and shook Suhasini's hand. When he could speak, he said, 'Auntie, I have come back to life just to taste your chow-chow bhath.' His friends stared at him enviously. Rajesh gave them a triumphant glance when Poornima vanished inside the house.

Sanjeevani, with the innocence of the young, asked him, 'Who beat you, Uncle?' Raghavendra did not want to drag his daughters into the sordid affairs of the locality but was too late to stop her question. He had himself never wondered about it, assuming that it had been the work of Nagaraj. Little did he know that Bindra had asked Rajesh the same question the previous night. And when he had heard what had happened, he had rushed out in anger.

Rajesh straightened himself and replied, 'I caught a bunch of thieves and one of them hit me with a stick. But I managed to defeat them and hand them over to the police.'

His friends laughed, provoking Rajesh to slap his thigh in appreciation of his own bravery.

By the time Poornima brought plates of chow-chow bhath for Rajesh and his friends, the girls were tired of him and went inside. The bhath was exactly the way he liked it. Salty upma and sweet kesari. As he left, he said, 'Don't worry Auntie, now that *I* am here.'

That twelfth-day morning, Prasanna left his home early. He walked into the innards of Mathikere Extension, where every curved street ended up intruding into new houses, searching for Shankar, wanting to find a residence in the place of a scrawled address.

Shankar lived in a two-storey building, whose many rooms had been partitioned into quarters. The stairs were narrow, and the walls and floors had been chipped in various places. To reach Shankar's quarters, Prasanna had to go through a narrow pathway with open doors on one side, rooms with anonymous outlines of faces staring out at him. He walked past lonely puddles of water waiting patiently for thirsty dogs to lap them up. When he got to Shankar's room, he found a white piece of paper stuck on the door. His name was written on it in a flowery script; underneath it somebody had scrawled: *World Famos Tailor*.

Shankar was woken from his sleep by Prasanna. Seeing him at the door, he was more scared than surprised.

Prasanna pushed past him into the room. There was an empty bottle of rum on the floor next to the bed. Prasanna sat in the only chair in that room. Shankar closed the door and sat on the bed. Prasanna glared at him as they sat in silence—Shankar with bowed head, looking for responses in his toes.

Suddenly Prasanna jumped up and whacked Shankar hard on his head, sending him sprawling on the bed.

'That was for Archana,' he said, taking his daughter's name for the first time since her death. 'And for shaming me.'

Shankar turned his body into a cocoon. He would not fight a father's anger. And hadn't he, by himself, agonised, grieved and drunk himself to tears the previous day? Hadn't Raghavendra's wounding words brought to life Archana herself? Hadn't he lain where Archana once had, *in secret*, finally finding a voice to ask for forgiveness? Prasanna could do what he wanted with him.

Prasanna grabbed his arm and pulled him to a sitting position. 'Come on, look at me. When I took you to the bar, you could have told me. You would have spared me the shame of hearing it from Raghavendra!'

Shankar looked at him. What could he tell Prasanna? That Archana's challenge had finally worked its charm? That he had taken her to Shahi twice—how foolish he had been to ignore all the staring eyes, those that would eventually find whispering tongues inside them. But caught in her spirit, her joy, what had he cared? Then, in his bed, in an unplanned moment of madness, as two teenagers who had forgotten the world in a few moments of passion. Later, when she had come to him, early one morning, drenched in the rain, fear in her womb, telling him she was pregnant—even then, it had only been a different kind of joy mixed with fear. He had immediately promised to marry her, but it was Prasanna who had found intolerable shame in her condition, who beat her, locked her up and drove her to death. How deeply Shankar had looked into his rum bottle for answers that would explain why Archana had taken the poison. He told himself that it was only a childish response to get her father's sympathy, and in that juvenile act she had completely forgotten him.

Shankar thought of all that he couldn't say, and began to cry instead.

Prasanna was aghast. How could Shankar cry so shamelessly? What sort of a man had he chosen to be his son-in-law? He slapped him again, much more gently, and said, 'Arre, what is all this drama? Forget it. I am only angry that Raghavendra is going around spreading rumours about you.'

Seeing an accusation in Shankar's eyes, he continued, 'I have no time left for *that* girl. She has gone, leaving me to carry all her shame and pain. I am not heartless, you see. I care for the future of Megha, and that is why I asked you to marry her.' He paused and then said, 'I am not to blame. It is only the society around us.'

Shankar got up, wiped his face with a towel that was hanging on the wall. He said, 'I am sorry. Truly sorry. I never expected that she would do . . . what she did. I agreed to marry Megha only because I thought it was one way of setting right the wrong I had done. If you want to cancel the marriage, that is fine with me.'

How calmly he spoke, how dignified he looked. And not a quiver of desire (*be honest, he felt it, didn't he?*) in his voice when he mentioned Megha.

Prasanna was impressed. He said, 'Eh, Shankar, I did not come here to talk about what is done. I only came to tell you that Raghavendra met me yesterday and told me about you. Seeing his nosy eyes, I knew he would do his best to stop your marriage with Megha.' His voice rose. 'I won't let that beggar do this to me. You understand?' When Shankar nodded, he continued, 'I came to tell you that I have fixed the marriage for tomorrow. I will show all these nosy bastards what I think of them! They want me to grieve for my daughter? I will give them a marriage instead!'

Shankar was aghast. To be married the next day! 'But what will Megha say? What about your wife?'

Prasanna dismissed the two women, expelling Shankar's worries through his nostrils. 'Megha should be happy. All said and done, you are a good match for her. And my wife? She will walk around in silence, groaning and moaning about her daughter. Anyway, they don't know what you've done. So why should you care?'

Shankar stared at him. He wanted to tell him that he had to call his parents, his friends and relatives for the marriage. That his father had wanted him to come back to their village in Kerala to get married when he was ready to do so.

Prasanna thought Shankar was having second thoughts. Belligerently, he said, 'Look, now you cannot back out.

I have already talked to a priest. I want the marriage performed tomorrow before people talk any more.' Struck by a passing thought, he added, 'Don't worry, it will be a grand function.'

Shankar drew on his last residue of self-respect. 'No, I need my parents to come. They have been wanting to get me married for a long time. I can't do it without them being here.'

Prasanna said calmly, 'If they come by tomorrow, that's fine. We can't postpone the marriage any longer. You should have thought of your parents when you made Archana pregnant.'

He got up to leave, then said, 'I need your help to make all the arrangements. Come to my house for lunch and I'll give you some work to do.' If his assistants had heard him then, they would surely have said: This will be one marriage where the groom has to do more than just take away the girl.

After Prasanna left, Shankar lay back on his bed in a daze. Everything was happening too fast. He looked around the room. Would this be his last day here?

As he got up to get ready, relieved and full of a pleasurable sense of anticipation, he had only one passing regret: he would have no time to stitch a blouse for Megha to wear at the wedding.

By that afternoon, a shamiana had come up on Prasanna's terrace. Some thought that it was for Archana's thirteenth-day ceremony, but they were only those who had not heard the impatient whispers. *You won't believe it . . .*

Shankar had lunch at Prasanna's house, for the first but not the last time. Hema served him hot food with cold eyes. Both Prasanna and Shankar, looking at her, had the same thought: *Did she know?* Prasanna dismissed this worry with a sweep of his hand that found a handful of rice in it. Shankar looked to hide it in sidelong glances that searched for Megha. When he couldn't see her anywhere, he asked Prasanna about her. Prasanna called out to her and Megha came from inside the kitchen, dressed in a cotton sari, the sweat from cooking coating her black eyes.

Prasanna said proudly, 'She cooked this meal,' but Shankar had eyes and ears only for her. He saw her, saw little Archana hidden inside her, and lowered his eyes.

That night, Prasanna turned on all the lights. He insisted that loud music be played, so as to drive away lingering suspicions and inauspicious ghosts. He even had a smile for Kumar and his friends, and invited them to lunch the next day. They were, of course, delighted to accept. But it must be said that three boys sat sadly at their window that night, looking longingly into Prasanna's house while listening to moody old Hindi songs.

That evening also saw a celebration in Raghavendra's house. Venkatappa had sent over groceries in a three-wheeler van. They were unloaded in Raghavendra's office room. The smell of rice, dal, spices, mixed with the motherly smell of jute bags, overwhelmed the house. The two girls excitedly poked around each bag, delighted that their game of shopkeeping was becoming real. Instead of toy containers, there were huge, heavy sacks of real groceries. Sanjeevani told her father, 'What is a shop without bottles full of chocolates?' Seeing him smile, she was emboldened to add, 'And lots of biscuit packets too.' It was her elder sister who smacked her and said, 'This shop is not for you, it's for others who will pay and buy.' *Little Poornima already.*

Since Marimuthu had chosen the next day for the pooja at home, Raghavendra went in search of Sunil to see if he could make a counter over the half wall. Sunil sent his boy—not the one who by now had a full halo behind his head. He cut away a large chunk of glass and placed a ready-made grill. It was a sloppy job, but it would have to do until Raghavendra found a proper carpenter to finish the job. If only he hadn't antagonised Prasanna!

Once again, in a monotony of repetition, it was Josephine who told Poornima about the wedding. When Poornima went to buy two extra packets of milk, for Rajesh had sent word that he wanted kheer that night, Josephine said, 'See how the world is. See what is happening? That carpenter came and asked us to arrange for twenty litres of milk for tomorrow. I asked him what for, and he said his daughter is marrying the tailor!' Her whisper made the words sound sacrilegious. 'I mean, thirteenth day for one and first night for another!' She laughed, delighted at her wit, and Poornima could only watch her in silence.

When she went back home, she told Raghavendra about it. He watched her animated gestures and felt a sense of guilt. By the time she finished, she realised the guilt was theirs to share. If only they (*no, she*) had not gone on a crusade for justice and let matters take their own winding course, the marriage would not have been held immediately. Who knows what might have gone wrong, given the nature of time? Had they sacrificed Megha to satisfy their own obsession over right and wrong? Why, for god's sake, why had she, and then he, felt the need to parade their knowledge as well as demand a price for possessing it?

They addressed these doubts to each other, although nothing was said. Raghavendra saw how troubled she had become. He held her hands and she lowered her eyes in response. They would have to find ways to atone for this too.

After a few minutes, he said, 'Knowing Prasanna, this was inevitable, independent of what we did. A man who refuses to accept he had a daughter just because she got pregnant—you think such a man would have cancelled the marriage?'

They held on to this image, made Prasanna an ogre in order to satisfy their own sense of justice.

As usual, Poornima had the last word, almost echoing Hema, when she finally found the strength to speak. 'What is the big deal about marriage? What does it matter who Megha marries? It will be the same life for her anyway.' Again, she managed to irritate Raghavendra by suggesting that her own lot in life was no better or worse than that of other married women. But he also realised that damning her own marriage was perhaps her way of atonement.

By late evening, the mood had lightened. Rajesh, with his friends following him faithfully, came to have the kheer.

Poornima had stood over the fire, boiling and stirring the milk for a very long time, till it had become thick.

Rajesh loved the kheer. He said, 'This is just like they make it in my village. This is so tasty.' But he still couldn't bring himself to say: Just like my mother's.

Raghavendra requested Rajesh's friends to help him bring down the nameboard for the agency. One of them climbed the ladder and removed the nails. Patil looked out from the opposite shop, hearing in that clatter the betrayal of Raghavendra. Baale Gowda too stood outside his door, staring at them. He had never thought Raghavendra would consort with *these North Indian boys*.

The board was softly but unsteadily lowered to the ground. After another round of kheer, they nailed the new one in. Rajesh was full of praise for it. 'This is great, Uncle,' he said again and again, keeping a watch on how many people stared at his bandaged head.

The board was finally up. Poornima read it proudly: Sri Krishna Provision Stores. She felt an immense sense of relief. She went inside and got a bedsheet. She asked the boys to cover the board with the sheet. They would hide their (*well-known!*) secret at least till the next day. After the pooja, it would be made visible to all literate eyes.

That night was for Bindra alone. He had a bath in the evening, put on freshly ironed pants and a shirt. He packed a small suitcase with clothes and other essential items. He shoved his pistol in the back of his pants, pulled on a loose jacket over his shirt, patted down his hair in front of the mirror, locked the door and left his room.

He walked to Guptaji's mess for dinner. He talked to his friends, who listened respectfully to what he had to say. He then went to the paanwallah below the B&R, and bought a 420 paan. He stood there masticating the paan until the tobacco swirled in, clearing his mind. He spat out the juice and asked the seller, 'Seen Nagaraj?' The paanwallah inclined his eyebrows towards the dark windows framed by leaking red lights inside the restaurant. Bindra nodded and crossed the road. His mechanic friend's garage was open till late in the night. The boy who worked there was completely covered in black grime. Each time he opened his mouth, he seemed to be grinning, although the boy had stopped smiling long ago.

Bindra went into the garage and sat on a chair away from the lights. The boy told him that the owner would come 'soon', but Bindra ignored him. He chewed the leftover pieces of betel nut and tobacco in his mouth and waited, watching the buses slumbering past, the motorbikes rushing up and down, and the little children leading their elders by the hand to the ice-cream shop nearby. It was only when he saw Nagaraj and his buddies come out of the restaurant that he got up. He spat all the accumulated saliva on a tree trunk that was vainly trying to grow beside the main road, then followed them. As expected, the trio went to Chikanna's house, their loud conversation and guffaws clearing the way ahead of them.

Bindra went back to his room, picked up the suitcase, and came back to the garage. He sent the boy to get an autorickshaw to take him to the railway station. Before the boy could crawl out from under a worn-out scooter, he left.

He walked briskly to Chikanna's house. It was past ten in the night. Inside the houses he passed, all those who were not yet asleep were lost in the enveloping sights and sounds of the TV. He lightly jumped over the gate, just another shadow within an arc. He crouched under the window and slowly peeped in. Three men were sitting in different corners, cigarette smoke hanging over their heads and drawing a noose around them. Bindra removed his pistol, checked to make sure it was loaded. He waited patiently till he saw Nagaraj get up and walk to a table to pour himself a drink.

Bindra lifted his pistol and shot Nagaraj through the open window. The creaking, rusting bullet sped swiftly, straight into Nagaraj's stomach. The glass fell, Nagaraj tumbled over his heaving paunch, and before the rolling thunder-sound of the shot had dissipated, Bindra had left.

Seeing Nagaraj fall, Chikanna finally lost his voice. He started sobbing, and it was left to the cop to shout at Chikanna's wife, who, without being told, rushed in with a bandage. When she saw that it was Nagaraj who lay bleeding on the ground, her trembling hands clutched her heart in joy. Chikanna and the cop carried Nagaraj to the hospital. Ironically, the bed that had been vacated by Rajesh was the one allotted to Nagaraj. The hospital at first refused to take a patient with a gunshot wound, but given that it was Nagaraj, and there was a cop with him, they quietly admitted him.

Bindra saw the auto waiting outside the garage and walked towards it, whistling. The auto driver looked impatient, as though he would have left any time now. The moment he saw Bindra, he began to say something, then kept quiet. Bindra nodded and greeted him in Hindi politely, then swung into the auto without a pause in his stride. He would take a train or a bus out of Bangalore and before anybody woke up to Nagaraj's moans, he would be on his way to Bihar. He was not running away—no, that he would never do—he was only leaving, having no desire to tempt the impatient hands of cops in case Nagaraj went to the police. He would be back in a few weeks, with more guns to sell and more people to protect. The cool night air of Bangalore embraced him and he sighed happily. The honour of his friend, of their whole community, had finally been restored.

Ironically, again, Nagaraj's fall meant Raghavendra's rise. When the residents of Mathikere Extension heard the news about Nagaraj, they presumed that the mild, myopic Raghavendra had something to do with it. Their respect for him grew and, if for no other reason, people would begin to flock to his shop. Just when Raghavendra shut down his detective agency, the people around him opened their troubles to him. That is fate, Poornima would have said, and—before she, once and for all, shut her mouth on the matter of justice—that is the way of justice too.

16

THE THIRTEENTH DAY OF ARCHANA'S DEATH WAS celebrated not in public by her father, but in secret by her mother. Hema had been devastated to hear that Megha was going to be married on what should have been the day of liberation for Archana's soul. Although not a highly ritualistic person, she believed that these rituals would ensure that the soul severed its ties to the earthly world and reached the abode of the gods. Hema knew, knew so well, how much Archana's soul needed the liberation. She could not forget the tortuous struggle of her daughter's last moments and believed that the rituals of the thirteenth day would finally give her peace. Instead, her husband had denied Archana even this small gesture. She slept in the hall every night after Archana's death, close to a small lamp they kept alight night and day to mark her presence. As she went to bed on the night of the twelfth day, days still defined by Archana's calendar, she realised that she was losing two daughters in a matter of thirteen days. That night, she decided that she and Megha would celebrate Archana's thirteenth day in their own way.

On the morning of the thirteenth day, they were both up by 3 a.m. For the first time in her life at Mathikere Extension, Hema did not start her day by taking a vessel to collect water. Instead, they walked to 'their' tap with Megha holding a small cloth bag. She stood there while her mother walked over to Poornima's tap. Poornima had just come to the tap, weary after having failed to persuade Raghavendra to get up and collect water. She was surprised to see Hema, who quietly told her to come over to her tap. Hema then went around to the other taps nearby and invited the women there to come with her.

At half past three that misty morning, a group of women could be seen sitting on the ground with vessels scattered around them. Hema's tap was closed and the mighty Cauvery river—isn't Cauvery a woman, after all?—waited impatiently too, at the mouth of the tap, to join the women. Hema told them, in a singsong Kannada mixed with Malayalam, about the thirteenth-day rituals. She told them that since she could not have the ceremony at home, she wanted to perform it with them. 'Only you will understand,' she told them. 'Only you as mothers will know what I am going through. What my little girl went through. Nothing is more important than her liberation today.'

She looked around at the women, and they looked back at her silently. In that moment, she felt a great sense of oneness with these strangers. She was seeing some of them for the first time, and with the others, she only had a fleeting acquaintance. She said, 'The ceremony for the dead are offerings to the soul, to let it go free, to make it leave us without any regret. I cannot let go of Archana so easily. But knowing that she cannot be with us anymore, I want to let her go. I want to offer this water from the Cauvery as ablution for her soul. I want you to all join me in offering water to the earth, the sky, the air, to all the creatures around us, with a prayer to liberate my little girl.'

Megha opened the cloth bag that she had brought along and took out five objects. She placed them on the ground in a circle.

Hema said, 'We did not perform any rituals for Archana's soul, all these days. It doesn't matter. In those rituals, we were supposed to offer Archana's favourite foods to her every day. Today, I am offering all these foods to Archana's soul in the presence of all of us. You, as mothers and women, understand this much better than those men and their priests. I made these dishes yesterday, one piece of each of her favourite dishes, for Archana alone. I am offering it to her, to the earth, to the river, in the hope that she is one with them at last.'

Hema opened the tap gently, and a stream of water impatiently gurgled out. It flowed over her hands, caressed her thoughts. She heard Cauvery herself promising deliverance for Archana. She cupped her hands under the tap and let the water flow out from her palms, with her fingers pointing towards the ground. She poured water on the food that was kept on the ground. In a clear voice, she said, 'This water I offer to the earth to release my little Archana. May she be happy wherever she is.' As she spoke, tears flowed down her cheeks, copiously, uncontrollably.

Megha got up and gathered water in her palms. She let it flow down to the ground saying, 'I am sorry that I could not save my sister. I am sorry that instead of the ceremony for her, I am going to get married. I could not save her and I cannot save myself.' She stood in silence, her sniffles threatening to become a flowing stream. Hema pulled her down gently next to her.

One after another, all the women performed the ritual of collecting water from the tap and offering it to the earth. Water flowed around their feet, over the food on the ground, into crevices in the stone underneath the tap. It lapped against the tails of the street dogs that sat silently watching the women. They all felt the comforting arms of the river around them, as though they were on the banks of the Cauvery, being embraced by the river goddess herself.

Poornima held Megha's hand and said, 'Megha, there is no need for you to feel guilty about getting married today. This is the way life is, the way the water flows in our lives. We all belong to the Cauvery and we flow with her. Whoever comes and goes in your life, remember, this water will always be with you.' So saying, she took some water in her palm and poured it over Megha's head.

The women sat around the tap without filling their vessels. They sat watching the sky, waiting for the sun to decide whether to appear or not. Waiting for the first carts that would soon begin the long trudge to the wholesale market. For the first birds to swoop down from the sky. For the lonely crow to come and sit on the tap, looking at all of them sitting at its feet. None of the women would collect water for their houses that day.

Before the first rays of the sun could light up the faces of the women, Hema got up. What they had done could only have been accomplished in the semi-darkness of that time of the night. She knew that once their faces became visible, she would not be able to share her grief with them. Seeing her get up, the other women stood too, some having to push themselves up with difficulty. Megha took out another packet from her bag and opened it. It was filled with many round balls. The fragrance of ghee, roasted gram and cashew filled the air.

Hema said, 'I made this specially for Archana and for us. This is the moment for celebrating her liberation. She is now free of all of us. Please take this offering as a token of gratitude from my dear daughter, Archana.' All the women put a sweet in their mouth and stood around in silence. Hema gave a piece each to the dogs and kept one for the crow on top of the tap.

'Now, Archana is gone. And it is time only for Megha. I want all of you to come to her wedding today. My husband has not invited any of our friends or neighbours. But I will not let Megha get married as if she has to hide in shame. Come to the wedding. Come and be with Megha.

I have decided that the food we serve today for lunch will be Archana's favourites. And Megha has decided to wear Archana's favourite dress. This is the way the two of us want to celebrate both the events. My husband cannot erase one daughter and get rid of the other so easily. So, please come and bless Megha that she can have a better life than her sister.'

Hema looked all around, as if imprinting the moment in her memory forever. Her eyes filled with tears as she said, 'I am leaving this place and going back to my mother's house in Kerala. I will not come back to live here. Megha will also leave immediately after the wedding. I don't know how to thank you all for having shared this moment with us. We don't know each other as individuals but we are all women, and we know what our feelings are. I will never forget what all of you have done for us today.' She walked away without looking back. Megha followed her, and the remaining women stood with vessels snuggled to their hips, watching them fade into the distance.

What of dear Raghavendra and his dream? Marimuthu came early that morning, dressed in a red silk dhoti with a flaming pillar of kumkum on his forehead. He broke a coconut and loudly recited prayers, beckoning everyone near and far to come and grace the occasion.

With a flourish, Rajesh pulled the bedsheet aside with the end of a stick, and the nameboard shone in the morning light. Rajesh's clothes looked as new as his bandage. His friends were still sleeping and would come later, casually astride the Yamaha. Bhaskar stood in a corner, waiting to slip away to his office at the first opportunity. The two girls had pulled out their silk langas with matching blouses, and their hair overflowed with white, fragrant jasmine. Poornima had not slept after she had come back from the ceremony with Hema and the women. Left to herself, she would have sat the whole day on the crumpled sofa, staring at the wall in front of her. *But duties first!*

She forced herself to get ready. She had decided to wear an old silk sari smelling of stale mothballs that she had worn only once, for the naming ceremony of their first daughter. To complete the picture: Raghavendra in a white dhoti and loose, overhanging shirt. None of them wore the same clothes they had worn to the opening of the now defunct Raagu's Detective Agency.

Josephine came with her fat cat in tow. She cheerfully waved to all her customers, sharp eyes looking to collect titbits. Baale Gowda stood outside Raghavendra's gate, even as his wife murmured from inside her house that Marimuthu was being unnecessarily loud, and asked no one in particular, 'Is god deaf?' Baale watched the activity around him with a benign smile, waiting to offer solace to any troubled soul nearby. He was sure that in all this euphoria of entrepreneurship, Raghavendra would not have the time to do anything about the water tap.

Chandru, forgotten Chandru, also came, once again with a toothbrush in his mouth. He spat in the gutter outside Raghavendra's house, punctuating each spit with a sceptical snort.

Patil and his family hid themselves deeper in their shop, and turned on their little TV.

Ahmed came over on the way to his shop. He looked at the board in surprise, and within his happy soul, a new desire (what else but to have his own grocery shop?) was born. In that moment of self-discovery, he waved to Poornima with a delighted smile.

And more people came: Sunil, Muthanna, Yediyurappa, all of whom had served as small stepping stones that finally made Raghavendra's desire come true.

But finally, fittingly, the warmest welcome was for Mr Paul, who walked in, swift and straight, carrying a bunch of flowers, which he gave to Poornima. He shook Raghavendra's hand, patted the girls' heads, met Yediyurappa and hired him on the spot.

Paul had finally forgiven Raghavendra for his momentary lapse of reason.

On this thirteenth day after Archana's death, Megha and Shankar were married. Shankar's parents had refused to come at such short notice. But they were worried about him getting married in such a hurry, with no prior warning. His father was convinced that he had been caught in some scandal that necessitated such an urgent marriage, and so they sent his elder brother to attend the ceremony. He reached Bangalore early in the morning by bus, and came to Prasanna's house directly, as he had been asked to do. Prasanna came out and greeted him as if he were the groom. The brother gave Prasanna a bag full of plantains, banana chips and pappadams saying, 'No marriage of ours can be done without Kerala produce, fresh from our land.' Shankar was dressed in a white dhoti and white shirt, whereas Megha wore the dress that had been Archana's favourite. He was wearing a gold chain prominently around his neck, courtesy of Prasanna. There was a smear of sandalwood paste on his forehead. He looked like the ready-made groom he was.

Prasanna had found a local priest who had been told clearly that this was going to be a very short wedding. Most of the unnecessary frills had been removed, as Prasanna wanted the ritual to be over as quickly as possible.

By eleven, the priest arrived. As instructed, he completed the rituals rapidly. Everything about the ceremony was odd. Shankar was dressed in a white dhoti and white shirt. When Shankar saw her coming out of the room, for a moment his heart stopped, for he saw not Megha but her sister walking towards him. As if the cosmos too had come to participate in the marriage, it was the same dress she had worn on that fateful day when they had ended up in his room. Prasanna, too, was shocked on seeing Megha in that dress for he had, just the previous evening, given her a special Kerala sari to be worn for the wedding. He looked at Hema in surprise, and she stared back defiantly. More surprises were in store for him. Megha refused to look him in the eye, but smiled at Shankar more easily. She seemed in good spirits, even telling the priest at one point to go slower.

But the biggest surprise for Prasanna was the steady stream of women who came to the wedding. Women he had seen on the streets, and those he hadn't, walked into the hall, smiling. They rushed to greet Hema and Megha as if they were old friends. Even more surprisingly, Hema and Megha reciprocated their warmth.

None of these women looked even once at Prasanna. It was as if he did not exist. Then Poornima walked in, carrying a present for Megha. She walked past Prasanna as if he was invisible. She smiled at Shankar, who was equally bemused by this sudden crowd of neighbourhood women. He, unlike Prasanna, not only knew some of them but also knew their blouse measurements. He turned his head towards Prasanna, who stood next to him, worried that he might have heard his thoughts.

Poornima had brought a sari for Megha. She had bought it some time ago, but had never used it. It was not a fancy sari, just a simple cotton sari made in Udupi. But she had liked it a lot and had kept it for a special occasion. When she had gone back to her house after the early morning ceremony at the water tap, she had been totally drained of all emotions. She had cried all the way back to her house, crying as if it was she who had lost a daughter and was giving another away in marriage. She did not lie on her bed and, instead, curled up on the creaky sofa in the hall. As she tried to sleep, unable to get her mind away from the haunting image of Hema, she saw herself in the mirror of the almirah. That was when she was reminded of the sari that was inside it.

When she gave the sari to Megha, she said, 'This is a special sari from Udupi. Wear it when you need the strength of Udupi Krishna to be with you.'

Prasanna looked out onto the road, expecting the men to troop in behind their wives. But that day, the road was bereft of men, even those who liked to lounge around all day in front of a shop or a bakery. In a way, he was thankful, for he was suddenly worried about feeding more people for lunch. By then, a few more people had come. Kumar and his friends had taken Prasanna's casual generosity for a genuine invitation, and turned up for the wedding lunch. When Kumar saw Archana's room for the first time, he could see her shimmering image at the window, brushing her oiled hair. From here, he could see the window of his own room through Archana's eyes. And he knew then that she had seen him, and in her own way, had acknowledged his presence.

Hema, poor, angry Hema, silently watched the proceedings. Only her concern for Megha's future sustained her, made her hold her peace. She would leave her husband and the house the next day, but today was for her two daughters. She rushed out to greet the women as they arrived, as if they were old friends or relatives. And they all hid their sadness, bundling them within the folds of their saris.

Hema had let Megha know that there would always be a place for her with her and her mother, as if it was inevitable that she too would leave someday. Her act of defiance, of leaving her husband, was only a small consolation for Hema. *Small consolation, yes,* she whispered to the picture of Archana encased inside herself, *but life is only made up of small consolations.*

Megha, silent Meghalatha, slightly excited but also slightly guilt-ridden. She had given in to the dictates of her father, even as she made a promise to herself that she would have nothing to do with him after marriage. She had no desire to live in Mathikere Extension any longer. She would leave the area as soon as possible. She knew that tailors, especially ladies' tailors, were in demand everywhere. This resolution was the only just offering she could make to her dear, departed sister.

And Shankar, anxious Shankar, who only smiled once during the brief ceremony, and that was when Megha had let the clouds part her lips into a smile. He was marrying Megha, and also her sister, finally living up to the promise he had made to Archana.

Prasanna was father personified that day. He ordered the cooks around, showed visitors to their places, sat on the veranda with people around him on rented plastic chairs, speaking loudly and joyously, as befitting a man who had finally got his daughter married. He had removed all traces of Archana from the house. Through this marriage, he had truly lost a daughter and gained a son.

On that evening of the thirteenth day, the rain came along with the setting sun, adding its own layer of darkness to the night. Raghavendra was sitting in his grocery shop—*finally!*—on a straight-backed wooden chair, staring out through the glass partition. Lights came on in Patil's tiny shop opposite their house. Raghavendra could not see

Patil, but could imagine him peering at his new competitor through his bifocals. The rain increased in intensity and the power went off. Poornima brought a lighted candle from the kitchen, and placed it on the table in front of Raghavendra. She sat on a plastic chair next to him. There had been no customers on the first day, not even Rajesh or his promised multitude of friends. Now, with the rain, no customers could be expected.

Suhasini and Sanjeevani came out of the hall and sat on a sack of groceries, balancing themselves on either side. The four of them sat looking at the steady rain, the sudden sound of a cycle braving the flowing water on the streets, a sharp honking from the main road, the whistle of a pressure cooker.

Poornima and Raghavendra looked at each other. They had thought that nothing had changed, but now they knew that everything had, in these last thirteen days. Their lives would not be the same again. Justice had intruded into their dreams, and they understood that everything that happened in the future would be contaminated with confused questions about right and wrong.

They knew, too, that it was not only they who had changed. Their lives only reflected the violent changes in the city, changes that would irrevocably erase the age of innocence in the life of Bangalore.

Also by Sundar Sarukkai